# INTERNAL AFFAIRS

*ALSO BY JERRY OSTER*

CLUB DEAD
SAINT MIKE
NOWHERE MAN
RANCHO MARIA
SWEET JUSTICE
MUNICIPAL BONDS
FINAL CUT (as Max Perry)
PORT WINE STAIN

# INTERNAL AFFAIRS

JERRY OSTER

BANTAM BOOKS
NEW YORK • TORONTO • LONDON • SYDNEY • AUCKLAND

Thanks to everyone at the Writers Room for the quiet and the energy.

The characters, events and institutions depicted in this book are wholly fictional or are used fictitiously. Any apparent resemblance to any person alive or dead, to any actual events, and to any actual institutions, is entirely coincidental.

INTERNAL AFFAIRS
*A Bantam Book / February 1990*

*Grateful acknowledgment is made to Leiver & Stoller for permission to reprint lyrics from "Black Denim and Motorcycle Boots" © 1955 Jerry Leiver Music and Mike Stoller Music.*



**Library of Congress Cataloging-in-Publication Data**

Oster, Jerry.
Internal affairs / Jerry Oster.
p. cm.
ISBN 0-553-05729-4
I. Title.
PS3565.S813I5 1990
813'.54—dc20 89-27477
CIP

*Published simultaneously in the United States and Canada*

*Bantam Books are published by Bantam Books, a division of Bantam Doubleday Dell Publishing Group, Inc. Its trademark, consisting of the words "Bantam Books" and the portrayal of a rooster, is Registered in U.S. Patent and Trademark Office and in other countries. Marca Registrada. Bantam Books, 666 Fifth Avenue, New York, New York 10103.*

PRINTED IN THE UNITED STATES OF AMERICA

RRD 0 9 8 7 6 5 4 3 2 1

*For Tenny Chonin*

# INTERNAL AFFAIRS

# 1

*Gimme fire.*

Somewhere back before he fried his brains—like the homeboy on TV saying this frying pan's drugs, this egg's your brains on drugs, any questions, asshole?—somewhere back then Monroe Riggs (street name World—why, his fried brains couldn't recall) read this poem about how everything might could go up in smoke—volcanoes, earthquakes, all that shit—or everything and everybody might could freeze solid.

*And as the poet asked himself, Which would I prefer? ask yourselves, Which would* you *prefer?* Miz Powell said—Miz Powell with that fresh fox Tina Turner voice, looking down at the poetry book she was reading, then up at the class to see was they paying attention or was they fucking around, waxing the bitches, diddling with their blades, their pieces, their works. *Ice is nice,* Miz Powell said the poet decided when he axed himself which would he prefer, *but gimme fire.* And the way she said it in that fresh fox voice and the way she looked at them in that fresh fox way, you knew when she said fire she meant fucking.

With his fried brains and all, World doesn't spend much time thinking about poems. But he's thinking about *that* poem right about now on account of right about now the poor fuckers in the apartment building across the street from his, the Raleigh it's called, after some old-time Mouseketeer or some shit, are dying in fire and smoke and flames and shit, and they don't look like they're fucking.

They're either dying in fire and smoke and flames and shit that's coming out of all the windows in the place it looks like just about, *or* they're dying by jumping out the windows and off the ledges and shit and smashing themselves all over the floor.

Here comes one now. An old lady. . . . Fuck.

Here comes a guy. . . . Shit, homes, your head popped like a melon, man.

Here comes two of them—a homeboy and a bitch holding on to each other like that'll make a diff— Oooh, man. Were they thinking about fucking? They were not thinking about fucking.

Yo, hey, check this out. This homeboy thinks if he holds a sheet by the corners like, like it's a parachute like, he'll float down nice and slow instead of popping his head like a melon all over the floor. . . . See, homes? Wrong.

*On account of I had a taste of desire, gimme fire*. That's how his fried brains remembered it went, the poem. *Ice is nice, but on account of I had a taste of desire, gimme fire*. Or some shit like that, meaning I balled some bitches so shit yeah I'd rather burn up than freeze to fucking death.

Yeah, well, tell it to the bitch up on the ledge there, Mister poet man, the one with her hair on fire and her dress and—

Holy shit.

That's Joy.

Joy Griffith.

Joy Griffith, the social worker, what a waste that is, her doing social work on the sorry fuckers in the Raleigh, she ought to be doing social work on him because the bitch is fine, homes. The bitch is *stupid* fresh.

Not no more, though. Shit.

Here comes another parachute asshole. This one's got nothing but a fucking towel. . . . Asshole.

Where'd Joy go? She ain't there. She jump? . . . Naw. . . . She go back inside? Shit. Send that bitch back inside, waiter. She ain't done enough.

*Ice is nice, but on account of I had a taste of desire, gimme fire*. Yeah, well, tell it to Joy Griffith, Mister poet man. Mister poet man asshole motherfucker.

After a while, after enough of this shit, World gets out his Super Cub and his glass pipe and blows a little jumbo, fries his brains a little more, the windows closed and the air conditioner going full blast on account of it's hotter than hell without the fire and with the fire it's hotter than hell and a half, does a little tube, Sally Jessy Raffy (''Women Allegedly Sexually Abused by Their Therapists''), so he doesn't have to listen to the sirens and the shortwave radios and the cops and firemen on bullhorns yelling at the poor fuckers don't jump, help is on the way, listening instead to the bitches tell Sally Jessy Raffy how their shrinks copped a feel.

And when Sally Jessy Raffy's over, World looks out the window again and no more poor fuckers're jumping out of windows and off ledges and shit, but some poor fuckers're most likely still burning up inside on account of smoke and fire and shit's still coming out of a lot of windows, but not as many as before. Most of the homeboys and bitches lamping and scoping the fire are gone home—to do some tube themselves, most likely, *The Price Is Right* or *Wheel of Fortune* or *Dukes of Hazzard,* most likely.

And on the news, which comes on in like this special bulletin like after Sally Jessy Raffy, they're already saying sixteen poor fuckers died in the fire in the Raleigh and they're saying the fire started on account of they was careless with a kerosene stove or a fire in a wastebasket or some shit like that, on account of there was no electricity or nothing in the Raleigh on account of it'd been empty for a year or more, the poor fuckers was just squatting.

But World, fried brains and all, wonders.

World wonders on account one of the homeboys and bitches still lamping and scoping the fire, he's been lamping there since the very first fire engines and cop cars rolled up, in the middle of *Geraldo* (''Kept Men''), he ain't even hardly moved except once when he walked down to the bodega on the corner and came back with a Sprite and a donut, is Bobby Liberty, Bobby Liberty who the word is you call if you need something burned, on account of like the statute in the harbor, which is how he got his name, Bobby always has a torch on him.

# 2

Charles Story wore two bracelets on his right wrist: one, made of copper, was a folk prophylactic against arthritis; the other, of silver from Senegal, a wedding present from his French-born wife (who in her youth—her *jeunesse*—played in a tennis tournament in Dakar staged to civilize the natives), was for ornament. The bracelets jingled together when Story moved his arm about, writing, making a point, hauling his fine, recalcitrant hair back from his forehead—a gesture he had crafted in his youth while under the influence of John F. Kennedy and that had become habitual; they made a pleasant, subtle noise, like a wind chime. On his appointment as Police Commissioner, Story had worried that the bracelets might be thought unmanly by the officers he would command; but the males, certainly, when in mufti dripped gold chains and bracelets, so that Story joked that perhaps he didn't wear *enough* jewelry.

Maybe because the joke had percolated the ranks, maybe because Story's right arm lay half across his chest and the copper and silver were conspicuous against his navy Lacoste shirt, Patrolman Lester Glatter, the first cop out of the first whitetop to respond to the 911 call from Story's townhouse on Seventieth between Park and Lex, noticed the bracelets (maybe because he was a rookie and still drafting his own fashion statement) even before he registered that their wearer, his boss, sprawled on a burgundy oriental rug in the parlor floor library, had a hole in his chest where the shirt's decorative reptile had been; before he registered that the middle finger of the boss's right hand had been severed and inserted in his mouth.

*Why me?* Glatter wondered, for he was smart and ambitious and could foresee no benefit to his career coming from his having his name somewhere on every single piece of paperwork an unprecedented misfortune like this would generate. *Aren't you the sorry son-of-a-bitch,* he would be asked for years to come, maybe for his lifetime, *who caught the nine-eleven when the PC got polished?* Every move he made, every step he took, second-guessers would be watching him.

The young cop's reaction was exactly that of Mayor Sidney Lyons on getting the news of Story's murder, *after* he had flipped through the late night newscasts and assured himself—the lead stories were all about the rain that had trashed the July Fourth weekend—that it had been a day without crises. Bridges crumbled, local sports teams stumbled, epidemics blew into town, the cost of a movie ticket got ever nearer that of swordfish, the Theater was still dead; the streets were home to a good-sized city's worth of people, while even more people (sadly, the kind you wanted as neighbors) flew to the suburbs' greener grasses; rival narcotics entrepreneurs executed one another alfresco (which would have been useful but for the innocent bystanders also felled); races, religions, sexes, and ages played a continuous hostile Ping-Pong of slurs and epithets; elected and appointed officials skimmed, peddled, and perjured; terminal gridlock was just around the corner—and for all of it his citizens, who didn't know a colossus among cities when they lived in it, blamed him. But they couldn't hold him responsible for the weather.

(Or could they? Lyons had just gotten a report from the Chief Meteorologist—who knew there *was* a Chief Meteorologist?—warning that the summer that had begun prematurely with the warmest March on record, and had produced the cruelest April, the hottest May and June, had legs that might extend its run until October. The rain, certainly, all two and a half inches of it, hadn't cooled things off at all, and that was probably his fault too, wasn't it?)

Sylvia Lyons answered the phone, the hotline direct from the Night Mayor's office at City Hall, flouting her husband's order that she keep her goddamn hands off that phone, it didn't do for the braves to have to tell the squaw why they were calling the chief. Engrossed in the latest Shirley MacLaine, Sylvia just said

"Darling," meaning not him but his press secretary, George Darling, passed Lyons the receiver, and went back to her book.

"Yes, George? . . . George?"

Darling was weeping, and while he got a grip, visions of catastrophes danced in Lyons's head: the Brooklyn Bridge had collapsed, the Queens-Midtown Tunnel had sprung a leak, the Mets were moving to Secaucus, Woody Allen to LA. One of his daughters (*Five* daughters—why him? His having a family had been instrumental in his election to succeed a man his campaign had pointed out often, and with innuendo, was a bachelor who lived all alone in a great big house, but why him?) was a *Hustler* centerfold.

"George, what the hell?"

Darling took a deep breath, then exhaled this: "Story's dead sir murdered shot in the heart around seven the ME thinks. A servant a houseboy got back to 119 from his day off around ten and found the body. Mrs. Story and their daughter're out in the Hamptons. Story came into town yesterday to do a talk show this morning. A Police airplane's gone to get them."

Lyons decided to laugh. It *was* a joke, right? On April Fool's Day, Darling had drawn a happy face with a felt-tipped pen on Lyons's forehead during his after-lunch nap. *That* had taken balls; this was kid stuff. "George, I just watched the *news*."

"Walsh and Amato didn't get to 119 until after ten," Darling said. "The precinct commander kept it under wraps until then, so it didn't make the late news. Everyone'll be live from 119 in the next half hour. Seven said they'd probably stay live all night and link right up with *GMA*. I think you should go straight to 119 rather than make a statement from the Mansion or the Hall. Hriniak's on his way there too I haven't said anything to the press of course but I assume he'll be acting PC."

Darling paused for breath and for confirmation of his assumption, but Lyons was thinking—about *GMA* and 119 and Walt Shinamato. He knew that *GMA* was *Good Morning America* and he supposed it was catchy to call it *GMA* instead of *Good Morning America,* but he didn't understand how 119 East Seventieth Street, Charles Story's townhouse, had become a metonym like, well, like City Hall. Okay, he under*stood* that it was thanks in part to trendmongering journalists like Ann Jones, the author of the cover story in that week's *City* magazine titled

"From 119 to 1 Police Plaza: Charles Story Takes His Primer on Privatization Downtown," but that didn't mean he liked it.

And who the hell was Walt Shinamato, and what did his not getting somewhere have to do with something's not getting on the late news? One of those gook coroners, Shinamato sounded like.

Then it came to him: Not Walt Shinamato. *Walsh* and *Amato,* the Chief of Department and the Chief of Detectives, the highest uniformed cop and the highest in clothes. (Cops didn't say *plain clothes,* Lyons had learned from listening to cops, they just said *clothes*. People could blame him for whatever they wanted, he was, as long as someone was saying something he wanted to hear, a good listener.)

Or maybe Hriniak, the First Deputy Commissioner, was higher than Amato. Hriniak wore clothes too—not *plain* clothes, expensive suits. (Sylvia picked Lyons's suits from off the rack at Syms and he knew an expensive suit when he saw one.) For that matter, maybe Hriniak was higher than Walsh. He must be, if Darling assumed Lyons would appoint Hriniak acting PC.

Whoever was highest, before Story's corpse was very much colder, all three of them would be bucking to be Story's permanent replacement—clawing, scratching, bobbing, weaving, kissing ass and kicking it, calling in favors, making deals, making promises, making threats. Wonderful: a mick, a wop and—a what?—a polack, probably. Uillean pipes, Sinatra, and a polka sounded cacophonically in Lyons's ears; the tune they played was *Why Me?*

*Why him?* Story's appointment had been criticized by the gamut of second-guessers—from cops who objected that he was a civilian to populists who protested that he was a millionaire to crackpots who were scandalized that he was on the list of best-dressed men (or that he married a former tennis player—a *foreign* former tennis player, a *divorced* foreign former tennis player; or that his stepdaughter played tournament tennis too, and was a fashion model besides; or that he lived in a townhouse, collected antique motorcycles and had his clothes (not *plain* clothes) made in England; or that he read books, and *wrote* them—books about how the top jobs in any municipality were best performed by businessmen, not career civil servants or politicians, books with words in them like *trust* and *excellence* and *responsibility* and *quality,* best-selling books). But it—Story's appointment—had been a brilliant solution to a nagging problem: Story's goddamn ubiquity. Didn't the son-of-a-bitch ever sleep?

If Story's likeness wasn't on the front page (*Realtor Offers to Build Public Swimming Pool*), then it was on the real estate page (*Story Slates Low-Income Units in Luxury High-Rise*), or the society page (*Gala at Story Residence Benefits Disease Victims*), or the split page with a jump to the sports page (*Developer Maps Major League Ballpark on Manhattan Landfill*), or on the editorial page, in a cartoon that accented Story's movie star good looks (not like the gross caricatures of Lyons that made him look like one of Dr. Seuss's humanoids) illustrating a thoughtful column (not like the crazed ranting columns that blamed Lyons for the price of tea in China) wondering whether Story aspired to be mayor or senator or president or Baseball Commissioner. Was he a man who would be king, or did he have his eye on God?

(And we're not even talking here about the *life-style* pieces: the *GQ* cover on what smart young billionaires are wearing; the *Vanity Fair* cover on the Long Island farm house that Story's architects, designers, and decorators made over into a palace; the simultaneous *City, Manhattan, Inc.,* and *Sports Illustrated* covers (who said there was no such thing as a media conspiracy?) on the yacht, equipped with Loran and depthsounder and twin Detroit diesels and twelve VHF radio telephones and sauna and wet bar and gymnasium and disco and helicopter pad and stock ticker, and guided missiles, probably, that Story bought from a Saudi prince with cash-flow problems. Not to mention the *Lear's* cover on how Lise Story juggled her roles as founder and CEO of a chain of health clubs for women executives, philanthropist, wife and mother, or the *Model, World Tennis,* and *Sassy* covers on Claire Langois's transition from world class junior tennis star to world class high fashion model. And, of course, the special *Lifestyles of the Rich and Famous,* aired in prime time, opposite *The Cosby Show* during the February sweeps, Robin Leach nearly levitating with apoplectic enthusiasm, just about the Storys.)

To put a ceiling on Charles Story's vaulting ambition Sidney Lyons had been powerless; but he could certainly scuttle a mayoral candidacy, at least for the time being, by making a virtue of the necessity of replacing retiring Police Commissioner Howard Nagle, and naming Story to succeed him. He could, as well, perhaps call Story's bluff by directing him to make his first task a study of the feasibility of the privately run Department he so eloquently and frequently mouthed off about. He could and he had ("I can look you in the eye, my fellow New Yorkers, and say without hesitation that today's appointment signals a new era in the history of the Police Department of this colossus among cities") and even his detractors had tipped their hats at his cunning.

So how the hell could Story go and get himself killed just when Lyons had gotten him out of his hair?

"Mister Mayor?"

"Yes, George, I heard you. Hriniak."

"Yes, sir. But another thing, sir—the only clue so far is the victim's, uh, finger."

Lyons's stomach tried to climb out through his mouth and he swallowed and swallowed to drive it back down. He supposed that meant he was getting good at this; the first time, called to the scene of the murder of a security guard at a welfare hotel in the east twenties, seeing the bloody shreds where the man's middle finger had been, seeing that bloody finger shoved in the man's face (What is that? A cigar? A turd? What *is* that?), he'd vomited on Chief Walsh's shoes.

Since then, there'd been four more murders, four more mutilations and humiliations in—what?—eight weeks, ten weeks, all because some malcontents who lived in sewers and subway tunnels and under bridges and wouldn't know what to do with a house or a job or a place in the society of a colossus among cities if they had one, which was why they didn't—all because they thought hacking people's fingers off and shoving them in their kissers was a colorful, sardonic way of saying fuck you to the system, to—let's face it, for Lyons was a man convinced that every sling, every arrow, had his name on it—to *him*.

The Hopeless, they called themselves, and the goddamn media picked it up and ran with it, *City*, naturally, leading the way, as if having a name made them into Robin Hoods or something, Butch Cassidys and Sundance Kids, instead of what they were, which was bums.

City Hall Park. Just a few lousy feet from the seat of government of this colossus among cities. Visible from his office window practically. A bunch of bums had been living there for years it seemed like even though he knew it was only last Thanksgiving. Hah—they probably thought that was funny, moving in with their sleeping bags and cardboard boxes on Thanksgiving Day. Defecating and urinating right out in the open where everybody could see them, where *he* could see them. Calling at him sometimes, when he held a press conference on the steps of the Hall to announce some new accomplishment, yelling *Siiid-ney, Siiiid-ney,* in the singsongy way fans yelled at Darryl Strawberry when they got worn out by his attitude, yelling it sometimes when he was *in*side the Hall, trying to get some work done. What did they know about work? Vets, they told the goddamn media they were, Vietnam vets. Bullshit. Did anybody check on it, did anybody call down to Washington for their service records? Of course not. Vets, bullshit. Pests. Derelicts. Bums.

Bums who defecated and urinated on the grounds of Gracie Mansion even, right outside the official mayoral residence, his goddamn *house*. (Lyons was out of bed and at the window now, stretching the phone cord to its limit, getting strange looks from Sylvia, his face pressed up against the glass, trying to see if anyone was defecating or urinating. He saw only his reflected face, and with the phone tucked into his shoulder couldn't budge the window, shut tight to keep in the mercifully conditioned air.) They had known better, the bums, than to move their sleeping bags and cardboard boxes onto the grounds of Gracie Mansion, but a bunch of them lived in Carl Schurz Park just south of the Mansion and they thought it was colorful and sardonic to soil his nest rather than theirs. Some nights he half-dreamed as he fell asleep of sneaking out of the mansion and down to the park and clubbing a few of them with a baseball bat. There had been a couple of attacks on sleeping homeless people in the past couple of weeks; the cops (predictably) blamed them on kids with nothing to do and no place cool to do it in, but Lyons was willing to bet the responsible parties were solid citizens fed up to here with bums and deadbeats. Who would know if he sneaked down and clubbed a few of them that it wasn't just the latest in what the newspapers would soon be calling a *series* of attacks? Who would care? Vets, bullshit. Bums.

Darling again: "And, uh, sir?"

"Just *say* it, George. Don't say *sir* all the goddamn time."

". . . Yes, sir. Sir, someone wrote wally on the rall."

"Someone did *what*?"

"I'm sorry, sir. Let me say it again: Someone . . . wrote Raleigh . . . on the wall."

*Rawley? Not that black girl from Poughkeepsie? Please God, not her and Al Sharkskin and the rest of them.* "Once more, George. Wrote *what*?"

"R-a-l-e-i-g-h. Raleigh. With a red marker from Story's desk, in big block letters."

Lyons could see them—the same childish capitals the illiterate ingrates of this colossus among cities used when they wrote him their niggling, complaining letters, on paper torn, usually, from their children's spiral notebooks because of course they wouldn't have anything like *writing* paper around the house. "George?"

"Yes, sir?"

"Why me?"

". . . Yes, sir."

# 3

At 119, at a few seconds past 4:11.33 by the digital watch his computer nerd daughter gave him for his birthday (it didn't have a thermometer on it, but the temperature was eighty-five if it was a degree, four in the morning or not; it did tell the date—5 July), Joe Cullen wondered, *Why me?*

The place was dense with cops. On-duty cops who'd heard the all-points and hauled ass to the scene from as far away as the Rockaways and Tottenville and Riverdale; off-duty cops, cops on vacation, cops on sick leave, suspended cops, retired cops, *dead* cops and un*born* cops, it seemed like, were all over the house, all over the sidewalk and street outside, spilling down the block both ways toward Park and toward Lex, the ones out of uniform dressed in Jams and gym shorts and T-shirts and tank tops, a little unsure, a lot of them, in uniform or out, whether a civilian PC (a multimillionaire civilian PC) was strictly speaking a brother-in-arms, but drawn nonetheless to the lodestone of a death in the Department.

Why then, with cops to spare, Cullen wondered, had he pulled this job? He got close to Captain Richie Maslosky, who was writing on a legal pad clipped to a clipboard, and jostled his elbow.

Maslosky didn't look up. ''What?''

''Why me?'' Cullen said.

Maslosky looked up. ''Correct me if I'm wrong, Joe, but there're probably guys who'd sell their mothers to babysit Vera Evans.'' Maslosky wrote something more, then looked at his watch, a regular old Timex with a face and numbers and hands, the kind Cullen had hoped he'd get when he'd said he wanted a watch, a watch that didn't show you the seconds slipping away, your life along with them. Did people who wore these watches make dates to fractions of seconds and inches—*Meet me twelve and a half feet from the northeast corner of Fifty-seventh and Broadway at 5:18.22?* "Her charter's due at La Guardia around seven. A limo's bringing her here. You should figure a first shift starting at eight. Make it seven-thirty."

Make it 7:29.59. "Captain, could you please talk to Walsh?"

Maslosky pointed his finger at Cullen's heart. "Correct me if I'm wrong, but didn't the PC just get polished? You think anybody's—"

"I'll talk to Walsh," Cullen said, and turned around and ran right into Walsh. And bounced off, for though half a foot shorter than Cullen and as thin as the cigarettes he perpetually smoked, Walsh was unyielding.

Walsh checked his gold braid, his medals, his uniform creases, for damage in the collision. He was perfect, the only man in the building with a jacket on, the only man in town who wasn't sweating. "Explain what to Walsh, Sergeant?"

"Sir, the PC and I—"

"Old buddies, I hear," Walsh said.

"Friends, yes."

"Queens?"

"Elmhurst."

"Elmhurst High?"

"Yes, sir."

"I went to Jamaica. Before your time."

"Yes, sir."

"Letters in basketball and baseball. You play any ball for Elmhurst?"

"No, sir. I was a juvenile delinquent."

Walsh looked Cullen up and down. In a wrinkled Haspel suit, Cullen was patently disorderly; was he also sarcastic and insubordinate? "So that's why you're a weasel now? For redemption?"

To make that make sense you would have to understand that this wasn't a conversation, it was a swordfight. Cullen was in IAU, the Internal Affairs Unit, the unit that polices the Police; Walsh, Chief of Department or not, was a hardliner who believed—who *knew*—that what IAU did—*all* IAU did—was trammel the Police and keep them from policing the people, the one and only group that needed a lesson in abiding by the law.

Once upon a time, in a newspaper interview, an IAU commander had called his men ferrets, hoping to paint a word picture of those engaged in a relentless search for Truth; someone—someone like Walsh—had known that a ferret is just a domesticated weasel and therefore synonymous with sneak. Weasel stuck where ferret had failed to adhere.

"How about Story?" Walsh said. "He a JD too?"

What was he thinking—that Story was polished as revenge for something that happened in a rumble thirty years ago? "He worked six hours a night six days a week at his dad's candy store and still found time to be an A student and a big man on campus."

Walsh squinted at Cullen, searching for more sarcasm, then looked around at the hallway's vaulted ceiling, at the modern art and the gold-framed mirrors and the scones or were they sconces, Cullen never could remember the difference. "Look what it got him, hard work."

Cullen thought about taking Walsh by the ear and dragging him into the study and poking his nose in the still-tacky blood on the carpet and saying, *Look what it got him, hard work.* Instead, he said, "Respectfully, sir, I'm too close to this. I don't have the perspective."

"We'll keep an eye on you, Sergeant," Walsh said. "We don't want any vendettas here." Before Cullen could explain that it wasn't about vendettas, Walsh added, "When're you going to clear the Dean thing?"

"The lawyers have it."

Walsh nodded. "Lawyers." He motioned at a uniformed flunky in his shadow and the flunky whipped out a brass ashtray, borrowed from Story's study (removed without authorization, if you wanted to get technical, from the crime scene). Walsh ground his butt out in it as if it were some lawyer's eye, and brushed the ash from his fingertips. "Then since you're not jammed up, Sergeant, do what I already told Captain Maslosky to tell you to do: keep an eye on Vera Evans, make sure the press isn't all over her, and the autograph crazies, make sure no copycats try and polish *her*. You probably knew her too, right, her being Story's kid sister?"

"Right . . . Sir."

"It'll be like old times for you then." And Walsh looked at

his watch, a watch with a face and numbers and hands, and made, predictably, of steel, and went away.

So, at 4:33.46, Cullen tried Amato, because whatever time it was it could never be like old times.

"How sorry I was, Sergeant, to learn that the PC was an old friend of yours. You have my deepest sympathy."

Cullen also had Amato's arm around his shoulders. Some were unnerved by Amato's roving hands (he'd gone to Notre Dame, for christ's sake, and been a Jesuit postulant; his nickname—he was roly-poly and tonsured by baldness—was Friar Tuck), but Cullen, a recovering ladies' man, recognized a fellow heterosexual. "I don't want to mislead you, Chief. I've already spoken to Captain Maslosky and Chief Walsh, and I've been told to follow orders."

"Then follow them you should, Sergeant." Amato let Cullen go and clasped his hands together abbatially.

"—but I feel I can input in more useful ways." *Input?* Cullen never said *input*. His partner, Neil Zimmerman, a late-model New Age cop, overcooked in the ovens of Modern Criminology, basted with sociologese and high-tech doubletalk, said *input*. *Input* and *impact* and *outreach* and *interface* and *greenlight*—all verbs, as was Cullen's personal favorite, *odometerize* ("It's six-tenths of a mile shorter to take Queens Boulevard to your house. I odometerized it").

"I understand, Sergeant, that you're upset. You want to be everywhere at once, do everything, you wind up feeling like you're nowhere, doing nothing." Amato's hand was on Cullen's elbow now, and he was guiding him toward the front door like a guest who'd overstayed. "A cop killing's always a delicate matter, and when it's the PC, well. . . . Chief Walsh sees it as the violent death of an officer in the line of duty, and feels as Chief of Department that it's in his bailiwick. To me—and it doesn't mean I don't feel the personal and fraternal loss—to me, it's plainly and simply a matter for the Detective Bureau. Ruth and Maslosky, they both want a piece of it." Powell Ruth headed the Homicide Bureau, Maslosky IAU; Amato was Ruth's rabbi, Walsh Maslosky's—it was terribly complicated.

"Someone like you, Sergeant"—Amato didn't say, didn't

have to, what Walsh hadn't said either, hadn't had to, that Hriniak, the First Dep, the man most likely to succeed Story, at least for the moment, was Cullen's rabbi—"Someone like you, well, he's got to fit in where he fits in, he's got to move with the flow, so that in the end. . . ." Amato had risen in the Department by letting sentences just slip away; he was impossible to pin down; when the buck was passed back to him, he was long gone. ("Getting a handle on Amato," Hriniak had said once over Dabs at a place in Yorkville, "is like trying to cuff a snake.")

"Oh, and by the way, Sergeant—any closer to clearing the Dean thing?"

"No, sir. The lawyers have it."

"Ah, yes. Well. . . ."

"Uh. . . ."

"Yes, Sergeant?"

But Cullen couldn't think what he'd been about to say. Amato worked on you that way; he lulled you, until you started drifting too, through smoke and fog.

"Well, then. . . ."

". . . Yes, sir."

# 4

"I had a root canal once that was more fun than this," Phil Hriniak said.

It was 4:47.19 . . . 20 . . . 21. Hriniak had survived being tossed by Mayor Sidney Lyons to the insatiable shark the press becomes on stories like this—quote unquote *good* stories. The one-time beat patrolman (*Yum!* the reporters had cried, envisioning the headline: FROM STREET COP TO TOP COP), in a dark blue suit, snow white shirt, maroon tie, black wing tips, looked like a mayor; Mayor Lyons, in an Adidas T-shirt, Sergio Valente jeans (too blue, too new, the jeans of a man who hated to relax), red Pumas, looked like a cop trying to look like a civilian.

"You did good," Cullen said.

"I'm sorry, Joe, about your buddy."

Cullen shrugged. "When a cop gets polished, even a cop I don't know, I figure his career was probably a lot like mine and therefore that somewhere sometime he helped someone—someone lost, someone locked out, someone who had a wallet boosted or a cat up a tree or a breather on the phone; I figure he'd done some good. I don't know *what* kind of person Chuck Story was. I haven't spent more than a few minutes with him in years; we didn't have a falling out, we just drifted."

Hriniak sniffed. "Aren't you the guy who's been crying for reassignment, saying he's too broke up to work on this case?"

"Walsh wants me to babysit Vera."

"Sounds like a good idea."

"Phil, it's a terrible idea."

"Not so loud with the 'Phils,' okay?"

"Commissioner, it's a terrible idea."

Hriniak hauled on the knot of his tie and unbuttoned his collar. "What do you think happened here?"

"You mean other than what it looks like?"

"All right."

"I've been hanging around here since midnight with not much to do but be in the way," Cullen said.

"But you've been listening."

"And heard someone from Crime Scene say the piece was a nine-millimeter Glock. A serious piece. Could mean a contract hit—the mutilation to throw us off."

"A contract put out by?"

"Someone who didn't like Story."

"Not a small group. A group that'd fill at least the Garden."

"At least. Maybe Shea."

Hriniak wrinkled his nose. "Any other ideas?"

Cullen shrugged. "There've been these assaults on homeless people."

"What about them?"

"Well, some people've been saying we should be doing more to protect them. We, the cops."

"Would those be the same people who said we should've done more to get the homeless off the streets and into shelters in the winter—we, the cops—or would they be the people who complained about all the overtime we charged the city for playing nursemaid—we the cops?"

"It's an imperfect world," Cullen said.

"So you think one of the assault victims or one of the people who thinks we should be doing more to prevent the assaults—we, the cops—got a Glock and polished Story?"

Cullen didn't bother to shake his head. Victims and their advocates rarely retaliated.

Hriniak watched a Crime Scene photographer setting up a tripod to take pictures of the defaced wall. "When people say 'the handwriting on the wall,' what're they talking about?"

"It's from the Bible. Belshazzar, the king of Babylon, threw a party and served the wine in gold and silver goblets taken from the temple. A disembodied hand wrote on a wall the words 'numbered, numbered, weighed, divided.' Daniel, a free-lance specialist in such things, was brought in to interpret. He said taking the goblets was a felony and that the message meant Belshazzar's time was up. That same night, Belshazzar was killed in a coup by the king of Persia, who later, on another matter, threw Daniel in the lion's den."

"I knew you'd know that, but how the *hell* do you know it?"

"I looked it up."

"Hanging around here with not much to do but be in the way?"

"At home, waiting for Zimmerman to pick me up. My car died."

"Where is Zimmerman?"

"He went to get something to eat." A power snack—sun-dried tomatoes and mozzarella, probably.

Hriniak said, "Have you heard on the street that the Raleigh was torched?"

"I haven't been on the street. I've been on the Dean thing. I read in the paper that Patrol said the fire started in a part of the basement the survivors say no one was squatting in."

"Did you read too that the owner of record's just a post office box, a front?"

"Not a first for New York real estate."

"Seen Tom Valentine lately?" Hriniak said.

Cullen leaned away a little from the implications of the question. "No."

"Thought you were pals—you, Valentine, Story. Went to high school together."

"And junior high."

"See what I mean?"

"And grammar school. But I still haven't seen Valentine lately."

"You know whether you've seen him or not, Joe, because you're a guy who looks things up and reads the papers that the social worker who died in the Raleigh was Valentine's old lady."

Cullen just waited.

"Don't you?" Hriniak said.

"Joy Griffith," Cullen said, to say something.

"You sure? I thought it was Joyce."

"Phil, what the fuck?"

"Keep your voice down, *Ser*geant," Hriniak said.

Cullen muttered: "What the fuck, Com*miss*ioner?"

Hriniak put his face close to Cullen's. "What the fuck? I'll tell you what the fuck. Valentine's old lady buys it in a fire at the Raleigh, of which nobody knows the owner. Story didn't give his real estate holdings to some charity when he was named PC; he put it in a trust. Story gets polished by someone who writes Raleigh on his wall, I say, 'Holy shit—maybe Story owned the Raleigh, had it torched.' That's what the fuck."

Hriniak had said all that in one breath and now took a deep one. "Let me remind you of some other recent events: after Patrol said the fire started, like you just said, in a part of the basement no one was squatting in, Valentine went Downtown with a bunch of homeless people and tried to get in to see Story and ask him to conduct a separate investigation. Story sent out a messenger—me—to say he wouldn't second-guess Patrol. Some of Valentine's people sat down in the lobby, the rest took off for the Brooklyn Bridge, stopped traffic, the usual. We busted them and some heads got busted too. It happens. You going to tell me the first thing you thought when you heard about the writing on the wall, be*fore* you looked it up, wasn't: Tom Valentine?"

Cullen breathed in and out through his nose.

"Are you?"

"No."

Hriniak flexed his shoulders like an athlete who's just scored a ten. He looked at his watch, a more expensive version of Maslosky's, suited to his rank, but still a watch with a face and numbers and hands, not displays and buttons and beeps. Cullen's computer nerd daughter had showed him how to set his watch to beep every hour on the hour, then showed him how to unset it so it wouldn't. While hanging around here with not much to do but be in the way, he'd set it to beep, but he couldn't remember how to unset it. In a little while, it was going to beep and guys who'd been wondering how come was Cullen from IAU so tight with the new PC were going to wonder how come did Cullen from IAU have to know what time it was every hour on the hour. "When does Vera get in?" Hriniak said.

Not *Vera*. Please not *Vera*. People weren't going to start *Vera*-ing him, were they? "Seven or so." Six fifty-nine, fifty-nine. "A charter."

"From LA."

"I guess. 'The Coast.' "

"Think she'll remember me? *One-horse* doesn't begin to describe the kind of world it is, does it? I know her because you were her brother's friend, I end up in her brother's shoes."

"Phil, please get me reassigned."

"Guys'd kill to babysit a movie star, Joe."

"Sell their mothers, Maslosky said."

"I wish people *would* sell their mothers. We could control it, surveill it; they'd have to move the merchandise, feed them, buy mahjong sets for them to play. Instead, they polish people, chop their fingers off, write on walls. . . . When're you going to clear the Dean thing?"

"Everyone's asking me that. It's everyone's favorite case."

"Of course it is. It's got sex, it's got violence, it's got a briefcase full of confidential documents."

"The lawyers have it. We'll all be dead before it's cleared. Phil, I'll sell my mother if you *don't* reassign me."

"My first directive as PC can't be pulling a cop off a bodyguard assignment just because the body happens to be his ex-girlfriend's. It's Walsh's call; I've got to go with it and so do you."

"You know she was never my girlfriend," Cullen said. "It didn't work out."

"Then what's your problem?" And Hriniak buttoned his collar and tightened his tie and walked away.

"Why you?" Ann Jones said, at 5:24.7 . . . 8 . . . 9.

"What do you mean?" Cullen said.

She twitched impatiently. "Ask a man something point-blank and he's guaranteed to beat around the bush. *Tootsie* was on HBO last night. It's the great American movie. There's a scene where Teri Garr comes to Dustin Hoffman's apartment to tell him he can't keep standing her up. He's in drag, so he jumps in the shower and yells, 'I can't come to the door. I'm in the shower. I've got soap in my eyes.' He finally lets her in, as himself, a towel around him, and says, 'Sandy, it was terrible. I was taking a shower and I got soap in my eyes.' She gives him the *best* look. It's a quintessential exchange: a woman saying 'I want you,' a man yelling, 'I've got soap in my eyes.' "

Cullen shifted around on the fender of the car they were using for bleachers, watching cops go in and out of 119. Ann was caffeined-up, and rolling.

"Whenever you talked about Story, you never said, 'my old buddy, Charlie.' I spent a month with him for my piece, and he never talked about you. I probably knew him better than you did. So why did you pull the job of babysitting his sister? Yes, I'm jealous. I wouldn't be normal if I weren't jealous of a movie star, especially one so . . . incandescent."

"I don't think of her as a movie star," Cullen said. "I think of her as Chuck Story's scrawny little kid sister."

"So you *do* think of her. . . . You called him Chuck? What did he call you? Joey?"

Cullen pointed down the block. "The guy in the yellow shirt is Tony Lippo, from Crime Scene."

"He did. He called you Joey, didn't he?"

"You should talk to Tony. You didn't hear it from me, but ask him if the killer left any messages. You know, graffiti."

Ann cocked her head.

"Graffit*o,* actually. Just one word. 'Raleigh.' "

Ann thought about it. "Tom Valentine. Your friend, Tom Valentine."

A theory that was attracting a crowd. "It doesn't make sense. The Raleigh fire wasn't arson, and even if it was arson, arson for what? Insurance money? To move the squatters out? Small-time. Story was big-time. Cheap. Story was not cheap."

"You just said you didn't know him all that well."

"I gave him the key to my house," Cullen said.

She flipped her hands helplessly. "You *what*?"

"When we were kids—Chuck and Tom and I. It was Chuck's idea. We exchanged keys, keys to our houses. Chuck lived in an apartment, Tom and I lived in houses, attached houses. We exchanged keys as a symbol of our . . . comradeship."

"Boyship," Ann said, then watched Cullen drifting into memory. "What?"

"Nothing."

"What, damn it?"

"At his wedding, Chuck's wedding, he gave me a key to his house—this house. It's in a drawer somewhere."

"Did he give one to Tom too?"

"If he did, it wouldn't mean Tom killed him. And it wouldn't mean Story had the Raleigh torched. I don't have to have known him well to know he had some integrity."

She touched his hand. "You're right, and I'm not trying to impugn your friend, but I spent a month with him, and I noticed one thing. I noticed that like a lot of men, he did one of two things when he got angry: he was silent or he raged."

Cullen got silent.

Ann hopped off the fender and stood in front of him. God, she looked good—a short-sleeved khaki bush jacket over a white cotton T-shirt with absolutely no words or pictures on it, khaki pants, leather huaraches, French braid, gap-toothed. (*Les dents du bonheur,* she called them, the teeth of happiness, after seeing a Channel 13 documentary that informed her she shared imperfect dentation with the likes of Cleopatra, the Wife of Bath, and Sandra Day O'Connor, as well as with the obvious, Lauren Hutton.) "So what did Story call you when you were kids?"

And smelled good too. "Do you always put on perfume when you go out to cover a murder?"

"Ysatis de Givenchy."

"I remember a Catullus poem from college about liking a woman's scent so much he wished he were *totum nasum*—all nose."

"What he wished—what all men wish—is that he were all cock. Did Story call you Joey?"

". . . Snake."

*"Snake?"* She said it so loudly that some cops and reporters and TV crewmen turned to look.

"We were kids."

"Snake Cullen." Ann laughed.

To keep her from telling anyone and everyone, Cullen said, "There's something new on the Dean thing. You didn't hear it from me, but the shooter left a briefcase in Dean's apartment."

"Really? How come you didn't tell me that before? You knew it, right?"

"I can't just hand you exclusives, Ann. People know we see each other."

"I hate that euphemism."

"People know we watch each other masturbate."

She actually blushed. "You *tell* people that?"

"The briefcase had confidential Department files in it."

"So the shooter *is* a cop."

"Not necessarily. There're civilian employees with access to those files.'' (Or as Zimmerman would put it, *had* put it: *Those files can be accessed by designated non-uniformed personnel.*)

''A quibble. It was someone in the Department, maybe someone high up, right?''

''You didn't hear it from me.''

''Files on what?''

''Maslosky won't let us see them.''

Ann found a piece of Trident in her pocket. She unwrapped it and put it in her mouth and got it going. ''How do you know the briefcase is the *shooter*'s briefcase?''

''Good point. We don't. We surmise it is, since it isn't Dean's.''

''I can print surmise.''

Cullen shrugged.

''Snake.''

''Don't call me that.''

''Weasel, then.'' She reached out to bat the word away. ''I'm sorry. I'm really sorry.''

Cullen put a hand in her pocket.

''Hey! Not here.''

''I want some gum.''

''I don't have any more.''

''Yes, you do.''

''Yes, I do.'' She took a piece out of the other pocket, unwrapped it, and put it in his mouth.

''Anyone who saw that will know we see each other,'' Cullen said.

Ann smiled and lightly touched him with the back of her hand.

He adjusted the collar of her bush jacket. ''I'm going to be busy for a while. I can't stick Zim and Bermúdez with all the overnights.''

''Guys'd probably kill their mothers for overnights with Vera Evans.''

''*Sell* their mothers is the metaphor of choice around here. I guess that's indicative of how you feel about your mother.''

''Or about Vera Evans.''

''Not a fan?''

''She's so . . . perfect.''

''To me, she's just Chuck Story's scrawny little kid sister.''

Ann touched Cullen's cheek. ''Is that why you shaved? The

reason I worry, Snake, is I used to be *my* brother's scrawny little kid sister, and look at me now.''

Two Crime Scene officers slung a rubber body bag out the door of 119 and into an ambulance.

''Ashes to ashes,'' Ann said. ''From son of a candy store owner to real estate tycoon to presidential timber to ashes.''

''Norman Podorhetz said the longest journey is the journey from Queens to Manhattan.''

''You're extravagantly overeducated. Can you get me an interview with Lise Story?''

''I hardly know her. I don't know her at all. I went to the wedding, but so did about a thousand others.''

''A thousand of their closest friends. Have you heard the rumors that Claire Langois has a cocaine jones, that that's why her tennis career flopped?''

''I didn't hear them, I read them in *City*.''

''*Touché*.''

Cullen lifted his chin at a ruckus down the block. ''Walsh is going to make a statement. You better go down there.''

Ann watched half a dozen young women with perfect hair and perfect clothes, each with a cameraman, soundman, and lighting man in tow, elbowing for position. ''Cappy and Tippy and Mopsy and Suzie, the yuppie newshounds. Newsbitches. And look who's with Walsh. Leah Levitt. *All* my favorite people're here.''

# 5

''God. Leah.''

Though she had the lights out and couldn't be seen, Mabel Parker yanked back from the window of apartment 5-C, 116 East Seventy-first Street, the *paradis* of the theater whose stage was the rear of 119 East Seventieth.

Sirens, the cackle of shortwave radios, the pulsing lights of bar flashers—all louder and brighter somehow, for being tucked down in the crevice of the next block—had awakened Mabel around midnight. She had dozed for a while—until twelve-thirty-two by the digital clock by the bed—until it was clear that whatever was going on wasn't going to be over any time soon. She got up and had a Carlton, and then another and another, and watched the show.

The performers were in the wings more often than not; Mabel never heard more than a few words at a time, and none of them illuminating; but when she saw through various windows at various times several major, major stars, she turned the clock radio to CBS to find out what was going on. Once she knew, she was captive. Even by the window, it was so hot hot hot that she hadn't put on even a T-shirt.

It had been years since Mabel saw *Rear Window,* and she remembered it imperfectly, but she was sure that the apartment opposite Jimmy Stewart's (Jimmy Stewart's, or Cary Grant's?), the murderer's apartment, had been much closer—closer, that is, than 119 was to 116, as she and Norman had begun to call this place after the Story townhouse began to be referred to so often in the newspapers by *its* address. Much closer because 116 had a kind of courtyard behind it (*courtyard* was too grand a name; it was a patch of cement) that adjoined the backyard of

119 (for which *backyard* was a name not grand enough, a swatch of velvety green grass with French trelliswork on the walls, teak lawn furniture—tables, chairs, Chippendale bench; an Italian market umbrella, tiered étagères, stone urn and trough planters and terra cotta pots; a glazed stone birdbath placed fancifully beneath a redwood foot bridge; a copper fountain, a blue-and-gold striped marquee. Six days a week, an oriental gardener coaxed and trimmed and babied the grass and shrubs and herbs and flowers with tools that gleamed like surgical instruments).

Or was the murderer's apartment closer to Jimmy Stewart's apartment only because Jimmy Stewart (Jimmy Stewart?) spied on it using a telephoto camera lens? (Jimmy Stewart or Cary Grant, Mabel remembered that he'd played a photographer.) Mabel wished she had a telephoto lens, but there was only the Pentax with the wide-angle lens, for Norman wasn't into telephoto shots, he was into closeups, big closeups.

There *was* the video camera with a zoom lens, but Mabel didn't want to move it from its place by the bed for fear that Norman might notice and holler at her. Not *might, would:* Norman noticed if she moved the magazines on the coffee table or tuned the radio to something other than jazz or put the toothpaste back in the left side of the medicine cabinet instead of the right side or ate jelly beans from the dish on top of the television or took a matchbook from the goblet on the window sill—noticed and commented, demanded an explanation, speculated on how an intelligent human being could do such a thing, wondered whether the *loving* thing wouldn't be to replace or replenish the item in question or return it to its proper place or leave it alone in the first place. Noticed and nagged.

Nag was what Norman said his wife did, which was why he was having an affair with Mabel, why he had gone to the trouble and expense of renting an apartment for them to have it in. The trouble and the expense and the risk (Norman was in arbitrage, and knew about risk), for in order that they might maximally optimize (Norman's phrase) their time together, their trysting place was in a building only four blocks from the building where Norman lived with his wife. (That building was a Park Avenue dowager; 116, analagously, was a widow in a cloth coat: the doorman doubled as porter, there was no elevator operator, the tenants were either fledglings still on the first few rungs of life's ladder or old farts who—acrophobes—had gratefully clambered off at middle management—in short, not people, though technically neighbors, Norman had to worry would spot him in the elevator and say, "Norm? Norm, buddy. How's the wife?") But Mabel often wondered if perhaps Norman weren't the nag, the critic, the second-guesser, the backseat driver, the kamikaze amazon ballbreaker—all the things he called his wife.

For instance, if Norman were there now, he'd be on her case for not minding her own business, for risking catching cold (*cold*—in this weather?), for exposing herself to peeping toms with nightsights or something ridiculous, something Norman. Norman, of course, wasn't there: he had gone home, as always, just when she would have liked to do it again; making a big deal, as always, out of removing the cassette from the video camera; putting the cassette in his Mädler leather portfolio along with the riding crop and the handcuffs and the starter's pistol (he claimed he watched the tapes at home while his wife slept beside him, but Mabel didn't believe him); pretending—this was getting tiresome, he did it so often—pretending first that he'd forgotten that she was still tied to the bed with the leather straps, then pretending that he was going to leave her that way.

But what would Norman do—it was fascinating to speculate on what a *risk* arbitrageur would do—what would he do if he knew what she'd seen some hours earlier while standing at the window waiting for him to arrive, smoking a Carlton, sipping an Amaretto (Amaretto di Mabel), wearing nothing but black patent leather heels with velvet bows and a black stretch lace body stocking, touching herself from time to time through the handy crotch opening just to get things warmed up?

It was just dark, but the hot dull clouds that lay like a hot dirty tarp over the city all weekend made it darker. The few townhouses on East Seventieth Street that had lights on had the spurious look of empty places whose switches had been thrown by automatic timers, or by servants who had then gone back below stairs; their occupants weren't the sort to spend even a cloudy rainy three-day weekend in town when they could spend it by the sea.

Mabel had been invited to the beach, to the house in Lonelyville, on Fire Island, of her former therapist, who had become, inexplicably, a good friend; to her parents' house in Jamesport; to her sister's (and her sister's husband's and their four children's and their three dogs' and their turtle's and guinea pig's and garter snake's) house in Sayville. She passed on all of them because Norman wasn't going out to Sag Harbor because his wife had a deadline to meet on the manuscript of her book about what an incredible woman she was.

What Mabel saw—or who—was a woman. A tallish, thinnish woman in a long tan lightweight raincoat and a soft-brimmed brown hat; white pants—painter's pants, or jeans; blue shoes—espadrilles, they looked like from this distance. The woman came out the back door of 119, which was up a short flight of wooden steps from the backyard and opened on a small porch that from this distance looked to be a kind of mud room for boots and old coats and the like, locked the door and went down the steps and crossed the yard and disappeared. She reappeared a moment later in the courtyard/patch of cement behind 116, went along the fence enclosing the courtyard, and disappeared again. It had taken Mabel a moment to get the screen up—Norman liked long fingernails and they made it difficult to prize the damn thing open—and when she had the woman was gone, but she had to have gone into a passageway that Mabel hadn't known was there, a passageway that probably led to a gate or door to the street.

A burglar, Mabel had thought. Then she'd thought: she wasn't carrying anything; her hands were in the pockets of her raincoat. Then thought: a jewel thief, the kind who knows exactly what he's looking for—*she's* looking for—and takes it and gets out. Then thought: the key, she had a key. She's a servant, a maid, a cleaning woman, a cook; she finished her work—she came in to clean or cook before the family returned from their weekend in the Hamptons or on the Vineyard or the Cape—and she took a shortcut to get to the subway at Seventy-fifth and Lex or her bus stop on Lex or Madison or Fifth.

Before Mabel could think anything else (could think, as she was thinking now, that that was no cook, that was a woman with style, a woman who looked after her figure, a woman who knew how to move), Norman knocked his usual dum dadum dum dum knock. And as usual, Mabel pretended she didn't know who it was and opened the door on the chain and there was Norman pretending to be a detective who wanted to ask her some questions about a murder in the building. Mabel let him in and he asked if she minded if he videotaped the interview and she said no and sat in the morris chair and draped one leg up over the arm while he set up the camera and got some things out of his portfolio. She asked if that was a riding crop he had and he said it was and she asked if he was a *mounted* policeman and he grinned and said only when he was off-duty. She asked if she could touch the riding crop and he said of course and she took it from him and lightly but not *too* lightly flicked at the back of one of his hands with it and he took the handcuffs and the starter's pistol out of the portfolio and said if she weren't careful he'd cuff her. Mabel knocked the pistol from his hand with the crop and lept on it before he could and pointed it at him and told him to cuff his own hands behind his back, threading the chain of the cuffs through the wrought-iron railing at one end of the sunken living room. Then she sat back down in the morris chair and draped a leg over each arm and slowly, slowly, slowly, taking ten or fifteen minutes sometimes, worked the handle of the riding crop up inside her through the handy crotch opening. As usual.

Knowing what she knew from listening to CBS, Mabel had more than the average citizen's obligation to report to the authorities that she'd seen someone furtive leaving the scene of a crime, for Mabel was an officer of the court, an assistant district attorney in the office of the New York County District Attorney. It was because she was an officer of the court that she recognized even from this distance some people the average citizen might not have: First Deputy Police Commissioner (now Acting Commissioner, according to CBS) Philip Hriniak, Chief of Department John Walsh, Chief of Detectives Anthony Amato, Captains Powell Ruth of Homicide and Richie Maslosky of IAU and a whole bunch of other cops she knew either by their first names or their last but not both:

Fast and Caldwell and Pietro and Janiak and Cullen and Zimmerman and Chonin and Nichols and Lippo and Glatter and Cassidy and Lorber and Schnurnberger and Feldbauer and Jansen and Sennish and Albert and Dutton and Banta and Bob and Tim and another Bob and Elvis and Lucy and Ty and Noel and Pigpen and Jim and Christine and Whitey and Mick and Nancy and a*nother* Bob and Jeffrey (not Jeff) and James (not Jim) and William (not Bill) and Amal.

Mabel recognized Mayor Sidney Lyons, of course, when he showed up at 119. She could hear his voice right now, coming out of the radio: ''*I can look you in the eye and say that Charles Story was the finest Police Commissioner this colossus among cities has ever been privileged to have . . .*'' And, of course, she recognized her boss, New York County District Attorney Levitt.

Leah Levitt.

Norman's wife.

# 6

At 6:03.53 . . . 54 . . . 55, the day was heatstruck already. ''Swing down through the park,'' Cullen said. ''We have time.''

''*Down* through the park?'' Zimmerman said.

''I want to have a look at the Raleigh.''

''You want to tell me what you're thinking?''

Six oh four.

''Joe?''

''Yeah?''

''You want to tell me what you're thinking?''

''Drive, Neil.''

Zimmerman drove. He turned the radio up louder: Sade. Lionel Richie, Billy Joel, now Sade. Next Chicago, probably; then Genesis, then Yes. Then Joe Cullen would become the first cop in the history of the Department to polish his partner for listening to Lite-FM.

The rule was, the driver got to pick the radio station. Cullen thought it a good rule (he'd formulated it), because he did most of the driving. Zimmerman wasn't comfortable with the Gran Furys from the motor pool, which was what they mostly used, or with Cullen's Reliant (they were nominal cars, he contended, in the way that, oh, shoes that weren't Weejuns or Top Siders or Reeboks were just shoes), and when he deigned to use his Saab Turbo 900 on a job (Cullen could forget about driving *it*), rather than take the Blaupunkt out of the trunk and lock it up and take it out and lock it up, Zimmerman preferred to listen through headphones to his Aiwa or his Sony Discman (Suzanne Vega or Nanci Griffith. Nanci Griffith, Jesus: Yuppie country music for people who'd never heard of Patsy Kline or Reba McIntire or Tanya Tucker). Cullen would slip on the phones of his credit-card-sized FM radio, nine dollars at a going-out-of-business place on Fifth Avenue, and listen to K-Rock or NEW or Country 103.

But hanging around outside 119 with nothing much to do but be in the way, Zimmerman had taken out the Blaupunkt to listen to WFAN, guys named Vinnie and Irv (and the occasional woman named Jewel or Fran) reaching out through the dark from Yonkers and Lodi and Ozone Park to play dueling clichés ("He not only strokes the pill, he's a magician with the glove, and he's got a rifle for an arm." "They got a pesky ball club that on a given day can hurt you in a lot of ways. To be a real contender, they need someone who can throw some bones in the paint.") with the overnight host ("I'm Steve, you're you")—justification, any sober judge would have agreed, for homicide, and *then,* when Steve signed off at five-thirty, Zimmerman had switched to soft rock.

"Sorry, Neil," Cullen said.

"Yeah."

"I'm a little tired."

"Yeah."

"One old friend killing another—if that's what happened—it's . . . it's tiring."

Zimmerman nodded. "But that's not what's on your mind."

Cullen was saved from having to go through the motions of telling Zimmerman not to tell *him* what was on *his* mind, thanks, by their arrival at the crisp black carapace that was what had been the Raleigh apartments. The sun, obtusely angled and coming from the rear, lighted up all the empty windows a splendid gold; little golden tornadoes of dust and ash swirled prettily on currents and downdrafts, unimpeded by things like floors and ceilings. If the Raleigh had looked like its neighbors—drab, dour, their windows wide open and thirsting for a breeze but blinded by yellowed ripped shades—then it looked better than it had.

Maybe that was why it had some . . . some occupants, if that was the word for people who had set up housekeeping in a place with only walls and barely those. A family, they looked like—mom and dad and little Suzie and Tiny Tim, his left leg, weighed down by a sorry-looking cast, dragging behind him as he hobbled through the rubble in a game of something-or-other with his sister.

"Jesus," Zimmerman said.

Cullen got out of the car, taking the heat full on the chest as if something like a safe had fallen on him from a very great height. He crossed the street and scuffed into what had been the Raleigh's lobby as if he weren't terrified that the whole place was going to come tumbling down around him.

"Howdy," the man said.

It was the first time in his life anyone had ever said howdy to him, but Cullen said howdy back without a blink. "You're not from around here." They had faces out of a Walker Evans photograph, narrow and wary.

"Miami." The man slumped as if caught in a lie. "Well, Eustis. Up 'bove 'rlando. But we come by way'f Miami."

Cullen saw the woman's lips move and thought she said, "Useless," and took that to be her variation on the name of their home town. "This neighborhood. . . . Well, it's mostly blacks and Hispanics. White people. . . ." He just shrugged. How to explain *his* home town's shortcomings.

Tiny Tim stepped front and center. He was awaiting new front teeth and lisped as well as drawled. "White folkths buthted my laig."

"Uh hunh. I'm, uh, sorry," Cullen said.

"College boys," the man said. "Kind of a game they play down in Miami. Drive 'round town busting up the homeless, setting their lean-tos afire. Thought you might be a couple for a minute there. Same kind of car they drive."

"I'm sure it is," Cullen said.

"You're a cop, ain't you," the man said. "Only a cop'd walk around here without being afeared."

*Oh, I'm afeared.* "How'd you wind up here? How'd you wind up in New York and how'd you wind up"—Cullen gestured around the war zone—"here?"

He was sorry he'd asked. They'd wound up in New York because a nice feller in Miami had offered the man gas money if he'd drive his van to New York and deliver it to another feller who'd pay him two thousand dollars and give him some kind of steady work. All the second feller had done was point a large handgun at his face and drive off with what even these innocents correctly concluded was a van full of narcotics. They'd wound up *here* because a nice feller in the Port of Authority bus station had taken what was left of the gas money in exchange for the address of a clean, cheap hotel.

Cullen gave the man ten dollars and wished him luck. He forbore telling him to steer clear of nice fellers, and that it wasn't only the likes of fraternity boys he should be wary of here in New York, it was the likes of junk bond traders, a couple of whom had been accused the other day of beating a homeless man near the South Street Seaport with squash rackets. He got back in the car and told Zimmerman they were going to be late, goddamn it.

"Do I want to know what went on back there?" Zimmerman said.

"No."

"Which means you can tell me what's on your mind."

Cullen didn't pretend he didn't know what Zimmerman was talking about. "Vera and I went out a few times a few hundred years ago. We went Dutch so I'm not sure if *dates* was what they were, if we had a friendship or a relationship—and anyway, the word relationship hadn't been invented yet. I was in college, working nights and weekends in a record store on Broadway just north of Times Square. That's where I met Hriniak: he was walking a beat in Midtown North and would stop by on his meal break to look at jazz records. He's a buff.

"She was Vera Story then, taking classes at The Actors Studio. She wanted sheet music for *Bye Bye Birdie*. It'd been only a couple of years since we'd seen each other, but they were the years between gawky and grownup—especially in her case; I barely recognized my buddy's kid sister, she barely recognized one of her brother's asshole friends. We talked, we had coffee, we took a walk, we went to some plays and lots of movies—musicals, dozens of musicals, at Theatre 80 St. Marks. We saw a ballgame—Yanks and Detroit, I don't know why I remember that; someone stole home, I don't remember who—we took more walks, we saw more movies, we drank more coffee, lots more."

Zimmerman waited, but that was it. "And then?"

"And then she moved to California, got married, got famous.

And I got flat feet.'' And got married. And *be*got children. And got restless. And got divorced.

''Why do I think you're leaving something out?''

''Not sex, if that's what you mean. We didn't sleep together. People often didn't, in those days. You probably can't imagine that. It wasn't morality that kept us virgins—or me, anyway; it was fear. Fear of pregnancy, fear of responsibility. Fear of the earth's moving—which we'd been both promised *and* warned might happen.''

Zimmerman didn't ask by whom. Despite his taste for music with no balls (his idea of raunchy was Fleetwood Mac and 10,000 Maniacs), for shmoozing sports, he had read some books. ''The guy she married was a director, yes?''

''Caleb Evans. He and Robert Altman were of a kind twenty years ago. He died two or three years ago.''

''And the marriage didn't last long, did it?''

''What's long?''

There was the usual inexplicable tie-up, too early and in the wrong direction, on the Triborough, and they speculated about that until they were well onto the Grand Central on the way to La Guardia. Then Zimmerman said, ''Speaking of the earth's moving, Amato asked me when we were going to clear the Dean thing.''

''He asked me too,'' Cullen said. ''So did Pavonelli.''

''Pavonelli? Pavonelli's a gun nut. That fits with the shooting range.''

''Walsh and Hriniak and Maslosky and Ruth asked too. And Nixon and Paltz and Kean. And Winerib. All the brass around.''

''The Dean thing,'' Zimmerman said.

Cullen agreed: ''The Dean thing.''

The Dean thing, though only three weeks old and far from being cleared, had partisans who thought it quite possibly the best case in the history of the Internal Affairs Unit, which had a long history of good cases:

Cops responding to neighbors' complaints about a domestic altercation on Prospect Place off Flatbush Avenue in Park Slope found themselves at the ajar door of a rookie cop, Officer Deborah Dean of the Two-Three, the granddaughter, daughter, sister, niece and cousin of cops. Deborah was flat on her back on a futon in the bedroom, wearing nothing but beige Chanel knockoff slingback pumps with black patent toes, lapis earrings, and a dab of Giorgio; she was bleeding from a bullet wound in her left shoulder.

Matching silk kimonos, a box of Koromex condoms, a bottle of medium-price California wine and two Pottery Barn tulip glasses, and a dildo from a shop called Come One Come All—you get the picture.

In his haste to leave before the cops (*more* cops) arrived, Deborah's lover-turned-assailant forgot his briefcase, an Atlas, one of a trillion like it, traceable only up to a point by its maker's markings but rendered very distinctive by its contents—confidential Police Department documents for the eyes only of only fifty-odd civilian employees. ("Correct me if I'm wrong," Richie Maslosky had said, "but this is like *lit*erally an internal affair." Cullen had said, "You're not wrong.")

Also in the briefcase, the only other tangible clue, was a brochure from an indoor shooting range in darkest New Jersey where customers could rent Uzis, grease guns, machineguns, machine pistols, Bren 10s, .45s, .38s, 9s—derringers, probably, if they were diffident—and shoot anything they cared to, as long as it wasn't animate and fit through the doors.

("Son," the owner of the range told Cullen on the phone when he asked if any of his customers were New York City cops, "I've got twenty-two galleries open twenty-four hours, seven days, fifty-two weeks. You get here after noon on a weekend, you got to park in the next county. What you notice about the folks that come in here ain't who they are but what they haul in with them, mostly stuff they bought and couldn't figure out how to make it work or it broke when they did: computers, VCRs, stereos, microwaves, TVs, toaster ovens, electric grills, compact disk players, fax machines, copiers, electronic typewriters, chain saws, lawn mowers, snowmobiles. Manuals and instruction books are a popular item. You're welcome to come down here, son, and see if there's anybody you recognize. And bring along something's got your dander up. Just remember—no wives, no large vee-hickles.")

Not surprisingly given that she was evidently outranked by her playmate, Deborah wouldn't finger him to the detectives who initially pulled the job; but the real fillip came when her attorney presented surgeons at Beekman Downtown, all gowned and gloved and ready to cut, with an order restraining them from extracting the bullet from his client's shoulder and handing it over to ballistics experts. The lawyer, Jimmy Freed, a civil libertarian's civil libertarian, had sold a judge his novel thesis that what the doctors were about to do would violate Deborah's rights guaranteed by the Fourth Amendment's prohibition against unreasonable search and seizure.

"In South Miami Beach, Florida," Freed had explained to Cullen and Zimmerman, "where my father, bless his ninety-three-year-old heart, once a member of the bar himself, now living a life of leisure, passes the time debating current political, historical and cultural events with fellow senior citizens, this is known as the No Vay Rule. There is no vay any judge would issue a warrant permitting a compelled surgical intrusion requiring general anesthesia absent a very, very, *very* strong showing of reasonable cause to believe the operation would produce evidence of a crime. And not *merely* evidence and not *merely* a crime. *Evidence* that is highly probative, important and substantial *and* that cannot be obtained in ways requiring less an intrusion of personal bodily integrity; a *crime* that is a very serious violation of the peace and dignity of the sovereign, so as to justify an operation to solve. No vay on the facts because there is no evidence that Deborah Dean was involved in any crime, no compelling need absent any other evidence that a crime was committed."

Mabel Parker, the assistant DA on the case because of the possible theft of confidential Department documents, shrugged and said, "Off the record? He's right."

"Isn't your client in pain?" Zimmerman said.

"What's a little pain," Freed said, "when you've got a chance to make jurisprudential history?"

And that was why the lawyers had the Dean thing, why they'd all be dead before it was cleared.

6:53.32 . . . 33 . . . 34. Eighty-seven degrees, eighty-five percent humidity, Wham on the radio, traffic inching as drivers going both ways gawked at a redhead in cutoffs and an undersized undershirt changing a tire on the median. Cullen's .38 hung heavy on his hip and he saw the headline:

COP GOES BERSERK
ON QUEENS PARKWAY

---

Opens fire on partner,
rubberneckers, radio.

---

Claims heat, wrist alarm
"Made me do it."

Zimmerman said, "Okay to brainstorm?"

Cullen would frequently have killed him for saying *brainstorm,* but this time he smiled and said sure and turned the radio off.

"Dean made a call from her apartment to Downtown almost every Tuesday for six months," Zimmerman said. "Freed'll try to make them look work-related, but we know Dean's work-related calls from home were to the Two-Three exclusively. The Tuesday calls were to confirm her Wednesday matinees. She was shot on a Wednesday, the neighbors remembered other arguments on other Wednesdays, Wednesday was someone's D-for-Doing-Dean Day.

"My thought is, we run Downtown's MUDS to see if there were frequent calls, occasional calls, *any* calls to Dean's apartment. The caller's our man."

6:56 . . . 57 . . . 58 . . . 59. Cullen covered his wrist to muffle the beep. "Downtown's a switchboard—a PBX or Centrex or whatever they're called. Are MUDS from a switchboard broken down by extension or is there just one list of calls from the main number? And however they're listed, did our man always use the same phone? If he works in a bullpen, he wouldn't talk openly, he'd use a phone someplace out of the way. If he had an office, he might not've wanted to risk a secretary or a clerk eavesdropping. There're pay phones on just about every floor; he might've used one of those. And who says he called Deborah at all?"

Zimmerman shrugged. "Just a thought."

"It's a good thought, but we have to refine it a little. To pull Downtown's MUDS we'd have to get an okay from at least Amato, who's not likely to approve quite so wild a goose chase."

''Especially since he's one of the geese.''

''Whoever the goose is, without the bullet in Deborah we can't subpoena his firearm, and anyway why bother, because for an absolute certainty whoever shot Deborah has by now ditched the piece. The score's going to be Dean Thing one, Us nothing.''

They pictured that for a while. Then Zimmerman said, ''So who polished Story? And why?''

Cullen said, ''Bob Grant, the *Post,* Morton Downey, Ed Koch when he was mayor telling people to 'just say no' to panhandlers, you and I because we do say no more than we say yes. That little kid back at the Raleigh had his leg broken by some joy-riding college kids; a prank gone out of control, but part of the backlash. People're fed up with it. They're fed up with drug pushers too, but drug pushers're dangerous. The homeless are harmless, so we're not afraid to let them know we hate them. And our hatred foments theirs. Cutting off someone's finger and shoving it in his mouth—man, that's *anger,* anger I can't even conceive of, anger I can't comprehend.''

''Want to hear something I can't comprehend?'' Zimmerman said.

''No.'' For Cullen knew that what he didn't comprehend was why, having driven all the way out to La Guardia, having flashed his badge at a guard to get through a restricted gate, having spotted the charter airline's hangar and headed toward it, he had been asked by Cullen's hand on his arm to come to a stop a long way away from the silver Falcon floating on mirage water on the broiling tarmac.

As they watched, the Falcon's hatch opened, a gangway swung into place, a woman in a black veiled pillbox hat, black suit, black shoes, black bag, descended. She looked cool and collected—as though she hadn't just arrived to mourn her murdered brother, as though she'd arrived somewhere more forgiving of black clothing than here in central Africa.

A woman in a gray suit—Deputy Police Commissioner Susan Price, the Department flack, representing the Department and the Administration (and, Cullen supposed, sisterhood)—stepped forward to greet the woman in black with a handshake, then stepped back. The woman in black walked—six quick strides; Cullen counted them—to a black Benz Pullman, nodded to the liveried chauffeur who held the door, and slipped inside. The chauffeur closed the door, got behind the wheel, and followed after the deputy commissioner's Chrysler.

"Want me to drive?" Cullen said.

Zimmerman shook his head. "I'd like you to be straight with me."

"Ah. Straight."

"You're still in love with her, Joe."

Cullen turned on the Blaupunkt and trolled the dial until he found something suitable—a year and a half-old oldie: Billy Ocean—"Get Outta My Dreams, Get Into My Car."

# 7

The Benz shimmied, yawned, spun.

The front end came around and around and around until it faced the Saab.

Zimmerman hit the brake, confused, thinking the Benz was coming right at him.

The Benz receded and Zimmerman stared after it for a moment before stepping on the gas again. ''What the fuck?''

The Benz spun again. And spun. And spun. This time, as the front end came about once more, Cullen saw that the windshield on the driver's side was shattered.

The front end hit a Federal Express van in the fast lane. The rear end swung into the van's path and the van clipped it. The Benz swung all the way around and bucked onto the median and down a small gully and smashed into a light pole.

Zimmerman whooped the siren and Cullen got the flasher on the roof, but the traffic on the left wouldn't give way, couldn't give way, so Zimmerman pulled off to the right.

Cullen was out the door before the Saab fully stopped. He slipped and darted and skipped between cars, showing his gun to drivers to startle them into stopping. Many of them risked frying their brains to let him know what they thought of him, rolling down their windows and sticking out their heads and calling him a scumfuckingbagcocksuckingmotherfucker. They—and others—leaned on their horns as though the horn buttons were his face.

Cullen caught a toe in the thick grass and tumbled into the gully, heels over head. He was sure he would break his neck, and nearly cried out, *No, God, please. Let me start all over again. Let me do it right.*

He rolled to his feet as if he'd meant to do it that way all along. James Bond, Bruce Lee, Rambo—he came from a long line of superheroes.

He yanked open the Benz's left front door and the driver fell into his arms like a clown doing a pratfall.

The driver had raspberry jelly for a face.

Cullen propped the driver up with a shoulder and turned off the ignition. He eased the driver down on the seat and backed out and grappled with the left rear door.

It was locked.

"Vera!"

He ducked down into the front seat again and pounded on the smoked glass partition. "Vera!"

He searched the dash for the switch, the lever, the button, the whatever the fuck, to open the glass. He couldn't find it. What did he know about stretch Benzes?

"Vera!"

He ran around to the right side and tried the rear door.

"Vera!"

The window opened a hand's breadth. He saw a pair of eyes bright with fright, then saw nothing but black.

"Vera? Vera, it's Joe Cullen. Are you all right?"

"What happened?" A very tiny voice.

"Vera, are you all right?"

"The driver. . . . Is he . . . ?"

Shit. The driver.

Cullen went back around to the driver's side. Zimmerman had the driver on his back on the seat. A knee on the floorboards, Zimmerman put his mouth over the driver's, puffed, turned his cheek to inhale. His eyes met Cullen's and he shook his head.

Cullen went back to the right rear door. The window was closed. He tapped on the glass.

"Vera? . . . Vera!"

Someone grasped Cullen's shoulder.

He whirled, reaching for his gun.

"Easy, now." A woman in a gray suit.

"Come on, lady. Just stay the fuck—"

"Cullen, right? The Dean thing. What the hell happened?"

Even out here? At a time like this? Then he recognized Deputy Commissioner Susan Price, her driver at her shoulder, a .44 Magnum in his hand, quite a piece for Public Affairs.

"Sorry. There were shots. From an overpass, I think. That one there." He waved without looking toward something he wasn't entirely sure was there.

"You call it in?" Susan Price didn't wait for an answer. "Jack, call in a shots fired—"

"I called it in." It was Zimmerman, his shirtfront and his suit covered with blood, blood on his face, his forehead, his eyebrows, his lips.

Susan Price jerked a thumb at the Benz. "She all right?"

Cullen raised his shoulders and shook his head.

"Jesus, Cullen." Susan Price rapped a knuckle on the rear window. "Miss Evans? It's Susan Price. . . .

"Miss Evans? . . .

"Vera?"

The window opened, as if she'd said the password. Susan Price bent down to it. "You okay?"

Cullen couldn't hear the answer. Zimmerman had a hand on his shoulder and was pulling him away.

On the overpass, just east of Steinway Street in Astoria—the shooter, confident of his aim as well as privy to schedules and routings, had sprayed in red paint:

RALEIGH 2

# 8

"Water *can*nons?" Leah Levitt said.

Mayor Sidney Lyons wanted to put his head down on the table and weep. Why him? He calls a crisis meeting to deal with a crisis without precedent and people keep interrupting him, dulling the edge of his preemptive response. "Not *can*nons, Mrs. District Attorney. Did I say *can*nons? I didn't *mean* cannons. I meant those trucks the garbagemen spray the streets with, they have—"

"Uh, Sanitmen, your honor." Sanitation Commissioner Thomas Turco sat forward in his chair. "The uniformed personnel of the Sanitation Department are to be referred to as Sanitmen, the term garbagemen being considered of a pejorative nature."

Why him? He calls a little meeting to deal with a crisis without precedent (screw the City Council, he called together a few people, that's all, a manageable number; it's in the City Charter that he's allowed. Somewhere) and people read regulations at him. "Tommy, Tommy, Tommy, I can look you in the eye and say there is not a single member of your department I would not be proud to have as a guest in my own home, so forgive me, please, under the extraordinary circumstances, a momentary lapse."

Lyons beamed at Turco, then at Leah Levitt, fighting to keep his eyes from fastening on her breasts, her excellent breasts. (Why him? Why a wife whose breasts. . . . Well, never mind how far from excellent they were. And anyway, Sylvia, her breasts, and their daughters, the harridan virgin spinster freeloaders, had gone to Sylvia's mother's in Lake Hopatcong. Doctor's orders—the heat was hazardous to Sylvia's health: that was the explanation cooked up for the public. Because they were scared shitless was the stark reality. If it should get out that the captain's family had abandoned ship, fleeing to Jersey, yet, *oy*.) "Leah, look." Lyons got up and went around his desk and stood behind her chair, where he wasn't tempted by her breasts and where she couldn't see right through him, something she was forever doing, usually in front of witnesses, another reason he'd kept the gathering small. "There're times when a situation demands that you do things you wouldn't usually do, wouldn't you agree?"

Leah Levitt turned to face him: her glare said he mustn't patronize her by hovering over her. "Civil liberties are not seasonal."

Shit. Why the hell hadn't *he* said that—not here, not to her, but to his citizens, where and when it counted. *I can look you in the eye, my fellow New Yorkers, and promise you that as long as Sidney Lyons is mayor of this colossus among cities, civil liberties will* not *be seasonal.* He needed new speechwriters, visionaries not drudges.

After this morning, he might need a new identity.

He had only been trying to prove a point by telling Betsy Barclay of *Good Morning, New York* (why did all women television newspersons have alliterative names and why, if *Good Morning America* was called *GMA* and didn't have a comma, wasn't *Good Morning, New York* called *GMNY* and why did it have a comma?) that not everyone with his hand out had his head on straight and his heart in the right place.

"I can look you in the eye, Betsy," he had said, "and tell you that many individuals who ap*pear* to be homeless, who ap*pear* to be needy, who ap*pear* unkempt and unwashed and in rags, are in *fact* dissemblers, charlatans, impostors—greedy hustlers who take advantage of our credibility and our compassion. Healthy, aggressive, clever, these . . . these *crim*inals is what they are, Betsy, are depleting the public's limited reservoir of charity and reducing the *truly* downtrodden to even worse circumstances.

"I'm thinking of a woman, Betsy, about your age, which I won't be so unchivalrous as to speculate on, attractive—pretty, almost—who haunts—I don't think that's too strong a word; she has a ghostly mien—who haunts a street corner just outside the

Municipal Building across from City Hall. I see her two or three times a week sometimes, sometimes two or three times a day, whenever my schedule takes me away from the Hall and I'm driven in or out of the driveway entrance closest to the Municipal Building. What this woman does, Betsy, is weep. Stands stock still, an empty delicatessen coffee container held out in front of her, and weeps. I'm told, by my staff, by police officers, by municipal employees, that she weeps for hours at a time. I myself have never seen her when she *wasn't* weeping. And while she weeps, passersby fill that coffee container with money—not just dimes and quarters, Betsy, bills, dollar bills, five and ten dollar bills, sometimes *twen*ty dollar bills, anything to stanch the flow of tears, to help that poor woman cope with her miserable condition.

"And of course *noth*ing does help, because there is *noth*ing the woman needs helping *with*. She's healthy, she's well-dressed and well-groomed, as well she might be given that she's probably making, at a conservative estimate, fifty or sixty dollars an hour. That works out to something in the neighborhood of five hundred dollars a day, Betsy, two thousand five hundred dollars a week—that part of town is lightly trafficked on the weekends, and she appears to take those days off. She's certainly earned it. She probably goes shopping, for some more of her designer dresses—which is what I would wager they are, Betsy"—were he not so afraid of losing—"Is this the kind of individual you have in mind when you refer, as you just did, to the, uh, *Hope*less?"

Having perfectly timed the commercial break, then having been saved from Betsy's followup or rebuttal by the need, as the show ran out, for a recap of the killing of Vera Evans's chauffeur, Lyons had been driven downtown by his Police Department driver, down Seventh Avenue and Broadway to Canal, then over to Centre Street and down Centre to City Hall.

Past the Municipal Building.

And there she was.

Not weeping at all, just half-sitting, half-leaning against one of the columns supporting the archway that formed the Muni's entrance, sipping a cup of coffee, eating a roll or a donut or a bagel like any other municipal employee with a few minutes to kill before going to work.

Lyons was discomfited to see that she didn't look as good as he'd thought, didn't look quite as he'd just described her to the early morning television audience: she was gaunter, her dress was dirtier—and might very well have been the dress she'd worn the day before and the day before that and the day before that, her hair was more disheveled, her ankles more swollen, her face and arms more weathered than, were he not so afraid of losing, he would have wagered.

Still, she didn't look *bad,* didn't look anywhere near as awful as plenty of others like her he'd seen around town. He would bet, were he not so afraid of losing, he would bet a *lot* of money that that dress *did* have a designer label, and not a fake one either, the real thing—because he had some training in these matters, Sylvia and the harridan virgin spinster freeloaders dropped a grand a month easy on dresses, designer dresses. And not on Orchard Street either, or in Jersey, where there were outlets, where there was no sales tax on clothes. Oh sure, Sylvia and the harridan virgin spinster freeloaders could go to the mattresses in Jersey, but shopping? Forget it.

"Tony." Lyons had leaned forward and touched the shoulder of his driver, Police Officer Anthony Casales. "Tony, pull over here a minute."

"Here?"

"Right here, Tony, right here. It's okay. I'll just be a minute."

"Sir, you want me to, uh . . . ?"

"Just stay here, Tony. I'll be fine. I just want to see something."

Casales pulled over and Lyons got out and walked over to the woman—not directly, but zigzag, so as not to frighten her. "Good morning."

The woman shivered, as if it weren't already eighty-five degrees, and held her arms close together in front of her, elbows nearly touching. She had finished the roll or donut or bagel or whatever it was, but she still had the container of coffee. She was going to use it to hold all the scratch she made when she started her weeping act, wasn't she?

"How are you this morning. Hot enough for you?"

The woman's teeth began to click together. Her coffee, so milky it was almost white, began to slosh out of the container she held under her chin.

"You be careful now, dear. You're spilling coffee on that pretty dress of yours," Lyons said.

The clicking became chattering. More and more coffee leapt from the container onto her dress.

"Here, let me wipe that off." Lyons took the handkerchief from the breast pocket of his suit coat and stepped close to the woman. Her dress—he didn't know what it was called; Sylvia and the harridan virgin spinster freeloaders would know—had a top that kind of overlapped, sort of, that was held together by a belt and a button or a snap on the inside of the dress, kind of. Anyway, the belt was gone and the button or snap had come undone and he could see *in* rather than *down* her dress and she wasn't wearing a bra and her breast was white and firm, not veiny and floppy, like he'd expected, like Sylvia's. Lyons glanced over at the Chrysler; Casales, windows up in air-conditioned comfort, read *Newsday,* just another cop in a coop, oblivious to what was going on around him. "Let me wipe that off. I won't hurt you. It's such a pretty dress. You're a very pretty young lady. Let me wipe that off."

Lyons touched the dress over her breast with his handkerchief, then with his fingertips.

The woman threw the coffee in Lyons's face.

He slapped her.

She ran, stumbling back under the archway.

Lyons ran after her, mopping the coffee from his face with the handkerchief. He caught her by the arm and yanked her to a stop. "Let me see that dress."

The woman screamed.

Lyons got a sort of half nelson on her and grappled at her collar. "Let me see that *dress*."

The woman kicked back at him, hissing and grunting.

Lyons changed his grip, putting one arm around the woman's waist and holding her tight against him as he found the dress's label and tried to smooth it out to read it. It was dark in here under the archway and he couldn't have made it out even if she weren't struggling. "It's a de*sign*er dress, isn't it?"

The woman clawed at his arm.

"*Isn't* it?"

The woman howled.

"*Isn't* it!?"

The woman reached behind her and grabbed him by the balls and sqeezed.

Lyons shrieked and thrust the woman away. He still held on to the dress, though, and it came away in his hands, it came off her. She stood there naked, no underwear, just her shoes. Brown, low-heeled shoes. The sole of the left shoe flapped loose.

Lyons took a step toward her. "I'm sorry."

The woman backed away. Her stomach was distended, her thighs were blubbery, she was filthy and bruised and bitten and beaten. He didn't want to look at her. He didn't want to see her ever again in his life.

Lyons took another step. "I'm so sorry."

The woman turned and ran, one sole flapping, through another archway and back into deeper shadows.

Lyons didn't run after her.

He shook out the dress and folded it neatly and placed it on a ledge of one of the columns supporting the archway. He took out his wallet and took out a twenty, then another, then another, and folded the bills lengthwise and smoothed the dress's label and fitted the bills under it:

The label said *Jaclyn Smith for K mart*.

# 9

"Your Honor, there's a tactical problem here that may be insurmountable."

Hriniak. Who the hell asked him what he thought? Or *if* he thought? He wasn't going to be another Charles Story, was he, a thinker, an innovator, the inspiration for magazine cover stories, a goddamn fixture, just about, on Sunday TV talk shows—*network* talk shows, half the time—a guy who could wrench the spotlight at meetings like this away from the guy who'd called the goddamn meeting and bathe in it himself, without breaking a sweat? Where were all the yes men, the what-a-brilliant-idea-your-Honor-how-could-I-have-argued-with-you-when-it-was-so-clear-that-I-was-wrong-and-while-I'm-kissing-your-ass-may-I-please-also-lick-your-boots men?

"Plain and simple, and with all due respect to Commissioner Turco"—

Look at him! Bowing and scraping to the *Gar*bage Commissioner, but to the Mayor? Oh, no, not to the Mayor.

—"Commissioner Turco's Sanitmen and women don't carry guns."

*Guns?* Of course they don't carry *guns*. They're *gar*bagemen. And garbage*women*. *Gar*bagemen and garbage*women* don't carry *guns*.

"And I'm sure Paul Verona will raise a strong objection to having his men and women—again, Commissioner Turco, no offense—to having his men and women driving sanitation trucks."

Of *course* Paul Verona, ballbreaking head of the ballbreaking Patrolmen's Benevolent Association, will object to his men and women driving Sanitation trucks, his men and women are New

York's ballbreaking so-called Finest and sanitation trucks are garbage trucks.

"Furthermore, Your Honor, we don't know what kind of firepower these people have available to them," Hriniak went on. And on and on. "The chauffeur, Janofsky, was killed with a Winchester pump, not a weapon you run into often in urban situations and an indication, I think, that we're up against people with some imagination if not sophistication when it comes to firearms. Until we know more about them, Your Honor, I would have to recommend strongly against the strategy you're proposing."

He *is* just like Story. Making recommendations nobody asked for, thinking too much, thinking all the time, thinking period. Why, why, why, why him? "Look. Ladies and gentlemen. My friends. I feel that in these times of crisis I'm entitled to look you in the eye and call you my friends. We're meeting, my friends, to deal with a crisis without precedent in the history of the City of New York. The Police Commissioner has been killed, his body unspeakably mutilated, a heinous attack has been perpetrated on his sister, a public personality of international renown, both incidents part of a larger pattern of mindless violence carried out by a pack of two-legged rodents gnawing away at the underpinnings of the colossus among cities—"

"Mister Mayor." Leah Levitt was on her feet and straightening her skirt. "Forgive me, I have to be in court in a few minutes before a judge who doesn't like to be kept waiting. No one's disputing the gravity of the situation. I'm simply saying you don't have probable cause—even if you did have the facilities to detain them—to arrest every homeless person in town as a suspect or a material witness in either of these incidents, *and* you may not use Sanitation Department water wagons—or fire trucks, if that thought occurs to anyone—to flush those people out. For better or for worse, there are a substantial number of people living in our streets, our parks, our public places—people who until we do something to improve their lot have a reasonable expectation that what passes for their homes shall be their castles. You'll get the Corporation Counsel's opinion on that, of course, Mister Mayor, but that's the opinion of the New York County District Attorney. Miss Parker here will represent me for the remainder of the meeting. Commissioners, Your Honor, I'll see you all at Saint Patrick's."

And out she walked, just like that, the bitch. Nearly perfect breasts, absolutely perfect bitchiness. And who was she to lecture him—*him*—who had marched on Selma, who had stood beside—well, be*hind*—his wife as she burned her bra on the Boardwalk in Atlantic City (even back then, her breasts, *oy*), on civil liberties?

And who was she to act like she gave a fuck if some *judge* got on her for being late? Wasn't her well-known obstinant refusal to let her assistants bargain for pleas responsible for a logjam in Criminal Court from here to Philadelphia, just about? Oh sure, she *said* she was concerned that defense attorneys who would have tried to plead Charles Manson to breaking and entering would turn her less-experienced assistant DAs to cream cheese and spread them on their bagels, but everyone knew she was just a hardass castrating bitch shrew. You could see it in her husband's face. What was his name, the Wall Street guy? Norman. *Nor*man, here *Nor*man, good boy *Nor*man, you poor pussywhipped son-of-a-bitch.

And who was she to tell him there were a sub*stan*tial number of people living on the streets, that their goddamn cardboard refrigerator boxes were their goddamn castles? It wasn't *his* fault that there were people living on the streets, it was the fault of greedy real estate developers. Like Charles Story. And anyway, many individuals who ap*pear* to be homeless, who ap*pear* to be needy, who ap*pear* unkempt and unwashed and in rags are in *fact* dissemblers, charlatans, impostors—greedy hustlers who take advantage of our credibility and our compassion.

And who was she to say someone would represent her for the rest of the meeting? Well now, okay, wait a minute, hey. Nice legs, this Mabel Parker, nice bod, nice smile. Bet she's always wanted to see the inside of Gracie Mansion—the Colonial bullshit, the wainscotting, the whatnots. The perfect opportunity, what with Sylvia and the harridan virgin spinster freeloaders gone to the mattresses in Jersey. Didn't these guys have to be somewhere? Like Story's funeral, for example, which would keep them busy for the rest of the day, with all the shit at Saint Patrick's and then going all the way out in Queens. Queens: he hated Queens, and the sad fact was that as chief executive of this colossus among cities he was going to have to go out there too. Why him? ''Phil?''

Hriniak hesitated, sure he'd heard his given name but unsure what it signified. ''Yes, sir?''

''Read the latest *Newsweek*?''

''. . . No.''

''*Road Warrior. Mad Max.* Seen those movies?''

Hriniak nodded. Seen them and gotten a kick out of them, but that wasn't what Lyons was creeping up on.

''Then you're aware that to have the City of New York of today compared with the world of tomorrow depicted in those movies—a postapocalypse world of perpetual gang warfare—is to be egregiously slandered. And yet just such an analogy occurred to the writer of *Newsweek*'s cover story. I. Will. Not''—Lyons punched his left hand with his balled-up right for emphasis—''have this colossus among cities made a mockery of by having it compared with an Aus*tral*ian movie''—compared with an Australian movie by a writer who also thought it was amusing to call New York ''a colostomy among cities.''

Hriniak tried to remember the things his son, who studied martial arts, had told him about clearing the mind. If he didn't clear his mind, he would laugh in Lyons's face. ''There's been some development, Your Honor. I intended to brief you immediately after this meeting. With your permission, I'll report to Commissioner Turco and to Miss Parker, as well.''

Report to the head *gar*bageman and an as*sis*tant district attorney as *well* as to him? Now just a goddamn minute. Lyons wanted to be briefed privately; that was what being mayor was all about—secret stuff. On the other hand, if Mabel Parker saw him getting some of the secret stuff, well, she couldn't help being impressed. ''Now, Tommy, now Miss Parker—you both understand that this is confidential, don't you? Nothing Commissioner Hriniak says is to go beyond the confines of this room.''

Turco nodded; the branches of his family tree heavy with mafiosi, he knew about *omertà*.

Mabel lighted another Carlton, her fourth since the meeting began, for Mabel was scared. A mongoose at a gathering of cobras, a shark in the shallows off Coney Island, a very large bull in a very small shop of breakable collectibles would be as welcome as was Leah Levitt around City Hall and Police Headquarters, and now Leah had gone off and left Mabel all by herself *in* City Hall with the Mayor and the PC. With men.

There were two groups of people in the world—Leah's fans and Leah's detractors. To the former, Leah was an innovator, a creator, an artist, almost, an advocate (as outlined in her polemic-in-progress, which she kept asking Mabel to "critique," six figures in advance and a sure best seller) of new technologies (closed circuit television to interview reluctant witnesses) and new strategies (community service as a condition of parole) for dealing with the oldest profession, crime, and its practitioners, but whose insights, sadly, fell on the deaf ears of the latter, longtime members of a hierarchy prejudiced against outsiders (Leah had been a state legislator), against boat-rockers (Leah had practically begged minority group members to knock on her door with their allegations of police brutality), and especially against women (Leah not only paid lip service to the rights of women, she hired the cunts). The former were women, the latter (who claimed that none of those things had anything to do with their enmity: Leah was simply impatient, unyielding and relentless) were men.

What the PC was saying frightened Mabel too:

"Crime Scene found a latent footprint in a flower bed right at the rear of Story's back yard. You'll remember it'd rained all weekend. There was water in the print, so it's pretty difficult without a lot more forensics to say when it was made or much about it. The best guess right now is that it was a woman's size ten or a man's eight. A rough-soled shoe, probably, like a sneaker or an espadrille. There's a gap in the fence right there—not a hole exactly, a kind of overlap of pieces of chain-link fencing put up at different times—between 119 and an apartment building behind it on Seventy-first Street. It's a tight squeeze, but a full-size person could go through the fence and out an alley alongside the apartment house. There's a gate with a panic lock leading to the street.

"We've canvassed the neighborhood for eyewitnesses—"

"A panic lock?" Mabel said, a test to see if there was panic in her voice.

"The kind with a bar you push, like in a movie theater," Hriniak said.

Mabel nodded and got out her Carltons and lighted a new one from the old.

Lyons wished he had matches or a lighter; he'd always wanted to light a woman's cigarette. Sylvia didn't smoke; Sylvia screamed across restaurants at strangers who were smoking. He wished he'd known what a panic lock was; he had thought Hriniak was saying a brand name—Pannig.

"We've canvassed the neighborhood for eyewitnesses," Hriniak said, "but so far we haven't turned up anyone who saw anyone leaving the house by the back door. It might be nothing at all; the print could've been made by one of our own investigators. We try to be careful about things like that, but when there're crowds of people the way there were at 119 the other night, and when the weather's the way it was, mistakes get made."

Lyons swelled up. "Mis*takes*? You're saying you may be committing manpower to a search whose fruit may be one of your *own* people? I'd call that more than a mis*take*, Commissioner Hriniak, I'd call that—"

"A second development"—Hriniak had discovered all by himself, without recourse to martial arts, that the way to keep his mind clear was to keep Lyons from talking—"is that a doorman on duty the night of the murder in a building at Seventieth and Lex has reported seeing a man walking west along the north side of Seventieth at around seven o'clock. The man stopped at a house about halfway down the block and rang the bell. The doorman was a good hundred yards away and it was darker than usual for the hour because of the weather, but he's pretty sure, the doorman, that it was 119 the man stopped at. It has a stoop while the houses right around it have steps *down* to their front doors. He was distracted for a moment, but when he looked again the man was gone—let into 119, the doorman assumed, because the man looked like someone paying a social call, not about to break and enter."

Lyons snorted. "A social call? You're looking me in the eye and suggesting someone Story invited for *cock*tails shot him, chopped his finger off and stuffed it in his mouth?"

"I haven't spoken to the doorman personally, Your Honor. I'm on my way to see him right now."

"And a*nother* thing"—Lyons was on a roll now, like Angela Lansbury—"You said this was around seven. The ME says

Story died between six-thirty and seven. Someone getting to Story's around seven would've been paying a social or business call on a dead man.'' He chuckled; he couldn't help himself.

Hriniak found that if he let his eyebrows droop down ever so slightly his mind stayed semi-clear even if Lyons couldn't be stopped from talking. ''Would you care to come with me, Your Honor? There's time before the funeral service. You can ask the doorman any questions that come to mind.''

''Well, I, er, uh. . . .'' Lyons strode to his desk, flipped the pages of his appointment calendar, which was still turned to yesterday's date; he'd been so undone by the incident at the Municipal Building that he hadn't noticed. He shook his head, snapped his fingers, shrugged his shoulders. ''I'm sorry, I just don't know if—''

''I'll be going then, Your Honor.'' Hriniak stood. ''I'll let you know at Saint Patrick's if there's anything further. Commissioner Turco. Miss Parker.''

Mabel tipped her head in farewell. She kind of wished Hriniak had asked her to come along, for she would have liked to hear more about Charles Story's social caller and to speculate on what his connection was, if any, with the tallish, thinnish woman in a tan raincoat, brown hat, white pants, blue shoes, who came out the back door of 119, locked it, went down the steps, crossed the yard, went through the back fence (leaving a footprint, kind of Cinderella-like), into the courtyard behind 116 and out the alley (unlocking the panic lock) leading to Seventy-first Street. Mabel was pretty much hooked on some popular sedatives these days and sometimes felt awfully logy, so she might not have been able to keep up her end of the speculation, but she still would have liked to be along for the ride.

# 10

Lightning, thunder, wind and rain, the entire tintinnabulous arsenal of a summer storm.

Hunkered on a jump seat of the first of a long line of long black limousines strung out behind the hearse ferrying Charles Story's corpse from Saint Patrick's Cathedral to the family plot at Saint Somebody or Other's somewhere in Queens, Joe Cullen bit the inside of his cheek to keep from smiling at the memory of a laugh he and his computer nerd daughter had shared a while back over an encyclopedia article she was reading for an Earth Science report: lightning (the subject of the article) rarely strikes twice, the author observed, and added dryly, once is usually sufficient.

Sufficient too, Cullen felt, was his participation in this emotional extravaganza: the several thousand limos (in addition to the dignitaries to be transported, there were moguls and wheelers and luminaries and doyens and doyennes and movers and rockers and emeriti and titans and players and laureates and dealers and pundits and shakers and rollers) were trailed by a million motorcycle cops on Electra Glides and Police 1000s and after them whitetops and blacktops and squad cars and cruisers with insignias of police departments from not only *le tout* northeast but (as you could bet tomorrow's newspapers would put it) from *as far away as* Texas and Wisconsin and Virginia and Indiana and Georgia and Ohio, moths to the flame of a fallen law enforcement officer's farewell; Emergency Services's helicopter rescue unit had been preparing one of those heart-rending Missing Man formation fly-overs, only to be stymied by the weather; names like those of the Grucci fireworks family's, like David Wolper's, had been pitched to the afternoon's organizers (*Would* pyrotechnics be appropriate? *Could* the Elvis imitators be mustered on such short notice and would their pomade melt in the heat?). It was time for a no-frills generic cop to jump off the caparisoned wagon.

It would be a soft landing, for everything had come to a perfect halt, frozen in place by some fender-bender, maybe, some clogged storm drain miles and miles away. (Or maybe the other day's redheaded tire-changer was still wrestling with her spare, her tiny undershirt entirely wet.)

"You know who's not here?" Cullen had said to Ann Jones as she climbed aboard one of the press buses outside Saint Patrick's, the sky above already a hot charcoal pregnant with electricity.

"Who?"

"Kurt Vonnegut and Jill Krementz."

Ann had laughed.

And she'd been a good sport about Cullen's pulling the job of riding shotgun in the lead limo, whose passengers were Mayor Lyons and the women in Charles Story's life: his widow, Lise; her daughter, Claire Langois; his sister, Vera Story Evans.

"Why me?" Cullen had said.

But Ann had said, "She'll be glad you're there."

Sidney Lyons wasn't glad. Sidney Lyons was furious. By rights, Sidney Lyons should have been on a jump seat in paradise. Oh, sure, out the window there was lightning, thunder, wind and rain, but in his mind's eye, Lyons could see greener grass, a rosy future somewhere far away from this hellhole of a colossus among cities he ruled, had actually aspired to rule from the time he was an envelope stuffer for the Bay Ridge Independent Democrats, a future above all free from Sylvia Ethel Saratsky Lyons, an American Express cardmember since 1957, Miss Emery Board of 1941–43, Miss Cockteaser of 1943–45 and again (after a frenzied decade of mating) of 1955 to the present, founder and chairperson of the World Anti-Fellatio Society, New York Telephone's Caller of the Year for forty consecutive years, the First Yenta, and from his darling daughters—Dawn, Deena, Roberta, Cindy (who dotted her *i* with a goddamn tiny smiling face) and Roxanne, the harridan virgin spinster freeloaders.

Good-bye to all that. Hail and farewell. He, Sydney Lewis Lyons, was now about to receive the payoff for sixty-four years of tooling along in the slow lane, was about to escape from the ordinary and feel the freshness and taste the difference and become the lover of not one but three surpassingly extraordinary women.

Where to begin? What did it matter? Look at this Lise Story. Beautiful in that tough, hard, muscular way (those calves!) that so many French women are beautiful. ("*Je suis vrai malheureusement,*" Lyons had said to her back at Saint Patrick's, boring all the way down through the strata of his past for a shard of seventh-grade French. Lise Story had frowned—she hadn't expected to hear her native tongue, after all—but had finally said, "Thank you.") Athletic, christ: she looked like she could still get out on the court and whip any one of these, ahem, *women* tennis stars of today. And not only that, did she have business acumen or what? Did she run a nationwide chain of exercise spas catering to your upscale professional women or did she not? And was she not her own best advertisement? Her beauty, her cosmopolitan sophistication, her selfless work on behalf of a dozen—a *score*—major, major charities—let's face it, he could look you in the eye and say Lise Story was one of the best-known, most-admired, most mir*ac*ulous women in this colossus among cities.

And this girl, this Claire Langois, Langois being—George Darling had explained it to him, he knew all this shit, it was a press secretary's job—her father's name, her natural father's, he was a tennis player too, also a fro—also French, this Claire Langois, not a girl at all, really, a woman, but also like some angel out of some painting by . . . by . . . Who's a French painter? Strong too, like her mother, muscular—those *legs*—but also delicate, fine, like, well, like a model, which was what she was when she wasn't playing tennis.

Okay, sure, he'd heard things, heard the rumors that Claire Langois could've been a lot better tennis player than she was if she'd spent less time running around with the Brat Pack (or was it the Black Pack? He hoped to *God* it wasn't the Black Pack) and metallic rock stars and guys who shaved every three days and glued broken dishes to chunks of wood and called it art and themselves artists.

One fatmouth gossip columnist quoted someone the other day (without attribution, natch, the way they were always doing about him) saying Claire Langois was "her mother's ghost." He'd heard all about that and it didn't matter to him, even if it was true, which he doubted. How could anyone with a face like that do things like that or hang out with people like that? So her eyes looked a little wild right now, so what? So she was staring into a corner of the limo down next to his very own feet and seemed to be seeing something there even though there wasn't anything there (or *was* there?), something that made her giggle, so what? Her stepfather got killed, for christ's sake, his goddamn finger got chopped off and stuck in his goddamn mouth by a bunch of two-legged rodents gnawing away at the underpinnings of this colossus among cities.

And last but certainly not least, Vera Evans, saving the best for last, the cream rising to the top, the dignity of her, look at her, the gravity, the authority, like a queen or something, like the Duchess of Windsor. And when she's on the screen—hell, there hasn't been anyone like her since—who?—Hepburn (either one), Bacall, Colbert, Stanwyck. Grace Kelly. She's Jane Fonda with a sense of humor, Streisand without the shtick, Cher minus the leather, the chains, the bellybutton, the boyfriend half her age. She's . . . She's . . . Words rarely fail him, but this time they do.

What a setup, what a gold mine. If only it weren't for this goddamn *cop,* Coleman. Coleman? Not only does he get into the limo at the last minute like he's going to steal it, take hostages (did he need headlines like this, Lyons thought, then thought he could *use* headlines like this), now the phone on the back of the front seat rings, he swings around and answers it, the cop, Coleman, like it's his car or something. *He* should answer it, he's the goddamn mayor, it's probably for him anyway, some secret stuff.

And now look at this. Look at this! The girl, Claire Langois, is getting out of the car in the middle of the LIE in the middle of a hurricane and running down the road. Hey, you can't do that! Hey, you, come back here! And look at this! Vera Evans is running after her.

He'll go after her—that's it! After both of them. He'll rescue them, sweep them up in his arms, ride off with them on his shining steed away from all this. He'll look them in the eye—eyes—him, Sidney Lyons, and say—

Shit.

There goes Coleman. There goes the goddamn cop.

* * *

The verge was graveled and Claire slipped to her knees as she tried to pull away from Vera. Cullen got his arms around Claire from behind and held her as tightly as he could without hurting her. She felt like quicksteel.

She bucked.

She pried at his clamped hands.

She made a sound, through clenched teeth, between a grunt and a whine.

She swiveled back and forth, swinging at him, missing.

She gave up and sagged in his arms, staring down at her bloody knees.

Vera took Claire from Cullen and helped her back to the limo. Cullen saw Zimmerman still half a dozen cars away making his way forward and got his eye and waved him back. Zimmerman gestured, *You sure?* and Cullen nodded and waved at him until he turned away.

Cullen faced the gale and let the wind and rain cool him. It didn't work; it never worked any more. Coolness was extinct. He looked for landmarks, but couldn't find any familiar ones and wondered where the hell in Queens they were anyway. Where the hell in America. In the Milky Way. He felt a hand on his shoulder and the shadow of an umbrella.

"Thank you, Joe." Vera's black straw hat had somehow stayed on and its brim snapped in the wind, but she made no move to hold it in place; she wasn't a woman Nature trifled with. How else could she not even be wet when he felt saved from drowning? She was cool; if he took her hand and held it to his face, it would cool him. Perhaps being cool was something she'd learned in Hollywood.

Cullen's watch alarm went off.

He pulled the cuff of his suit jacket down over the watch and grasped it and tried to strangle it.

Vera raised her eyebrows. "Noon?"

The suit, gray, pin-striped, was a year-rounder, meaning his only good suit and too warm for this weather and he had sweated his light blue shirt dark blue. "I think so, yes." He didn't let go of the watch, or look at it.

"We're running late."

Today, or ever? "The phone call was about an accident on the ramp to the Clearview. We should be moving soon."

She nodded, then kept on nodding, as if he'd said something very wise.

"I'm sorry for your loss, Vera."

Did her shoulders twitch just a little in reaction to his formality?

"And I'm sorry about the other day. I should've . . . I don't know."

She cocked her head. "The other day?"

"The driver. Coming from the airport. It's irrational. I feel I could've kept it from happening. Pounding on the window. I was frustrated. But I'm sure I frightened you more."

Slowly, there was a break in the clouds of her personal weather. "That was *you*?"

He flipped a hand. "Yeah. I mean I . . ." Shucks, ma'am. T'weren't nuthin'.

She touched his elbow, then held his hand. "Joe, I didn't recognize you. You understand that I *was* scared. Confused, disoriented. I had *no* idea. . . ."

"Hell, there's no reason. . . ."

She'd given over the umbrella to him and embraced his left arm in both of hers. She walked with him—pulled him almost—farther along the verge, past the cars of ordinary folks trapped in the same logjam, as if moving him away from something she didn't want him to see.

"It's been a long time," Vera said.

"Twenty-five years, three months, a day or two."

She stopped and faced him. She had gray eyes. Had she always had gray eyes? "Oh, Joe."

Rain on the umbrella like idle fingertips on a tabletop. Ba ruppa duppa duppa dup. "I haven't been counting. It's the twenty-fifth anniversary of lots of things for me—graduation from City, starting at the academy. . . ." Missing you.

"You got married, I heard from Chuck."

"For ten years, until five years ago."

"Join the club. The divorced, I mean."

He nodded; he'd known what she meant, and he suspected that she thought the *club* was The Married, and that its rules were burdensome.

Vera said, "Kids too, I heard."

"James, fifteen, a sophomore at Juilliard. He's a pianist, a classical pianist, theoretically, but his hero, thanks to my taking him to Theatre 80 St. Marks last winter to see *To Have and Have Not,* is Hoagy Carmichael. And I was worried about the effect Bacall would have on him. Stephanie, known as Tenny, a computer nerd, is twelve. They live with their mother and her second husband in Riverdale. He. . . ."

Vera put her head closer, as if she might not have heard. "He what?"

"He was her high school sweetheart. Theodore Roosevelt. In the Bronx? They should've acted on their first impulse."

"If they'd married back then, there wouldn't be a James or a Tenny."

"I suppose."

"It sounds as if you've let your kids grow up in their own ways. One would think she'd be the pianist and he the computer nerd." She laughed. "Computer nerd."

Cullen look back over his shoulder toward a shout and saw Vera coming toward them. So it was a dream after all. But starting when?

"Vera!"

Vera—the Vera beside him; there were two Veras—turned too, and raised a hand in greeting to the Vera who approached.

No. She was younger, the woman who approached. Same height, same weight, same spring in her step and swivel in her hips, same classy clothes and perfect hat, but younger. Her youth was especially manifest in her eyes, in their bewilderment.

Vera—no bewilderment in her eyes, just experience, control—took the younger woman by the arm and drew her in under the umbrella. "Nicky, come. Joe, this is Nicky Potter, my more-than-assistant, my life-support system. Nicky, Joe Cullen, the old friend of Chuck's I've told you about. Nicky, it's extraordinary—Joe was the policeman who helped when the poor driver was killed."

More bewilderment—maybe because *helped* lacked an object. But just for a moment; Nicky quickly sorted it out: "A terrible thing. I'm glad to meet you. This traffic." The distress was gone from Nicky's eyes; talking to strangers was her forte.

"Joe says we'll be moving soon," Vera said. "There was an accident."

"At the Clearview," Cullen said, and would have given both arms not to have. A road nerd.

"I hope nothing serious," Nicky said.

He shook his head. "I don't think so. Just. . . ." An accident. Ba ruppa duppa duppa dup.

Meanwhile, in other cars trapped in the jam, people rubbed

condensation from their windows and asked each other, *Isn't that Vera Evans? Look, Vera Evans. Ohmigod, it's Vera Evans. I don't believe it. I can't believe it. It's Vera Evans.*

*Which one? Which one?*

*The tall one.*

*They're both tall.*

*The good-looking one.*

*They're both good-looking.*

*The one on the* right, *then.*

*I think she's the one on the left.*

*Then who's the one on the right?*

*I don't know. Who's the guy?*

*Some movie star.*

*No, he's not good-looking enough.*

*I think he's cute.*

*Cute, maybe, but not good-looking.*

Vera turned Nicky around and pointed her at the lead limousine. "Have a look at Claire, please, Nicky. Tell her I'll be right there. It got terribly close for a moment there and she got claustrophobic. Leave the windows open if necessary."

"Nice to meet you," Nicky said. "Is it *Officer* Cullen?"

"Sergeant. Joe."

Nicky noted that on her mental Rolodex. "Nice to meet you, Joe. Vera's talked about you."

Sure. An old friend of Chuck's. "Nize t'meet ya."

Ba ruppa duppa duppa dup.

Vera looked at Cullen and smiled and looked away and stopped smiling.

Cullen said, "That was Phil Hriniak on the phone."

A frown, then: "No? Really? Oh, yes, of course, I heard from Susan Price. Phil's acting commissioner. It's *such* a coincidence."

"Phil says . . ."

"Says what?"

"He says it's a one-horse world."

Vera smiled. "Have you two stayed friends all these years?"

"It's one of those friendships where we don't see each other that often, but when we do get together we pick up in mid-sentence, practically, from where we left off."

Again, that nod, nod, nodding at his sagacity. "I've had friends like that, but none right now."

Ba ruppa duppa duppa dup.

"So Theatre 80's still there," Vera said.

"Still there," Cullen said. "When the weather got warm—it's been warm since March—a lot of the homeless moved into the parks."

Vera stared. What had that followed from?

"Hriniak said there's been a report of a sighting, in Van Cortlandt Park in the Bronx, of a suspect in Chuck's murder."

Her eyes were locked onto his eyes now. Her nostrils rose and fell.

"I don't know how much New York news reaches you in California—"

"Who, Joe? Who's the suspect?"

"—You may've heard of what's being called the Raleigh fire."

"I know some people died, yes. What does that have to do—"

"One of them was a social worker named Joy Griffith—"

"A friend of Tom's, yes. I know about this."

"His fiancée, I think, more accurately."

Vera grabbed the wrist of the hand that held the umbrella—ba ruppa duppa duppa dup—and shook it. "All *right,* Joe, his fianc*ée*. So *what*?"

"A doorman—this is from Hriniak too—a doorman on duty near 119 the night Chuck died saw someone going in Chuck's door. A man. Around seven. He didn't break in, he was let in or let himself in. The doorman's not absolutely sure about the time. He can't even be absolutely sure, since he was half a block away, that it *was* 119—"

"Well, goddamn it, Joe, then why—"

"What he is absolutely sure about," Cullen said, "and the reason he noticed the man at that distance in the first place, was that the man was unusually tall, six-six or so."

Vera took a big breath and let it out. "Six feet, six inches tall?"

"Yes."

"Well?"

"Hriniak said Tom hasn't been seen—at his home or at his office—since early on the afternoon Chuck died. Except for this sighting in Van Cortlandt—if Tom is who it was."

Vera looked over Cullen's shoulder at nothing for a long time. Then she locked onto his eyes again. "You suspect Tom Valentine of *murdering* my brother?"

Cullen wanted to say, Not *me*; the *cops*. But he said, "Yes."

# 11

As the storm pummeled the Bronx, Monk Monsky stood out in it and raged back at it.

*Newsweek* hadn't been far off, Tom Valentine thought. In paratrooper boots, fatigue pants, a Megadeth T-shirt with the sleeves ripped off, a black scrap of something tied around his forehead, Monsky did look like one of the futurethugs from *Road Warrior*.

"You motherfucker, Valentine. You wanna bring the whole motherfucking police department down on us? Hunh, do ya, hunh?"

"Take it easy, Monk."

Monsky hopscotched back into the lean-to where Valentine squatted. "Don't tell *me* to take it easy, motherfucker."

Valentine thought about killing Monsky. But then he'd thought that many times before and had always concluded that it would do more harm than good—although often, as now, he couldn't have said for sure why. "Here's the thing, Monk—"

"Don't tell *me* here's the thing." Monsky was on his knees, his wet face a foot from Valentine's, his breath a miasma. "The Monkster's who says *here*'s the thing, *Val*entine. The Monkster tells *you* here's the thing, *Val*entine, you don't tell The Monkster here's the thing. You dig, *Val*entine?"

"Here's the thing, Monk." Valentine doodled in the damp earth with the blade of his Swiss Army knife. "I need two days' food and water, a ground cloth, a sweatshirt, insect repellent, a trenching tool, matches, a flashlight, a pack. That's all. No big deal. I'll be out of here in five minutes if you'll just shut up and—"

That set the Monkster off again and Valentine ducked his head and shut his mind to him and wished he could shut his ears. In Vietnam, Warren Caldwell Monsky had been Monk because Monk's the kind of nickname you get when you've got a last name like Monsky and because he was quiet, almost shy, the kind of guy you sometimes didn't know was there until your eyes had adjusted to the dark, your ears to the natural heartbeat of the place. And when he did talk, what he said was, well, monklike—short and soft and pithy.

In Vietnam, Warren Caldwell (Monk) Monsky, Shaker Heights, Andover, Yale, had been the best friend of Thomas George Valentine, Elmhurst, Elmhurst High, Syracuse. Shaker Heights–Andover–Yale wasn't a frequent route to Vietnam, any more than was Elmhurst–Elmhurst High–Syracuse, and although Shaker Heights–Andover–Yale would not, stateside, have spoken—except down—to Elmhurst–Elmhurst High–Syracuse, there had been an immediate recognition, in country, that their differences from everyone else were greater than their differences from each other.

And there was their fundamental similarity: namely, that after Shaker Heights–Andover–Yale, and after Elmhurst–Elmhurst High–Syracuse had come not the logical, preordained, desirable next step (in the case of Shaker Heights–Andover–Yale, med school—at Yale or Harvard or Columbia; in the case of Elmhurst–Elmhurst High–Syracuse, the National Basketball Association). What had come was a step off the edge, into the abyss, the pits, Hell.

In the case of Shaker Heights–Andover–Yale, the push over the edge was provided by marijuana, acid, mescaline, angel dust and 'ludes—and all kinds of things Warren Caldwell Monsky had forgotten the names of, and the effects, but that came with the territory when you were the son of a doctor of medicine; in the case of Elmhurst–Elmhurst High–Syracuse, the impetus was plain old beer. Schaefer—The One Beer To Have When You're Having More Than One. And Tommy Valentine was never not having more than one. Things didn't look right to Tommy Valentine until he'd had more than one, until he'd had eight or ten or twelve or twenty-four, things weren't . . . balanced.

(Here's a good one, right? A pisser. You listening? Pan

American Games. Drug tests. You play a game, afterwards you drop your dick in a mason jar, they test your piss for steroids, diuretics, uppers, all that shit. Only you've just gone the full forty-eight sweating like a pig, you don't have a drop of piss left in you. You're not the only one, every starter on both sides plus the top men off the bench is sweating like a pig too, doesn't have a drop of piss left in him. The solution? The farsighted organizers of this international athletic competition invite you to step right up and partake of your choice of beverages, your *preferencia de bebidas,* or something like that: orange juice, apple juice, mineral water, tap water, club soda, seltzer, soda pop, milk, beer. Sure, go ahead, hell, have a beer, son, drink up, get your johnson working again after the hell of an effort you just made on behalf of the U.S. of A. Have two. Have another. Hell, yes.)

So instead of Shaker Heights–Andover–Yale–P&S (say)–Mount Sinai–Park Avenue–Gin Lane–wife named Pidge–kids named Bradley and Alexandra–Weimaraner–Benz–Meadow Club–blah, blah, blah, it was Shaker Heights–Andover–Yale–Nam. And instead of Elmhurst–Elmhurst High–Syracuse–Knicks–East End Avenue–condos in Key West and Aspen–models–Porsche–stewardesses–actresses–dancers–Hall of Fame–best-selling autobiography–CBS Sports–blah, blah, blah, it was Elmhurst–Elmhurst High–Syracuse–Nam. Two lives motherfucking converging. Two minds with a single motherfucking thought, which was no motherfucking thought at all.

And after Nam—

"*Val*entine."

—after Nam—

"*You* shut up, Valentine. The fuck're you to ask me for anything? The fuck're *doing* here? You think I don't know what you're doing here, Valentine? You think I haven't fucking figured it out? You're setting us up, you're bringing the heat down on us. The heat wants to talk to you, Valentine. They think you polished Story. What they don't know, what *I* know, 'cause I'm a lot fucking smarter than they are, is you polished him and whacked off his finger so it'd look like *we* polished him, so the heat'll come down on us. We might've done it, don't think we wouldn't. Revenge for the Raleigh, just like you made it look."

Monsky had begun in anger, his face close to Valentine's again. But what he was accusing Valentine of was ripping him off and to be ripped off is to be honored. He tried not to grin, tried not to feel guilty pleasure, but he couldn't help it. He jerked a thumb at his chest. "*My* idea, polishing the fuckers. *My* idea, whacking their fingers off. They deserved it. I mean, who're we talking about here, man? That hotel security guard. A rent-a-cop. Lower than whale shit, man. Women'd go downstairs to get food for their kids, he wouldn't let them back up unless they gave him a blow job. Polishing him was a public fucking service, man.

"That crackhead rolling people sleeping in the tunnels in Grand Central. I mean, shit, man, how the fuck can you rob people who don't have fucking nothing? That college kid, nobody could figure out what he was doing living in Tompkins Square. What he was *doing*, man, was raping women. Shit, I should've cut his dick off.

"That caseworker, that real estate goon. I mean, shit, man, these're people who prey on people who have nothing left but their dignity."

Monsky turned the anger back up now, feeling not ripped off but mocked. "So I don't fucking ap*prec*iate you polishing Story and whacking his finger off to make it look like *we* polished him. We might've polished him, so I don't fucking ap*prec*iate you making it look like we wouldn't."

"Give it a rest, Monk," Valentine said.

Monsky jabbed at Valentine's nose with the heel of his hand. Valentine parried with his forearm, put his hand on the off-balance Monksy's chest, and pushed him over backwards. He went out of the lean-to and stood up straight. The rain was still dense, but the storm had passed by. The parched golf course in whose fifth hole rough the camp had been pitched had gulped up the torrents of water and was nearly brown again. The Hopeless—a dozen, twenty, thirty, too pathetically few to be called a band—had come out of their lean-tos, their makeshift tents, and stood hugging themselves, rocking, mindless.

"Hello, Tom."

Valentine turned and looked down at the tiny figure in a camouflage poncho, the hood up and pulled low. "Hello, Tina."

"Long time."

"Oh yeah." And then again maybe not so long since so much of it he didn't remember, he'd been anesthetized. After Nam. . . .

"I was sorry to hear about your old lady, Tom."

Valentine nodded. He looked back toward the lean-to, where Monsky was thrashing about, looking, Valentine knew, for his works, knew it because after Nam, after Shaker Heights–Andover–Yale–Nam and after Elmhurst–Elmhurst High–Syracuse–Nam, Monsky and Valentine had become one guy, Shakerheightselmhurstandoverelmhursthighyalesyracusenamnammonskyvalentine-valentinemonksy. Monskentine, Valensky. The baddest mother-fucker in all the land, forever wild, forever high on marijuana-acidmescalineangeldustludesandschaefertheonebeertohave-whenyourehavingmorethanone, sharing butts, sharing burgers, sharing chicks, sharing tokes and tabs and works, sharing three or four or five six-packs. Or eight. Or ten. Until Valentine crashed in flames. And Monsky, somehow (who knew how?), all his engines billowing smoke, spinning and tumbling and buffeting and auguring, kept somehow (who knew the *fuck* how?) on flying. "Tina, things're going to get real bad; it's time to move out."

Tina laughed, and the hood of the poncho slipped back off her face. "Out? Tom, I'm not *in*."

Valentine wanted to turn away, and struggled not to. It wasn't Tina, it was what was left of her. Her face was purpled with bruises; one cheekbone had been caved in; her lips were clotted blood; some teeth were cracked, others were gone. He held his breath and put his hand alongside her face. "Who did this? Did Monk?"

Tina laughed. "Monk? Monk's a pussycat."

"Who beat you up like this, Tina?"

She took his hand in hers—her middle finger was knobbed from having broken and mended poorly—and kept it next to her face. "It's open season on the homeless, Tom. Haven't you heard? I got beat up last week down in Grand Central. By some kids. Or maybe they weren't kids. Maybe they were grownups."

"Some of these bruises are old, Teen."

She smiled. "Oh, them."

He tried again: "Get out, Tina. While you can."

She laughed again. "Tom, Tom, Tom. I told you. I am not in. I am not in. I am not in. I am not in."

So she was a crisp too. Well, then, he'd done all he could, hadn't he? Or was it up to him now to take her away with him, kicking and screaming, probably, for old time's sake? He assumed that they had an old time together, he and Tina—why else would she be talking to him if they hadn't?—but he couldn't be sure; so much of it he didn't remember.

Monsky was back now, twitching and jerking a little, but stabilized. Shit, he'd wanted to, he could've done the rap that'd made him a household motherfucking name, a face known all over the motherfucking world, picture in motherfucking *Newsweek: Ladies and gentlemen, brothers and sisters, if I could just have your motherfucking attention for a moment, please, I'd like to call your attention to a few motherfucking facts:*

Uno: *Every motherfucking year, half a motherfucking million units of low-income housing go condo, go co-op, get torched, get wrecked.*

Dos: *Rents for the poor have gone up thirty motherfucking percent in this decade.*

Tres: *There are ten motherfucking million families that pay more than half their motherfucking income on rent.*

Cuatro: *Twenty-seven percent of Americans are children. Forty motherfucking percent of motherfucking poor people are children.*

*You get it? You motherfucking dig? We are raising a motherfucking generation that may never in their lives have a motherfucking place to motherfucking live. We have put a motherfucking lock on the motherfucking door of the motherfucking American Dream.*

If he'd wanted to he could have, but he didn't motherfucking want to, he was motherfucking tired. "T-T-T-Tommy, look. I'm sorry. Sure, sure you can have whatever you need. Whatever we got, I mean. We don't got a lot. What we got is y-yours."

"Monk?"

"What, Tommy, what?"

They dapped: fist, fist, palm, palm, forefinger, forefinger, clench, break, down low real slow. "Monk."

"T-Tommy."

"It's over, baby."

"Nah, it ain't over, Tommy. It ain't even started yet. That was beautiful, polishing Story. You did a beautiful thing. Hey, man, you know I'm wrecked about your old lady, man. I mean, I am *mother*fucking wrecked."

"Yeah."

"I am, man. I mean it. *Mother*fucking wrecked."

"Monk?"

"Yeah, Tommy?"

"Be careful, will you? The shit is going to hit the fan in ways you can't even begin to understand."

Monsky smiled a smile that back before Valentine first met him, back in his Shaker Heights–Andover–Yale days, had transformed people into puddles of compliance. "What else is new, T-Tommy?"

"Nothing, I guess."

"We've seen it all, homes."

"I guess we have."

"And done a lot of it."

"I guess."

"And what we ain't, we've lied and said we did."

Valentine smiled.

Fist, fist, palm, palm, forefinger, forefinger, clench, break, down low real slow.

"Be cool, homes."

"Be cool, Monk."

"Jayce here'll fix you up. You know Jayce?"

Jayce's face was so filthy that Valentine wasn't sure of his race. From his eyes, he was sure that he'd killed. "Jayce."

"Valentine."

"You need heat, Tommy?" Monksy said.

Valentine stretched just a little so he could assure himself of the cool weight taped to the small of his back. "I'm okay for heat."

Monsky backed toward his lean-to. "Later, Tommy."

"Later."

"I love you, babes."

". . . I love you, Monk."

# 12

''You've probably never even heard of this song,'' Cullen said. ''I haven't thought of it in years:

'' 'He wore black denim trousers and motorcycle boots
'' 'And a black leather jacket with an eagle on the back.
'' 'He had a hopped up 'cycle that took off like a gun.
'' 'That fool was the terror of Highway 101.' ''

Predictably, Zimmerman squirmed. This was proto-speed metal. ''And that was *your* song?''

Charles Story had been praised and buried. Twelve bagpipers had scared the shit out of the cemetery's wildlife and the few very young children in the cortège. Three hundred police officers had stood with their backs to the goings-on, a ramshackle fence within the weathered but true wrought-iron cemetery fence, guarding against unpleasant surprises. They hadn't even seen—nor had *any*one been prepared for—the unpleasant surprise that occurred when Claire Langois jumped down next to her stepfather's casket and hurled back out of his grave the red long-stemmed rose her mother had just dropped in, nearly nicking the Archbishop of New York, the celebrant of the funeral mass, with a thorn. Cullen, as usual, had gone down to get Claire; as usual, she had gotten all pliant in his arms. It had been over in an instant; no one had discussed it afterwards; just possibly, it hadn't happened at all.

The trek back to Manhattan had been merely tedious, the Storyettes (the collective minted by cops hanging around with not much to do but be in the way to embrace Lise Story, Claire

Langois, Vera Evans and Nicky Potter) had been tucked into 119 for the night, Keith Bermúdez had the watch (along with a dozen others, for events had demanded reinforcements and their original threesome had been augmented), Cullen and Zimmerman had gone to Katz's for heartburn (power heartburn—and Zimmerman hadn't embarrassed Cullen by asking for radicchio and arugula salad), then had driven over the Williamsburg (as ever, expecting The Collapse), and dropped down to Brooklyn Heights.

To see a man about the Dean thing.

They sat on two benches on the Esplanade, gazing at downtown, which didn't look like Manhattan anymore, it looked like Atlanta, or Toronto, full of hypermodern buildings that curved and cantilevered and reflected one another, at the bridges, at the Statue of Liberty way out in the harbor about the size of a model of itself. It was nearly midnight by the clock on the Watchtower Building and Cullen got ready for his wrist alarm to go off. How could people live like this, with Time's wingéd chariot not just hurrying near but running right over them? The noon storm had cooled things down only a few degrees for only a few minutes, then the heat had come back on just a little bit hotter, in case anyone had forgotten what hot was. It was still hot now; the Esplanade felt tacky, the wood of the bench rotten.

Farther along, where light from the cobra head street lamps didn't reach, there would usually have been the motionless mounds that for years now had signified that someone had set up ersatz housekeeping; but the strip was bare, for the word was out on the street that out on the street was not a safe place to be.

After leaving 119, driving down Fifth Avenue (Zimmerman's choice; it went with the Saab better than Lex), stopped for a light alongside the statue of Sherman across from the Plaza Hotel, they had watched a young green beat cop driving a feral woman away from the sidewalk café that had opened a few weeks ago around the Pulitzer Fountain and was already nearly old hat.

The young cop had a paunch and had sweated a Rorschach onto his uniform shirt; he jogged and shuffled and skipped and hopped after the woman, who was nimble as a monkey. With one hand he stilled the bouncing of his service revolver, his nightstick, his summons pad, his flashlight, his handcuffs, with the other he held on to his hat. His face was drenched with perspiration—and with tears of frustration too, probably, for the woman taunted him as she darted and weaved and sidestepped. Her clothes were rags, her hair a tumbleweed, her limbs blackened by sun and grime. But she was no crone; she was quick and light and youthful.

The spectators—and those trying not to watch—sat stiffly on those delicate little slatted chairs you see in photographs by Brassaï and Cartier-Bresson and Lartigue—French park chairs; they wore white or black or black and white; they were sleek, brown, tight; they cared about the price of nothing and knew the value of everything; they were, simply, perfect—and perfectly helpless.

The woman—she was a girl, really, Cullen grew surer the longer he watched—wasn't traveling light; she had her life in a teetering pile on a supermarket shopping cart. The cop, the poor fat green cop, was smart enough to recognize that the cart and its stuff meant something to her, and that to feign impounding it would lure her to where he could grab her.

Lure her he did, putting a foot up on the cart's left rear wheel, taking out his summons book, as if about to give the contraption a ticket; grab her he did, when she came sidling toward him—or grab at her. She leaped backwards, monkeylike, and into the path of a taxi that had turned right onto Fifth from Fifty-ninth. The taxi wasn't up to speed, but it tossed the woman—the girl—into the air. She landed flat on her back on the asphalt with a splat that knocked the wind out of everyone who saw her. A streetcorner's worth of the world sighed.

Then, slowly but unmistakably, inexorably, inevitably, the streetcorner began to giggle. To snicker. To applaud. To cheer and cheer and cheer. On its feet now, tipping over those French park chairs, some of them, in their enthusiasm, the onlookers gave a standing O, raised their glasses, punched the humid air with celebratory fists. Celebrating what? The poor dumb fat green cop? The cabbie, a sixties throwback with a ponytail, tie-dyed shirt, bell-bottoms, granny glasses? Who knew? Not celebrating the filthy, dirty, inconsiderate, crazy bitch, that was for goddamn sure.

The light had changed just then and Zimmerman had aimed to

pull over on the right. Cullen had reached across and put his hand on the wheel. "Make the left."

"Joe."

"Make the left. There's nothing we can do."

"We saw it happening. We could've done something."

"What?"

"We could've *done* something."

"What?"

"Stop saying, 'What?' for christ's sake. We *could* have done something."

"Make the fucking left, Neil."

Zimmerman breathed out through his nose, made the left and drove all the way to Second without speaking. He made the right onto Second and said, "There wasn't a fucking thing we could've done."

"It wasn't my song as much as *The Wild One* was my movie," Cullen said. "I may be wrong but I think the song may have been a takeoff, almost, a parody. But the movie was the real thing and there was nothing anybody could tell *me,* I *was* Marlon Brando. Tommy Valentine—Tommy was the jock among the three of us—Tommy got interested in roller hockey around that time and tried to get the rest of us to buy sticks. The sticks cost the same as a motorcycle hat—a soft hat with a plastic brim and a sort of headband across the top. Kind of like motorcycle cops still wear. I *had* to have one of those hats. There was a kid—Ira something—on the fence; he couldn't decide whether to go for the hockey stick or the hat. I convinced him the hat was a better long-term investment; Tommy suffered *my* craziness, but he wouldn't talk to Ira for months after that."

His watch went off—computer nerd midnight two minutes after the Jehovah's Witnesses'.

"That was junior high. By high school, I'd refined my act a little. I wasn't Brando anymore, I was James Dean—which meant, most of all, that I could get away (to myself, if not to the guys I hung out with) with reading books. Tommy was a big man on campus, varsity hoops and baseball, president of this club, treasurer of that one, most likely to, most inevitably, most assuredly, always tossing the ball appropriate to the season in the air, always with a flock of adoring girls in his wake.

"And there was Chuck. If Tommy was a jock and I was a rock—that was the term; *rocky* was the adjective—Chuck Story was something we didn't have a name for. Nowadays, he'd be a hustler, a player. He was a player; he was in on the action, but more than that he *made* the action. He worked after school and on weekends at his father's candy store, but it wasn't like he was a soda jerk, a bus boy. He was like . . . Vincent Sardi. No. What's the name of the maître d' at the Post and Coach?"

"Chick."

"Chick. He was like Chick. Imagine Chick without the tuxedo. Chick in a blue button-down oxford shirt, no tie, chinos—chinos with a little belt that buckled in the back; they're making a comeback, I couldn't believe it—white wool socks, penny loafers. That was what Chuck always wore. Tom too. Ivy League, we called it. Sort of like the way you dress."

Zimmerman just sniffed. He was outfitted by Paul Stuart, J. Crew, Banana Republic (Banana World, Cullen called it, to get Zimmerman going, Bananas "R" Us); maybe there was a scrap or two from Lands' End or L.L. Bean. White wool socks indeed. "And you actually *wore* a black leather jacket with an eagle on the back?"

"I wore black shirts with the collar turned up, unbuttoned at the neck to show a white T-shirt; pegged black pants with white piping down the legs; skinny, very, very skinny belts buckled over on the hip; black pointy-toed shoes with taps on the heels, and a black satin jacket with yellow stripes around the shoulders and my name"—Snake, but Zimmerman wasn't ready for Snake—"in yellow script on the breast. It was against the rules to wear jackets with gang names on them in school, but it was well-known as the jacket of the Cougars. The colors, but I don't think the word had been coined. . . ."

He could feel the jacket's smooth weight—it was too light for winter, too heavy for summer, but he'd worn it year round nonetheless—could hear the metal taps, could appreciate the trimly tapered slacks. He had a kinetic memory of tweaking the points of his jacket's collar, drawing the long, narrow comb from his right hip pocket, combing back his ducktail haircut, caressing his Elvis pompadour with his left hand till it looked . . . just right, caressing it with his right hand, returning comb to pocket nonchalantly, tweaking his collar points, smiling his minimalist Jimmy Dean–Elvis–Brando smile at his reflection in the windshield of a car parked along Roosevelt Avenue or the window of Sid and Cy's Nosh Box on Queens Boulevard or the window of Chuck and Vera Story's old man's candy store—did it have a name? It was always just *the candy store*—on Elmhurst Avenue, his reflection smiling back as if saying, *Yeah, Snake, you are one good-looking cat.*

"I was what I was because my dad was a subway motorman. In the winter, there were days when he never saw the sun. At the end of every run, he'd walk to the middle of the train and talk to the conductor for a couple of minutes, then go on to what had been the back of the train and was now the front. On his lunch break he usually read the paper. That was the extent of his interaction with anybody but me and my mother. I spent a whole day when I was about eleven riding with him, and after that I pledged to myself that I'd never follow in his footsteps. In my arrogant ignorance the only way I could see to make sure I didn't was to be unlike him in every way I could: he was quiet, I was noisy; he was decent, I was a thug; he was honest, I stole—nothing major, but compulsively. I like to think that he's lived long enough to see that I turned out okay, but he's never really understood the divorce: the necessity for it, sure—he and my mother fight twice a day, and always did; first thing in the morning and at dinner—but not the actuality of it.

"Chuck's father had the candy store. His mother—and Vera's—had died when Chuck was twelve or thirteen. Tom's dad was a salesman of some kind, on the road a lot, so I don't remember him very well. He was tall—so was Tom's mother—and not very friendly to us—or maybe it was just that he *was* so tall. Why am I telling you this, Neil?"

" 'Advocate for Homeless Polishes Boyhood Friend. Cop Buddy Investigates.' You're compelled to make it make sense."

He who couldn't even turn off his wrist alarm. Cullen looked at his watch: 00:04.24 . . . 25 . . . 26.

"Where was Vera Evans in all of this?" Zimmerman said. "Vera Story. Did she work in the candy store too?"

"I barely remember her in junior high and high school. She's two years younger, I guess, than Chuck and Tom and I, and at that age that's a lot. She was kind of plain and kind of gawky. And she was very, very shy. Yes, she worked in the candy store. They lived right upstairs. The candy store was on the ground floor of a six-story building, the Storys lived on the. . . ."

Zimmerman looked over. "What's wrong?"

"Nothing, I just . . ."

"What, Joe?"

Cullen shook his head. "I can't remember what floor they lived on, that's all. . . . I remember the apartment. I'd go up to see Chuck. I don't remember Vera being around much. But I don't remember what floor it was on. . . . The moment that stands out in my memory was her appearance in a play. One of those awful things young amateurs do—*The Late George Apley* or something. Vera'd been the stage manager, the girl playing the ingenue got appendicitis, Vera went on in her place. She was extraordinary—even punks like me knew it. It was like *All About Eve:* wallflower to toast-of-the-town in one night. Except it was more like Cinderella because it was for one night only. There were other plays, but Vera wasn't in them; there were parties and dances and Vera wasn't at them. . . . I don't know why."

"And after high school?" Zimmerman said.

And after high school Cullen didn't want to talk about, and he was glad he wouldn't have to—or not now anyway, for he saw a solid young black almost pimp-rolling along the Esplanade toward them.

"Dar*nelle*?" Cullen said.

"Darelle," Zimmerman said.

# 13

Darelle Dean, that is, not a singer exactly, but a man with something to tell them in exchange, for sure, for whatever slack they could cut for his sister, Deborah Dean of the Dean Thing.

Darelle stopped, keeping two benches between him and them, in case they *weren't* good guys. He wore a black and gold Russell singlet, black nylon Nike running shorts just a little too prodigious in the genital area for comfort (honky comfort), white knee socks with black and yellow bands, white Air Jordans, fat yellow laces untied à la mode. "Would you gentlemen be Misters Cullen and Zimmerman?" His voice—a James Earl Jones voice—didn't go with the threads.

"Good morning, Officer," Cullen said. "I'm Sergeant Joe Cullen. This is Detective Neil Zimmerman. What's up?"

"I believe Detective Bermúdez told you I called."

"He told us you called."

"We grew up on the same turf, Keith and I. Soundview. He's a few years older, but I was big for my age, so I played ball with the older kids."

"He said something about that."

"I imagine he said I'm in the One-Nine."

"He did."

"I imagine he said I'm Deborah Dean's brother." Just for a moment, his diction lapsed. "Ya know, the Dean Thang."

Cullen smiled and nodded. "Yup."

"Okay to sit?"

Cullen gestured welcomingly. "Hey."

Darelle sat on a third bench. "Hot."

Cullen smiled and propped an ankle on a knee and spread his arms along the back of his bench. *His* bench.

"Either of you out in that storm today?"

"Man," Zimmerman said.

Cullen said, "Whew."

"At the height of it," Darelle said, "I was on the phone—I'm on the switchboard Fridays—taking a call I thought you might be interested in hearing about. I was scared out of my wits because a cousin of mine was killed while talking on the phone during an electrical storm."

"I've read about that," Cullen said—had had it read to him, actually, by the computer nerd. "The lightning hits the ground or a house or a tree and the phone's like an outlet for the surge."

"The thought occurred to me," Darelle said, "that maybe I was safe, that I wouldn't get struck, because my cousin already had. She lived in Georgia, but we *were* family. Do you understand what I'm saying?"

Zimmerman said, "You mean, lightning doesn't strike twice?"

"Precisely," Darelle said.

"Once is usually sufficient." Cullen held up a hand. "I don't mean to make light of your cousin's death."

Darelle shook his head. "It's undoubtedly true. Once is undoubtedly usually sufficient."

"About the call, Darelle," Zimmerman said.

Cullen looked at Zimmerman and nodded thanks. He didn't like being the bad cop all the time, the guy who told singers and witnesses and anybody else who was wasting their time to get to the point; who put the notes up on the office refrigerator saying IF YOU TAKE ICE, *COCKSUCKER*, MAKE ICE; who sent the fatty pastrami back to the kitchen. It was the way he sometimes had to be, as well, with Hoagy Carmichael and the computer nerd ("James, in the cupboard there's one dish and two glasses that you haven't used yet. So don't wash anything—okay?—until you've gotten them dirty too"). And it was good for Zimmerman that he do it himself; it was part of his development, his evolution from tadpole to bullfrog in the pond of life. Or some fucking thing.

All business, Darelle said, "The call came in on a line that isn't listed in the phone book, it's what the Captain calls the slimeball number because when he's calling from home or the street the only way he can remember it is that the digits spell slimeball—without the final *L*'s. It's for precinct business only, not for calls from the public, not for personal calls, in or out.

"The caller was a woman. Young and white'd be my guess. She said she'd seen a woman—five-eight or so, one twenty-five or so, wearing a long tan raincoat, her hair tucked up in a brown felt soft-brimmed hat, white pants, blue shoes—canvas shoes like sneakers or espadrilles—coming out of 119 East Seven-Oh, the PC's house, between seven and seven-thirty the night he got polished." This time, Darelle Dean made the appeasing gesture. "No offense, Sarge. I know y'all grew up on the same turf."

Cullen hated being called Sarge; it made him feel grizzled and paunchy, whereas he was merely graying and softening. "So the alleged witness couldn't tell the woman's age or race or hair color because the hat hid her features?"

"That's correct."

"But she was sure it was a woman."

"She didn't betray any uncertainty."

"And the five-eight or so, the one twenty-five or so, the felt soft-brimmed hat—that's information the alleged eyewitness gave or information you pried out of her?"

"Gave it as though it was information she's used to giving, as though she's used to noting such details—which I needn't point out to you gentlemen most people aren't."

"Did she say where she was, Darelle?" Zimmerman said. "That she could see this woman leaving 119? Was she on the street or in another building on the block?"

"She didn't say. All she said I've just told you, pretty much in her words."

"And then she hung up?" Cullen said.

"And then she hung up," Darelle said. "I know you gentlemen're thinking that means I couldn't start a trace and you'd be right about that—but for the good fortune that, as part of a pilot program co-sponsored by the phone company, the precinct has had Exec-Call installed."

"Exec-Call?" Zimmerman said, and Cullen was thankful once more because he didn't like to be the prompter all the time, either, the guy who wouldn't let things move at their own rhythms, who was always trying to get the punch-line without the buildup.

"A machine, much like an answering machine, that, when

the phone rings, displays the number the call is coming from. It's someone you owe money, someone you'd rather not talk to for whatever reason, you just let it ring or switch on your answering machine. In addition, the machine can be programmed to block altogether calls from as many as six numbers. Another feature: if you get a busy signal, the machine automatically redials the number for half an hour; it automatically calls back the last number to call you whether or not you answered the call. And so on. An extraordinary machine. I plan to get one for myself as soon as it goes on the market. The phone company sales rep who set it all up at the precinct is going to arrange a discount."

Cullen hadn't interrupted because he knew Zimmerman would insist on hearing all about it later so it might as well be sooner. Other cops squirreled copies of *Playboy* and *Penthouse* in their desk drawers; Zimmerman had in his catalogues from Brookstone, The Sharper Image, D.F. Sanders, Sointu, State of the Art, Williams Sonoma. And he didn't just jerk off to them, he consumed from them. You already know about the Saab, the Blaupunkt, the Aiwa, the Sony Discman, but not about the Metro One cellular phone and the Knight Hawk II car alarm; about the Copy-Jack 96 pocket copier, Lamy pen, Porsche Design personal agenda, Braun platinum-plated rechargeable shaver, Becker aluminum calculator, Serengeti Drivers, Tech anodized rubber-handled tools (hammer, Phillips and standard screwdriver, needle and snub nose pliers)—all with their special pockets and niches and grooves and slots and slits in the Halliburton aluminum briefcase; about the Braun coffee grinder, the Krups coffee maker, the Europiccola espresso machine, the Yafa halogen desk lamp, the Corby pants press, the Sony DiscJockey, the Panasonic television/VCR (for taping episodes of *thirtysomething*), the StumpJumper Epic mountain bike, the Precor Fitness Climber 718e, the Pro Trainer Heart Monitor, the Soehnle scale, the Interplak, the Sound Soother 2 (to block out, Cullen imagined, the din of other Sound Soother 2s resounding through the upper East Side as the yuppies nestled all snug on their futons).

"So you traced the call to where, Darelle?" Cullen said.

"Pay phone. Seven-Oh and Lex."

"And a white top went around there but there was nobody home."

"It's a pair of phones, open to the street, not a booth per se. It took about ten minutes to free up a unit. Some power lines went down in the storm over on Eight-One and Second. While the unit was responding, I used the automatic call-back feature, on the chance someone could pick up and describe the previous user. No one answered. When the unit got there, there was a male Hispanic on the other phone. The Captain told the unit to ask him if he'd seen anyone, but to otherwise let him be."

"What else did the Captain do?"

"He told me to call Chief Walsh."

"And?"

"It took a while to reach him. I called Downtown at first, forgetting that he would be at the PC's funeral. I finally reached him in his car." Darelle's voice was less authoritative, and his manner; he knew he was getting to the tricky part, the part where it stands up straight and tall all by itself or it all comes crashing down. "I didn't hear what Walsh and the Captain said."

"But you have an idea," Cullen said.

"Well. . . ."

"Go for it, Darelle," Zimmerman said.

"Walsh. . . ."

They waited.

"Walsh told the Captain that since Tom Valentine was clearly the perp who polished the PC, it would be a waste of time and manpower to follow up on a crackpot phone call. He reminded the captain that Crime Scene and Homicide and his own precinct Squad had canvased the neighborhood without turning up anyone other than the doorman who observed Valentine in the vicinity of Story's house."

Cullen stood up and stretched. He walked to the railing of the Esplanade, held onto the spikes, braced his feet, leaned way back. A humpbacked moon he hadn't noticed looked straight down at him from the zenith. It was sweating too, like the three of them, like everything. He pulled himself up and shook his head to clear it and sat back down. "This, uh, slimeball number, Darelle—do you ever get calls from civilians on it?"

"I'm only on the switchboard Fridays."

"I understand that."

"PDs call, looking for an arresting officer. DAs too. Every now and again, the feds call. I took a call once from Rudolph Giuliani himself. Civilian clerks call from Personnel or Payroll or Procurement. The Killer *P*'s, the Captain calls them. The Captain's a funny homeboy, sometimes."

Cullen and Zimmerman smiled.

Then a long pause. It was 00:37.57 . . . 58 . . . 59. 00:38.

Zimmerman sat forward on his bench, elbows on his knees. "A PD, a DA, a fed, would know that nine-eleven calls, that calls to the special information numbers, get taped. A PD, a DA, a fed, would know that a voice on a tape might be IDed by a cop, another PD or DA or fed."

Cullen nodded.

Darelle said, "That's correct."

"A PD, a DA, a fed, would be good at giving descriptions," Zimmerman said.

Cullen nodded.

Darelle said, "That's correct."

"A PD, a DA, a fed, knowing the slimeball number, might also know about the Exec-Call, and would know to call from a pay phone," Zimmerman said.

Cullen smiled. Exec-Call: Zimmerman was already planning to get a demonstration.

"That's correct."

"A woman making a call from a pay phone on the street in a thunderstorm might've been noticed," Zimmerman said. "By storekeepers, doormen, a mailman, a bus starter."

Cullen nodded.

"That's correct."

Zimmerman sat back.

"Thanks, Officer Dean," Cullen said.

"I just thought, hearing that you and Tom Valentine grew up on the same turf too, Sarge, that you might want to know that there might be a witness who might help him out. That's a lot of mights, I realize. And since you and the PC grew up on the same turf too, well, it's complicated, I guess."

"It is complicated, but thanks. . . . I'm afraid we don't have anything for you."

"Hey, that's okay. That's not why I'm here."

"But there is something maybe you could do for us, and it might end *up* being something from us to you."

"What's that, Sarge?"

*Don't call me Sarge*. "We have your sister's phone records. She made regular calls to the main number Downtown, to—let's be straight about it—to the guy who shot her. You don't have any reason to believe that the guy who shot her *wasn't* brass, do you?"

Darelle shook his head.

"Neither do we. Detective Zimmerman had the idea that we check Downtown's phone records to see if there were regular calls to your sister's home phone. It's a big job, and if we go through channels to get authorization for it, well, we might tip the perp. You mentioned a sales rep at the phone company; are you tight with him?"

"Uh, it's a her, Sarge."

"Okay, well. Do you have a good relationship with her?"

"Uh, well, uh . . ."

Cullen looked past Zimmerman at Darelle. He was grinning. "I see."

"Yeah."

"There's nothing wrong with that, Darelle."

"I wasn't sure, Sarge. I mean, you homeboys're IAU. I thought maybe it wasn't such a good idea to, you know, fraternize, with a business rep involved in a special pilot program."

"I think you're all right, Darelle."

"Good. Good. I'm glad. I hoped I was."

"So maybe you could ask your friend, Darelle, if there's a simple way to run a trace like this. You see, we don't know whether the calls—if there were calls—were dialed direct or went through the main switchboard or what. Also, now that I think of it, maybe your friend could get us the MUDS of the public phones in the building too, because maybe the guy who shot Deborah used one of them."

"I'm sure she can, Sarge. She's a supremely competent woman."

They all stood up and shook hands and Darelle almost pimp-rolled back along the Esplanade (except now it looked like the walk of a man who was fraternizing with a supremely competent woman) and faded into the dark. Cullen and Zimmerman took one last look around at downtown, at the bridges, at the Statue of Liberty way out in the harbor. It was twelve-fifty-five by the Watchtower Clock.

"Long day," Zimmerman said.

Cullen said, "Long day."

"Long tomorrow."

"It's already tomorrow."

"You want a lift home?"

Cullen made cameo appearances at home these days. The plants the computer nerd kept insisting he needed for a balanced ecosystem were dying; bills and supermarket flyers and missing children and sweepstakes prizes were ankle-deep behind the door, where he left them lying because what was the point of picking them up, there was no real mail down there; there would be dust on the dust; the leftovers in the refrigerator would have multiplied and would be plotting to overpower him and escape when he opened the door—irrefutable evidence, your Honor, that there is no Joe Cullen living here. Nor is it, I hasten to remind the Court, his first offense.

"Drop me at Ann's," Cullen said.

# 14

''You know''—Cullen was barely in the door of Ann's apartment, the ground floor rear of a brownstone on Riverside just across from the Soldiers and Sailors monument—''you're never home.''

''I don't live here,'' Cullen attempted. ''I mean, it's true. I *am* never home. But I don't live *here*, so it's not that I'm not *home*, it's that I'm not *here*.''

She stared at him through tortoiseshell glasses—she'd been sitting in the garden writing by the light from the open french door on her Toshiba laptop—hands on hips. She had bare feet and wore a big T-shirt that had originally said:

*Nick and Kathryn's Wedding*
*6 June 1982*
*Washington, CT, 06793*

Across the hem of the sleeve, jock-style, it said *Bridesmaid*. With a laundry marker, after the wedding date, Ann had added *15 Feb 1987*, the day Nick and Kathryn's divorce became final (''It was the Zip Code that jinxed it,'' Ann theorized. ''Who would commemorate their nuptial *Zip* Code?''), and drawn a small grave and tombstone. She wore just panties under the shirt. ''Would you like to run that by me again?''

''I'd like a beer.'' He went into the kitchen and opened a Corona and took the bottle into the bathroom and stripped and got into the shower.

Ann came in. She pulled the curtain back a bit and sat on the toilet seat. She poured some beer into a plastic glass from the toothbrush holder and sipped it. "So what are we to make of young Claire Langois's erratic behavior these days?"

"Her stepfather was murdered and mutilated. Her aunt's driver was killed by a sniper."

"And of your heroics? God, you've just been everywhere, haven't you? Like Errol Flynn or something."

Cullen let the water beat on his neck.

"Haven't you?"

God knows why—or maybe it was perfectly obvious since he was standing in a shower with water beating on his neck, but Cullen's mind was on a funny little old building on Greenwich Street, just south of Spring, around the corner from the Ear Inn, his and Ann's place, that bore this cryptic sign: *Water Spilled From Source To Use*. The closest they'd come to exegesis was that it was a variation on *There's many a slip twixt the cup and the lip*, whoever the hell had said *that*.

"*Haven't* you?"

Cullen ripped the shower curtain all the way open. "God damn it, Ann, I'm exhausted, so take your complaints that I don't want to live together and shove them up your ass."

She winced; they were vulgar to each other, but not cruel, and they tended to argue about what they were arguing about and not displace and misplace. "Turn the water off, please. Or shut the curtain. Everything's getting wet." She got up and made a big deal out of brushing some drops off the glass of the frame holding her favorite *New Yorker* cartoon, a Cline—sinuate yuppie woman to sinuate yuppie man: *"Call me when you stop growing."*

Cullen (whose favorite *New Yorker* cartoon was from another generation almost, a Steinberg of two men facing each other as in a duel, the one on the right bearing the names, written in flowery script, Raskolnikov, Rodion, Emma Bovary, Pavel Ivanovich, Chichikov, Candide, Ahab, Leopold Bloom, Papageno, Julien Sorel, Gulliver, the man on the left the name Kim Novak) drew the curtain all the way and deliberately stayed in the shower another five minutes by his computer nerd water-resistant-to-a-hundred-feet watch, even though he was so tired he could barely stand. Ann wasn't there when he got out but she brought him a big plush clean bath sheet and a brand-new beer in a frosted glass.

"I'm sorry," Ann said.

"*I'm* sorry."

They kissed, rather experimentally. The bath sheet made him nervous: it was the kind of luxurious necessity men never buy and mistrust women for having the self-indulgence to buy; it was *stuff* and men don't have stuff and that's why men don't like to move in with women—it bares their poverty. ("So this is where you live," Ann had said the first time he took her to Kew Gardens. She had meant, *So this is how . . .*) And the frosted glass was fraught too; in Zimmerman's freezer—Ann had been to a party at his apartment—there were *nothing* but frosting glasses and ice cube trays, as, down below, there were nothing but six-packs of Sam Adams and smart little plastic containers from smart little gourmet take-outs. Was she trying to tell him . . . ? What was she trying to tell him?

"I went around to East Seventieth this afternoon, just to see what the posh, as they say in the tabloids, Upper East Side looks like in the daytime. I might as well have been in Williamsburg—Brooklyn *or* Virginia. That's how different life up there is from the life you and I lead. Very few men—they're all trading bonds or operating on brains. Lots of women who from their gait and the bags in their hands are just out shopping—and not even varsity shopping; Tampax and cute little strands of pearls that caught their eyes—but are dressed *up*, even in this weather. Little kids with serious names—Hudson and Samantha—with au pairs and nannies, never with their mothers. A sense that everyone there is only there for a minute, until they can get back to East Hampton. Antique stores you're afraid to walk by forget about go in, you might break something. Doctors' offices—lots of plastic and reconstructive surgery; obscure organizations—theosophy, stuff like that. Ever known a theosophat? Hunter College. The Mali mission. Name a city in Mali."

"Timbuktu."

She tisked, annoyed that he knew. "I'd like your reaction to something. To two things."

Cullen disappeared under the bath sheet and rubbed his hair dry. He'd rather have her tell him that toweling wasn't good for his hair, he should just comb it dry, than hear the next part. Finally, there was nothing to do but reappear.

Ann smiled. "Hello."

"Hello."

"You shouldn't towel your hair like that, you should just comb it."

"Ann, please. I'm exhausted. I'm going to fall on my face."

"Does that mean no sex?"

"Yes. No. Maybe. In the morning. I don't know. Just tell me what you have to tell me. Please."

"When Story was appointed PC, he formed a trust to run Corinthian Holdings. You know that."

Cullen sat on the edge of the tub and sipped the beer. Corinthian, Doric, Ionic—long ago and far away he had been taught that they were the—what was the word?—*orders* of Greek architecture. Why had he been taught that and what was the difference between and among them? He didn't have a clue. *Water Spilled From Source To Use.*

"Lyons has been pushing the SportsDome to distract the citizenry from some of the problems that threaten to overwhelm this colossus among cities in the last decade of the twentieth century," Ann said. "Everyone thought the dome would be built, if it were built, downtown, on yet more landfill, where it would be merely ugly and intrusive and environmentally unsound. Lyons surprised everyone by approving the Clinton site, which will be ugly and intrusive and environmentally unsound *and* will displace thousands of people, most of whom will be unable to afford any new housing at all forget about equivalent housing. You know that too.

"What you don't know, what I just found out today, was that Story, knowing which way Lyons was leaning, signaled Corinthian that that little nondescript patch of Manhattan had the site of a stately pleasure dome been decreed and would be worth owning a piece of—preferably pie*ces*. Corinthian put together a phony—Don't shake your head at me like that."

"I'm shaking my head because your source is wrong. Your source is the phony."

"My source," Ann said, "is a source to write home about. He also says—I use the masculine pronoun merely for convenience; my source could easily be a woman—he also says that word is out among those who earn their livings by applying matches to edifices that there's work to be had in Clinton, one simply has to send one's résumé or whatever they have—ashes, probably—one simply has to haul one's ashes over to a man known as Marks. That's not his name; it refers to the scars on his face, merit badges, I suppose, earned in the school of hard knocks. Marks is the conduit to those who want what buildings flambéed and my source contends that he was at one point last month looking for someone who would flambée the Raleigh. . . . Earth to Cullen."

Cullen had been sinking deeper and deeper into a swimming pool in a David Hockney poster on the wall. (*Water Spilled From Source To Use.*) With what was left of his energy, he resurfaced. "Have you talked with Marks?"

She shook her head. "He wants five yards just for a sit-down."

"Ann, please stop talking like a player. Journalists aren't players, they're spectators."

"I'm sorry." Ann squatted down between his legs. "I didn't mean to make light of what you've done. You're a wonderful, wonderful cop. What you did with Claire Langois—both times, what you and Neil did when the driver got shot, they were wonderful things to do. Yes, I'm a spectator, and sometimes spectators like to talk like players; we always get a laugh out of it at ball games." She put her hands on his thighs as she talked, working her fingers under the bath sheet across his lap. It felt good.

"What's the second thing?" Cullen said.

Ann sat cross-legged on the bathmat, her elbows on his knees. "The second thing is did you check their alibis?"

"Whose alibis?"

"Claire's and her mother's."

"Claire's?"

"And her mother's."

"Alibis isn't exactly the word you're looking for. They were a hundred miles away."

"So they say."

Cullen brushed her elbows off him and wrapped himself up in the bath sheet. "Christ, Ann. Not everyone's a suspect."

"Why not?"

He couldn't answer that. "Lise and Claire were flown back from East Hampton by a police airplane. They'd driven there from their house in Sag Harbor."

"Saga*pon*ack."

"Wherever."

"Were they alone in Sagaponack? Did they have house guests? Are there servants or neighbors who could confirm that they were there?"

"Ann, con*firm*ing that they were there hasn't been on anybody's mind. Chuck was killed, they were notified and fetched, so what the fuck do you mean 'con*firm*'?"

" 'Fetched.' How quaint."

"Fuck you."

She stuck her chin out. "Yeah, well, fuck *this:* someone saw Lise Story on the LIE at about six o'clock on the Fourth—the morning of the day Story was killed. Driving west in a white Benz with someone beside her who was probably Claire Langois but she was asleep and her head was turned away so he couldn't see for sure."

"You use the masculine pronoun merely for convenience; your source could easily be a woman."

She gave him a dirty look. "Someone who works at the magazine. He has a place in Remsenburg, he had to come in for a funeral, another AIDS funeral."

"Who?"

"Does it really matter?"

"Yes."

". . . John Anthony."

"John *An*thony?"

"Just because you don't always agree with his movie reviews, Joseph—"

"I *never* agree with John Anthony's movie reviews. And the reason I *never* agree with John Anthony's movie reviews is that he's frequently in error about what went on right in front of him on a very, very big screen—a screen that's standing stock-still and so is he. With the result that I'm inclined to doubt anything John Anthony has to say about what was happening—who was driving, who was sleeping, who was doing anything at all—in a car—what kind of car it was—going sixty miles an hour."

"More like eighty, John said. He barely got a glimpse of them."

"Ann."

"Don't worry. Before I print it, I'll confirm it."

Cullen had an inspiration. "What exit?"

Ann looked triumphant. "What exit of the LIE did he see them at? I knew you'd ask that. Lake Success. Right at the city limit. So, yes, they came all the way in—or at least that far."

"You're not disputing that they were on the East End when the plane came to get them?"

"Of course not."

"But you're suggesting they might've driven in that morning, then driven back out sometime later that day."

"Yes."

"But you're not suggesting they might've driven in that morning, hung around until evening, killed Story, then driven back out in time to be picked up by the plane."

"Don't be stupid," Ann said, doing her imitation of Bronson Pinchot in *Beverly Hills Cop. Dunt be stiyoopid.*

A pause.

"I'm sorry I shouted."

"*I'm* sorry." Ann got her hands under the bath sheet again and squeezed his thighs.

And caressed them.

She pulled the sheet away and yanked it from under him and shoved it under the sink. "Umm."

"Ann."

She got on her knees and licked him.

This was one of his fantasies, except in the fantasy he was standing under the shower and she hauled open the curtain and sat on the edge of the tub, her bare feet in the tub, her legs wide apart, wearing a low-cut red dress with a full skirt bunched up over her thighs, the dress getting wetter and wetter, her hair getting wetter and wetter, drinking the water that ran off him as she sucked him. "Ann."

Without letting go of him, she reached down crosshanded and pulled the big T-shirt up over her neck, her head. Deftly, breaking the link only fractionally, she pulled her arms out and tossed the T-shirt after the towel, then took him back in her mouth again. He tapped on her shoulder. "Ann?"

She looked up at him, which was in the fantasy, except that in the fantasy she looked pleased with herself not annoyed.

"Please."

She stopped and let out a huff and sat back on her haunches. "Please *what*?"

"I want you to drop it."

She looked down at his erection and back up at him. "*Drop* it?"

"So Lise and Claire drove in, so what? Maybe, just maybe, they drove to Forest Hills, to the West Side Tennis Club. To play tennis. Tennis is something both of them play rather well."

That was pretty clever, he had to admit, especially given the conditions under which he'd concocted it, and Ann was on her feet now, as far away from him as she could get without leaving the bathroom, up against the door over which hung a replica of a Manganaro's six-foot hero. ("I've been looking for a six-foot hero all my life," she had told the manager in begging him to let her buy the sign. "This may be the closest I get.") "You'd do anything for her, wouldn't you?" *Snake*.

His answer, had he been permitted to answer, had he not been shoved backwards, more by fear and surprise than by an actual force (though the blast was loud enough to *have* force), into the bathtub, and smacked the back of his head and an elbow against the porcelain, and sprained a wrist trying to soften the fall—his answer would have been that all he'd done so far in this matter had been his duty, a duty Ann knew full well he had tried very hard to evade; that all he'd done he hadn't done *for* anybody—his training didn't teach him to be selective, it taught him to react, to assess, to analyze, to select modes of response based not on personal biases—pro or con—but on his own awareness and understanding of his skills and abilities blah blah blah and so on and so forth. In short, his answer, had he been permitted to answer (*Water Spilled From Source To Use*), would have been bullshit followed by more bullshit topped with bullshit.

The fire bomb tossed through the wide-open door from Ann's garden, though its shock wave clobbered the door she leaned against, thrusting her up against the towel rack, spared her from having to listen to that.

# 15

The dream is always the same:

*He enters without knocking, but not without forewarning: the creak of his bedroom door; the tap-tap-tap of his slippers on the parquetry; the whump of the bathroom door, swollen from his shower of a quarter hour ago (he's ever so clean; showers nightly); the arrogant splatter of urine; the toilet's gasp; the door again, the tap-tap-tap; the click of her latch. A gap of silence, then the hiss of his clothing, of his breath.*

*Now he's at her bedside, on her bed, on her, in her—so quickly it knocks her breath away. He used to wheedle, coax her to want him, to make . . . love; now he just takes. He comes, teeth clenched, grunting.*

*He used to ask hopefully if it was "all right" (sometimes "good") for her; now he just leaves.*

*Then she cries herself to sleep.*

*Every night.*

# 16

"So tell me, Sergeant Cullen, the fuck do people you're with keep getting polished, or almost?" Hriniak stood on the top step of the Soldiers and Sailors, watching dawn tint Riverside Park, the Hudson, Jersey, hot pink.

Across the street, the last Emergency Service van grumbled away from Ann's building, the last TV crew packed up a station wagon, the last nosy neighbors, empty coffee mugs in their hands, scuffed and muled and flip-flopped back to their apartment houses, raring, in spite of their sleepiness, to get to work and recount how they'd been *this* close to Cappy and Tippy and Mopsy and Suzie, the yuppie newshounds—newsbitches. Hriniak's driver leaned on the fender of a Lincoln Towncar, reading a Spanish scandal sheet: *ESTRELLAS DE "DYNASTY" PUGNAN*.

Hriniak looked ever more mayoral, in a gray suit this time, a suit for ending a day not starting one. Why wasn't he sweating? Was he taking Hollywood pills—cool in a bottle? Or was it just that he was a cool jazz fan?

Cullen was sweating, and had his suit coat off, his tie hanging loose, shirt sleeves rolled up above his elbows. Naked when the bomb burst in air, he hadn't consciously dressed *up* to ride the ambulance to Roosevelt Hospital, but he had put on the extra suit and clean dress shirt he kept at Ann's, rather than a T-shirt and Jams or jeans she'd insisted he also leave so that she could tell herself that hers was a place where he sometimes let his hair down. So—what?—so Hoagy Carmichael and the computer nerd wouldn't see the tabloid photographs and the television footage and be embarrassed that their dad went out with a woman fifteen years younger than he and tried to dress away the difference?

Cullen finished his hundredth or so container of coffee in the last couple of hours and walked down the steps to throw it in a trash can that would have been picked clean by scavengers who would have been prowling the park's perimeter at this hour were it not out on the street that out on the street was not a safe place to be. "Come on, Phil. Can I *call* you Phil?" Cullen waited to be called insubordinate, but Hriniak chuckled. "I'm not the link; the link is Story. The chauffeur, Janofsky, was driving Story's sister, Ann was finding out stuff about Story. That I was around was a coincidence."

"Stuff about Story," Hriniak said, "which she won't tell me because she says it's privileged, and neither will you because why?"

Because Ann was high on notoriety. Sitting cross-legged on a gurney in a hallway outside the emergency room, holding an icepack to the bruise on her chest from the towel bar, bright-eyed with fatigue and excitement, she had said, "You were wrong, Cullen—I am a player."

"Before you leave for the Coast to make a movie deal, who's your unimpeachable source?"

She cocked her head. "A *mov*ie deal."

"Ann."

"You'll try and arrest him."

"I'll just *talk* to him. Unless you think *he* threw the bomb, in which case I'll kill him."

She touched his arm. "My hero. And anyway, the bomb squad guys said the device flashed out too soon to've been a serious bomb. It was like a firecracker, meant as a warning. It didn't even singe my rug, damn it. I could've gotten a new dhurrie with the insurance money."

Cullen put his hands up in surrender: *the device*. "You met Prager; he's a good man; it's his investigation. But I'll say this: If you don't cooperate with him, you'll lose all your credibility."

She did John Wayne: "You'll never work in this town again, pilgrim." Then frowned: "What an unlikely speech to come out of your mouth, you who would have me suppress what I know about Lise and—"

Cullen stepped close to her and put his hand over her mouth. "Don't say a word about that to Prager. *I*'ll look into that and *I*'ll decide if it's worth pursuing." He took his hand away and kissed her.

She was like the ice in her fist at first; then she let her lips part and took his tongue and gave him hers. She breathed in his ear, "I miss you."

"You've got to trust me." Whatever that meant. Trust him (*Snake*) to look into and to decide but not to run off with Vera Evans, *estrella de cine*? *You'd do anything for her, wouldn't you?* had been Ann's last words before the *device* exploded, and so far it looked as though the answer was at least, *Well*. . . .

Ann wouldn't let him go. "I'm scared, Joe."

"Rita and Bruce're coming to get you, right?"

Ann nodded into his shoulder. Rita (Ann's best friend since college) and her husband, Bruce, were body builders who ran a combination gym/health food snack bar/workout togs boutique. "I'll stay with them until I can face going home. I'll work out all day long. The next time you see me, I'll look like Arnold Schwarzenegger."

"And do whatever Prager tells you to do. . . . There're reporters out there, you know."

She couldn't help it, she checked her outfit: a big workshirt, washed nearly white, blue jeans ditto rent at the knees. She'd changed too, perhaps so as not to embarrass Nick and Kathryn, her divorced friends. "I won't tell them about us, don't worry."

He waved a hand as though it had never ever crossed his mind, but there was that image of Hoagy Carmichael and the computer nerd—their mother, hands on hips in the background—staring at the kitchen radio over their granola. "If there was ever a time to say 'no comment,' this is the time."

That cock of her head again. "No comment. I like the sound of it." Then she sat up straighter, indignant in advance: "That goes for you too, cowboy. You keep your mouth shut about what I told you."

"I promise," Cullen said.

To Hriniak, on the steps of the Soldiers and Sailors in the hot pink morning, the promise to Ann barely two hours old, Cullen broke it: "I don't know her source, but her information is that Story tipped Corinthian Holdings that Lyons had picked Clinton for the SportsDome. Corinthian bought up . . . The value. . . ."

He petered out, then stopped altogether, for Hriniak was shaking his head with amusement and resignation and bewilderment combined that another human being, a fellow member of the Force yet, could be so fucking gullible.

"What?" Cullen said.

Hriniak laughed and snorted.

Cullen grabbed his coat off the balustrade, whipped it over his shoulder, and started down the steps. "Fuck you." It was too hot to be mocked.

"He was working undercover, asshole."

Cullen stopped and turned. "Story?"

Hriniak shrugged. "Why not? Who would expect a weasel that high up? It was beautiful."

"Beautiful?" Cullen said. He'd never heard Hriniak use the term.

"The fuck're you, Joe, some kind of judge, some kind of moral fucking umpire?"

"I don't like it when civilians play cop, that's all. Look what it got Ann."

Hriniak waved a hand as he turned away. "That's not what you don't like. What you don't like is you weren't in the picture. It was none of your fucking business, people with more at stake and more knowledge and more experience set it up, people—ci*vil*ians—who want to make this a city that can be lived in again, but you're pissed off 'cause they didn't ask your permission."

"I don't know what you're talking about."

"You're a detective sergeant, you're not supposed to know."

They stood as they were for a long time, in a tableau of mistrust and contempt, but their postures were awkward, not adamant, for neither knew how they'd gotten to this point, what lay down the block, around the corner, into next week. Finally, Cullen understood *some*thing and unfroze and moved up the steps. He put a hand on Hriniak's shoulder. "I'm sorry, Phil. You weren't in the picture either, were you?"

"Fuck it," Hriniak said. "I'm out. Not soon, but soon enough. Nobody was in the picture—not me, not Walsh, not Amato. Maslosky sure wasn't in it even though it had IAU written all over it. Story and Lyons dreamed it up. It was a complete rogue operation—no records, only verbal reports, clean as a whistle. They were after a heavy, heavy hitter, someone—don't ask me names, I don't know names, I wasn't in the picture—someone who had the arm on someone at Corinthian, who would take what Corinthian got tipped and run with it before Corinthian could. It backfired: Story tipped Corinthian that the site for the Dome would be Clinton, they put together a paper corporation to buy up the Raleigh, they waited for the heavy, heavy hitter to make his move, instead the Raleigh got torched, Story looked like the bad guy. With Story polished, he can't defend himself, Lyons can deny knowing anything about it, plus he'll say, See? I looked you in the eye and told you having a civilian police department was a stupid idea, but I gave it a chance, but now maybe you'll believe me, look what it got us, a fucking amateur playing cop. . . .

"I was Story's first dep, I'll go. Walsh, Amato, they may go, they may not. Maslosky, Ruth, Ingram, Intaglia, Nixon, Pavonelli, Kean, Paltz, Winerib—Lyons can clean the Department out as far down as he wants, he can have a field day, guys nobody ever heard of'll end up brass, you'll probably be Chief of Department."

Would he stop sweating then? Cullen was bathed in it now, as if he were guilty of something—something other than having broken his promise to Ann, than having tried to deflect her curiosity about why Lise Story had been driving on the LIE at six o'clock in the morning on the day of Charles Story's murder, driving west in a white Benz with someone beside her who was probably Claire Langois. Cullen fought off an urge to draw his piece from his shoulder holster and kill the sun.

"What do you hear about Detroit?" Hriniak said. "I hear they're looking for a Chief. Good sports town, I guess. Christ, I grew up hating them—the Pistons, the Tigers, the Red Wings, the Lions. Bobby Layne. I *hated* Bobby Layne. He wouldn't wear a face mask, I rooted every week someone would yank his nose off. Lee Iacocca. My first car was a plain old Dodge, before they had so many different models, I got no complaints about my Wagoneer, but I *hate* Lee Iacocca, that smug look on his face, marrying that stewardess like he's a regular guy, then dumping her. And that writer, the mystery guy, always writes about Detroit, about cops with skinny girl friends with big tits who can say smartass things, cook a gourmet dinner, *and* give the cop head all at the same time. Leroy Leonard—I *hate* Leroy Leonard."

If he wrote about women like that, instead of women who act like players—who *are* players—and make you make promises you're just going to have to break, Cullen hated him too. "I'm going to take a week."

Hriniak stared. "To do what—check out Detroit?"

"To look into things on my own. Report to you if there's anything to report, otherwise just take the loss."

"Come on, Joe. In the movies, cops do that. In real life, you sharpen a pencil, you report to *some*body."

"Just a week. I'm on hold anyway, with the Dean thing, because of the lawyers."

"You call fire bombs and snipers polishing innocent civilians being on hold? I should have a permanent detail on your ass twenty-four hours a day, sweeping up the broken glass, hauling away the bodies, maybe lucking into a perp or two."

"Just a week. With Zim. Take us off the 119 watch."

"It's Walsh's call, Joe. I'm still the PC, I got to be professional, I can't deep six Walsh's call."

"Then I won't tell you about it," Cullen said.

"Just like in the movies. Someone's got to do for you at 119."

"Bermúdez. He loves stakeouts."

"Fuck's he going to do—work triples?"

"He loves stakeouts."

"Don't tell me about it."

Cullen slung his coat over his shoulder, in defiance of the late PC's (Cullen's old buddy's) directive, yet to be rescinded by his successor (another of Cullen's old buddies), that detectives were to keep their jackets on however hot it got. "See you around, Phil."

Hriniak scuffed at the marble. "Like in the movies."

"IAU, Bermúdez."

"Keith, Joe."

"*José*. *¿Qué tal*, baby? Hey, you all right, homes?"

"I'm all right."

"Ann, she's all right? Where are you, homes, in the subway or something?"

"In a pay phone. They're digging up the street. Ann's all right too. What're you doing in the office, K? I thought you'd be home. I only called to have Cindy tell you to call me when you checked in."

"I came by to pick up my check. Want me to slip yours in your locker?"

"Just leave it on the desk."

"Joe, I left a tarantula on your desk, somebody'd take it."

Cullen laughed. "Put Zim's in my locker too, please, would you, K? K, I need a favor. Zim and I're going to take some personal time. Can you do for us at 119? For a week, max. Anybody asks, tell them you owed us, we hate stakeouts. You can work out with anybody who needs the OT to take the other shifts."

"Hey, I'll take them. I love stakeouts. But listen, *amigo*, I can't do it Saturday night. My uncle's getting married, my mother's brother. For the fourth time, the other three died, you think I should look into it, maybe he's polishing his wives? Nah, I'm just kidding, they got sick, they died, that's all, tough luck. Saturday's the wedding, Friday's his bachelor party. Bachelor, my ass, he's a fucking *espada*, a swordsman. I'm okay for the party, it's Saturday I couldn't work for you."

"I'll work Saturday then," Cullen said.

'Thanks, *hermano*."

"Thank you, Keith."

"What you're up to anything I should know about?"

"Nope."

Bermúdez laughed. "I didn't think so."

"*Hasta pronto*," Cullen said.

"Later, homes."

# 17

"May we call you Mabel?" Cullen passed the basket of sconces (or were they scones? he could never remember) to Mabel Parker.

Zimmerman passed the butter.

Mabel sipped her orange juice and glanced around Windows on the World. "You guys have breakfast here often?"

Cullen laughed. "Call me Joe. This is—"

"Neil." Zimmerman invaded Cullen's airspace, and took over the conversation, which didn't surprise Cullen in that Mabel was fresh but did surprise him in that her name was Mabel. Zimmerman's women were fresh but had names like Brooke and Tandy and Tree and Townsend, last-name-sounding names. Except sometimes their names *were* last names *and* were the names they went by. It was very confusing.

To Mabel (he could call her Parker) Zimmerman was singing the song he'd learned from Darelle Dean: ". . . a call to the precinct from a woman saying she saw someone leaving Story's house around seven the night he was pol— The night he was killed. Tall, thin, wearing a raincoat, a hat, slacks, sneakers. The witness didn't see the woman's face and couldn't make a guesstimate of her age. The officer who took the call thought she meant the woman left by the *front* door. That would've made for a crowd since Tom Valentine was also spotted near or at the front door around the same time. No action's been taken on this tip because Valentine's everybody's favorite candidate for perp.

"What you haven't heard, what nobody's heard because it hasn't been made public, is Crime Scene found a footprint in a flower bed between Story's *back* yard and the courtyard of an apartment building on Seventy-first Street. We're entertaining the possibility—we find it an enter*tain*ing possibility''—Zimmerman smiled, but Mabel was staring out the window toward Pennsylvania—''that the caller was in that building or another building on Seventy-first and saw the woman leaving by the *back* way.

''The call was made at the height of that thunderstorm the other day. It came in on an unlisted line—''

''It was a woman's footprint, then?'' Mabel said by way of dragging herself back to the table.

''A woman's ten, a man's eight. A small foot,'' Zimmerman said.

Mabel got out her Carltons.

''The call came in on an unlisted line reserved for precinct business, known to Department personnel, others in law enforcement, people like yourself.''

Mabel got two fingernails into a Carlton and prized it kicking and screaming out of the pack.

''I don't think this is the smoking section, Mabel,'' Zimmerman said.

Mabel lighted the Carlton and blew the smoke out of the side of her mouth over her shoulder. ''I don't have a lot of time, Zimmerman. Get on with it.''

(He was grinning. She'd called him Zimmerman. He was in love.)

''The language the caller used to describe the woman was arguably that of a trained professional. Combined with the knowledge of an inside number, well, we're wondering if maybe the witness wasn't someone with some legal or law enforcement background who saw *some*thing, but not enough to really want to come forward and risk her reputation.''

Mabel blew smoke right at him this time. ''Too bad the cop wasn't fast enough to trace the call.''

(The grin got bigger. He *had*, the son-of-a-bitch. He'd had an Exec-Call demonstration and ordered one for his apartment.)

''I'll spare you all the details,'' Zimmerman said. (The details would come later, over dinner at Mortimer's or M.K., then back to Zim's place, or Parker's, for tofutti all rooty or Ben and

Jerry's or whatever the fuck, coffee ground on the Braun, brewed in the Krups or maybe the Europiccola, a dram of Drambuie, some Keith Jarrett or Kitaro on the DiscJockey, turn the Yafa down low, adjourn in due course to the futon, in the afterglow instruction in the use of the Interplak [except she wouldn't need instruction, would she, she probably had her own, carried her own spare brush head around in her bag to plug in wherever she landed for the night], switch on the Sound Soother 2, good night ladies, milkman's on his way.) "The short of it is the call *was* traced to a pay phone at Seventieth and Lex. By the time a conditions car got over there, the caller was gone."

"Obviously," Mabel said.

"Obviously."

(He was going to die, his grin was so big—die of a split-open face.)

"There's a drugstore on the corner. Taubman's. When the storm came blowing through, the pharmacist, Taubman junior, took a look out the window at the people running, the wind blowing over trash cans, signs swinging. He noticed one of his customers on the phone."

*Of course he did, the dirty old man. My skirt was up around my crotch, my blouse was sticking to me like a wet T-shirt contestant's.* "Pretty circumstantial, Zim."

(Overload. Grin overload. Sound the general alarm.)

"Maybe, but worth a little investment of time, I figure. Taubman junior doesn't know her name, but she's a regular. Once a week at least, sometimes twice, she buys condoms. Fourex. Rolled."

A rapier of smoke. A stiletto. "She's not worried about AIDS then."

The grin warped just a little. "Oh? How's that?"

"Natural skins are pervious to the HIV virus. Rubbers aren't."

The sick look of a man who had hoped for once to have a virgin—an experienced virgin, to be sure, but a virgin nonetheless. Gradually, Zimmerman regrouped. "Taubman junior gave a good description: curly brown hair"—

*Wavy. Auburn.*

—"Five-five, one twenty-five"—

*Five-five and a half, one-twenty-one before this high-calorie breakfast.*

—"Early thirties"—

*Twenty-nine. Well, just turned thirty, not long enough ago to actually* be *thirty.*

—"Not married. No ring and—"

"Lots of women don't wear rings anymore."

The grin lost its flaccidity. "No ring *and* she always buys just the three-pack of condoms. He said, Taubman junior, that she reminds him of the little old ladies, widows, who go to the supermarket every day and buy one lamb chop. They're afraid if they buy three or four to keep in the freezer, if they plan ahead, then die, they'll be out the money they spent. She's afraid—"

"She's afraid if she buys a dozen she won't get laid so she must not be married because married women get laid all the time? Get real, guys." Mabel jabbed her cigarette out and hurled the pack into her pocketbook. "All right, gentlemen. I've listened to your *tip*. What the fuck, in the few seconds of patience I have remaining, do you want in return?"

Cullen sat forward to bear the brunt for a while. "Are there any investigations in your office of the Raleigh fire or any other recent fires in Clinton?"

Mabel laced her fingers together and rested them on the edge of the table, a woman of experience addressing hyperactive little boys. "It's not my case, but I do know—as would you if you'd simply asked—that Patrol found no evidence of arson at the Raleigh."

Cullen nodded. "We're talking, of course, about torches whose signature would be no signature."

Mabel looked at him from under her lashes. "Everyone's heard by now that Ann Jones had a fire bomb delivered early this morning while in the company of a certain police officer. I trust everyone's okay."

Cullen's aches were history, but he realized just now that there *had* been some lasting damage: his computer nerd watch hadn't beeped in hours. It was keeping time okay—8:38.21 . . . 22 . . . 23—but the alarm had been disabled, probably when he walloped his wrist on the bottom of the bathtub. "Fine, yes, thanks."

"And is there a connection between that incident and your question to me?"

Cullen took the promise and ripped it to shreds. "Ann has a source who was paid to torch the Raleigh." (So he exaggerated a little, so what? *Water Spilled From Source To Use*.)

"Paid by whom?" Mabel asked, looking, in her eyes, in the way she held her head, as though she suspected he exaggerated.

Cullen spread his hands. "I was hoping for your help on that too."

Mabel sat way back in her chair, Leah Levitt style, putting the maximum distance between her and people who were getting a little wearisome. "So we're not really trading here at all. You want to know who had the Raleigh torched and you want to know what 'trained professional,' what person 'with some legal or law enforcement background' might've seen someone leaving Story's house? How the hell would I know anything like that?"

Zimmerman returned from the penalty box. "Not 'person' —woman. We know it was a woman. What we wonder for starters is, is there a woman in your office who lives in that neighborhood. We can't get addresses without raising eyebrows."

Mabel raised hers. "You want confidential information on people who aren't suspects in the slightest, they're only 'trained professionals'?"

"No one's a suspect, Mabel," Cullen said. "We're trying to catch a killer." He pushed his chair back, finished his coffee, motioned with his head at Zimmerman, stood. "You have our number."

Mabel watched them go. Good exit. Good guys. *Cute* guys. Nice bodies, nice dressers, nice manners, nice eyes. Not guys who got it right every time they tried to understand how a woman's mind worked, but not total pigs and not wimps either. A kind of guy Mabel rarely met any more, had turned off when she had met them because as nice as they were (too nice a lot of the time to pick up that she was addicted to vodka, nicotine, cocaine, and those popular sedatives) they were cynical enough and hip enough to know that she was addicted to money.

Mabel met guys to whom women addicted to money clung like lint; guys whose shirts cost more than the nice guys' suits; guys who tickled your palm with their middle fingers when they shook your hand and dared you with their eyes to make something of it in front of their wives and the rich powerful friends who were introducing you and *their* wives, who like the guys' wives knew exactly what was going on and couldn't say anything because otherwise they'd be out in the street; guys who smelled of cigars and aftershave and would have said, if you'd called them on it, that they were priceless cigars, priceless aftershave, but who didn't possess among them the nose to know they still stank; guys who tipped the bellhops at the hotels they took you to (after taking you to dinner and a show) before they finally sprung for an apartment (so they wouldn't have to take you anywhere, just meet you and ball you) with a here-kid-I-don't-know-if-this-is-a-ten-or-a-twenty-or-a-hundred-and-I-don't-give-a-fuck-just-take-it-and-scram gesture, peeling the bill off the roll and taking the bellhop by the elbow and cramming the bill into his hand, looking out the window while they did it, like they'd taken the room for its view of the park, thinking the bellhop's impressed and never even once seeing the contempt in the bellhop's eyes, the pity, almost, for the dirty old man—not to mention the bewilderment and a little bit of contempt that someone with her looks, her class, had to sell herself, because that's what it amounted to, to a sleazebag like this; guys like Norman Levitt, Leah's husband.

Mabel watched them go and wished they'd come back and buy her a bloody mary—so what if it was eight forty-five in the morning, you had to start sometime, right?—and then another and another, until she was loose enough to tell them she was the woman they were looking for. Well, not *the* woman—not the tallish, thinnish woman in a long tan lightweight raincoat and a soft-brimmed brown hat, white pants, blue espadrilles, who not very long after Charles Story was murdered came out the back door of 119, locked it, went down the steps, crossed the yard, went through a hole in the fence into the courtyard or patch of cement or whatever it was behind 116, went along another fence and down a passageway and out a gate—a gate with a panic lock—to the street. Not *that* woman, but the woman with the curly brown hair (wavy auburn, really), five-five, one twenty-five (five-five and a half, one-twenty-one, really), early thirties (just turned thirty, really, not long enough ago to actually *be* thirty), not married, always buys one lamb chop, one bottle of beer, one can of tuna fish, a pint of milk, three Fourexes, the smallest size of everything possible because she's afraid if she buys more, if she plans ahead, then dies, she'll be out the money she spent, okay a neurotic, an addict, a screwed-up, strung-out piece of trim, but still, I mean guys, hey, what's so bad, what's so terrible, wouldn't you, couldn't you, won't you . . . ? Please.

Please.

# 18

''Hi, Con.''

''Joe? Kids, it's Daddy. Joe, are you all right?''

Shouts of *Daddy, Daddy, thank god you're okay*? Nope. Shouts of nothing. Something like a mumble sounding like *We still goah ah duh Metz gay?*

''Of course you're still going to the Mets game,'' Connie said. ''Joe, you're still taking the kids to the Mets game, aren't you?''

The Mets game. Saturday night. When he'd said he'd work for Bermúdez. Shit. ''You bet.''

''Are you still in the hospital, Joe?''

''I'm at the office. I'm fine.''

''Who's this woman, Joe? How long've you been seeing her?''

''Not long.'' A year. ''I'm not really seeing her.'' She just gives me head in the shower and if I don't go off, fire bombs do.

''Where did you meet her?'' One of Connie's favorite questions, as if introduction were destiny. And maybe, in a one-horse world, it was: she and Cullen had met in Washington Square Park, where every clement morning at eleven and afternoon at four Connie Carrera, teacher/idealist, had brought the children from a nursery school on West Fourth Street and where, in the morning or in the afternoon and sometimes both, Joe Cullen, a rookie beat cop in the Six in those days, would saunter past and hang around and talk as if he had all day, as if crime went on hold when he felt like flirting; and seventeen years later, here they still were—he footloose, she nurturing kids.

''She's a reporter. For *City* magazine.'' Who had written

about one of his and Zimmerman's better jobs. The Case of the Schizophrenic Cop, *City* had called Ann's piece, which won a Silurians award and whose lead is worth repeating:

> Everyone who knew him knew Harris Schwartz spent his Thursday nights at a faux cajun joint in Chelsea, playing rubboard in a zydeco band under the *nom de musique* Bois Sec d'Evenrude. No one, arguably, should have been *that* surprised that on Tuesdays, Harris, a cop with three decorations for valor, three kids, and a wife who is often mistaken for Valerie Bertinelli, shaved his legs, put on a bunny outfit, answered to Roxanne, and served drinks at a cocktail lounge at Newark Airport.

"The kids've never met her; they've never even heard of her. What is she, some kind of secret?"

*What am I, some kind of secret?* Ann had said more than a few times, or words to that effect, when the subject of meeting Hoagy and the nerd had come up—when she'd brought it up. "Con, I don't think—"

"Kids don't miss anything, Joe. You know that. They find out something in this kind of way, they know you're ambivalent."

He had never said he wasn't ambivalent. He wasn't ambivalent about being ambivalent. "Can I talk to them?"

"Have you had it?" Connie said.

"Had what?"

"Don't make me say it. They're right here."

"Had . . . *sex*?" He was instantaneously sorry he'd said that. He could've said something like, oh, *Had a meaningful, thoughtful dialogue on our innermost feelings?*

"A *blood* test," Connie said through rigid lips.

"You mean . . . ?"

*"Yes."*

"I'm not sure it's any of your business—"

"The children's *health* is my business."

"—but neither Ann nor I is in any of the risk groups"—though Ann had suggested that the wait for the AIDS antibodies test results might be salutary, had suggested it with hindsight and rue after their first time in bed, for which they'd skipped dessert after their first dinner together—"Can I talk to the kids?"

There was the unambivalent sound of the phone's being put down hard on a hard surface. Then Hoagy Carmichael got on.

"Hi, Dad."

"Hi, James. How're you?"

" 'Kay."

"What're you up to?"

"Having breakfast."

"How about later? Any plans?"

"No."

"Going to practice?"

"Yeah."

"Going swimming?"

"Yeah."

"Tennis?"

"Yeah."

"At night, right? When it's not so hot?"

"Right."

"How's everything? Everything all right?"

"Yeah."

"You sure?"

"Yeah."

"Anything you want to tell me, ask me?"

"Like what?"

". . . Tenny there?"

"Hang on."

The unambivalent sound of the phone's being let fall to the floor, then let dangle at the end of its cord, knock knock knocking against a cabinet door.

"Dad?"

"Hi, Ten."

"How's your watch?"

"Great. I love this watch, Tenny. I don't know how I did without it."

"That all?"

"Is what all? Hey, that's a pretty big reaction to a birthday present."

"No, I mean, like is that all you called to say?"

". . . Do you have someplace to be?"

"No."

"Something better to do?"

"No."

"So what're you doing?"

"I'm talking to you."

*One, two, three, four, five.* "What else is new?"

"I'm learning Quattro. It's out there."

*Out there*, he'd learned when he'd asked *out where?*, having replaced *stupid* which had replaced *savage* which had replaced *rad* which had replaced *to the max* which had replaced. . . . He'd forgotten. "Everything else okay?"

"What do you mean?"

"Just . . . Nothing. Are you having a good time?"

"Doing what?"

"Now that school's out, *Steph*anie."

"Don't call me that, Dad."

"Sorry. It's just that I don't understand why, when what I do all day is try and get answers from people who don't— Oh, never mind."

"What?"

"Nothing."

"Daddy, you like hate it when *I* do that."

"I know."

"What, then?"

"Forget it. Really. It's nothing."

"Like here's Mom, okay then? Bye."

"Ten— Shit."

"I beg your pardon," Connie said.

"Hi."

"Are you all right, Joe?"

"Yes, I said I was all right."

"Don't get testy. This bomb—it has to do with Tom Valentine, doesn't it? Your girlfriend's writing something about the Raleigh, isn't she, and someone threw the bomb to scare her into backing off, didn't they?"

Had every chance listener to the morning news put it together so deftly, or just the cops' ex-wives? "It wasn't really a bomb. And she's not my girlfriend."

The unambivalent sound of tongue against teeth, of an ex-wife's disbelief. "I drove Doug to the station this morning.

His car's in the shop. There were cops all around Van Cortlandt Park. I heard on the radio they arrested some guy Tom was in Vietnam with, one of the Hopeless, Monsky or something. They think he killed those people—the ones whose fingers were cut off. They don't really think Tom's hiding there, do they?"

"I guess maybe they do."

"But you don't."

"Connie, I haven't really. . . ."

"What?"

"Nothing."

"What, Joe?"

". . . ."

*"What?"*

Cullen stretched out a leg and shut the door with his foot. Zimmerman was down at Missing Persons getting some tips on what power tennis racquet to buy from Schuyler Barnwell or Barnwell Schuyler, Cullen could never remember which, who had somehow stumbled into the Police Department from Princeton, where he'd played Number One.

"When we were kids, Tom was fascinated with Jamaica Bay. There're islands there, I guess. Some are submerged at high tide, others are . . . I don't know if habitable's the word, but you can walk around on them. He loved saying the names. Pumpkin Patch is one I remember. He went out there a lot one summer"—a summer Joe Cullen, the juvenile delinquent, the wild one, the rebel without a cause, had spent shoplifting forty-fives from record stores along Queens Boulevard—"with somebody's cousin who lived in Howard Beach and had a boat."

"And you think that's where he is?"

"He could be anywhere."

"Joe?"

"Yes?"

"Be careful."

". . . How're the kids?"

"You just *talked* to them."

"That's why I'm asking."

Connie laughed. "I have to go."

"John *Anth*ony?" Zimmerman thought movie critic was *the* job to have, thought John Anthony second by a nose to Pauline

Kael in perspicacity, perspicuousness, erudition, wit, and spleen.

"They could've been going anywhere," Cullen said. "They could've had an urge for . . . I don't know—lox from Zabar's. They're rich people; they don't think, they don't plan, they don't ask if it's convenient or affordable."

Zimmerman shook his head. "It would've come out. It would've been remarked on—the irony that they made a round trip into the city on impulse, then had to come all the way back in again because of a tragedy."

Cullen shook *his* head. "It would've come out *if* they'd been suspected of being something other than what they are, which is victims. Since they *are* victims, since they've done nothing suspicious, they haven't been subject to interrogation. Which is as it should be. We're not talking about alibis."

After a while, Zimmerman said. "What?"

"What what?"

"I thought you were going to say something else."

"I was thinking I've got to get my car fixed." Connie's husband, Doug, Hoagy's and the nerd's stepfather, at least had his car in the shop; Cullen's car was parked in front of his building, accumulating tickets.

"I thought you said it was a lost cause."

"What's a lost cause is my affording a new car, or even a not-very-decent used one."

"If you moved in with Ann you wouldn't need a car. You could bike to work and use a car from the motor pool on the job. Or ride with me."

"I don't have a bike," Cullen said.

"I'll sell you mine."

"Not your StumpHumper? I thought you loved that bike. I thought you slept with it."

"Stump*Jumper*. I've got my eye on a track bike. A LeMond."

"What about tennis?"

"What about it?"

"Where do you get the time? Where do you get the energy?"

Zimmerman shrugged the shrug of a man whose tank of energy needed only an occasional topping off. "Barns, believe it or not, plays with wood—a Bancroft Super Winner. When he smelled that synthetics were going to drive wood out of the market, he bought fifty frames. He stores them in a kind of humidor he built; every couple of years, he pulls out a new one."

"And lights it up?"

"He won't sell me one, so I think I'll probably go with a Donnay."

Cullen thought a Donnay was a car. "Has Ann been on my case to you?"

"I have eyes, Joe. She wants more of you."

"She's got a lot—and she doesn't have my dirty laundry."

"Freud's conundrum? 'What does a woman want?' The answer is: everything under one roof—including dirty laundry."

Cullen looked over at Zimmerman. "You figured that out and Freud couldn't?"

Zimmerman picked up a ringing phone. "IAU, Zimmerman. Wait one." He covered the mouthpiece. "The bottom line"—

*Oh, christ, not the* bottom *line.*

—"is that you don't give a fuck about Lise and Claire's mystery tour on the LIE. You know there's an explanation for it that has nothing to do with Story's getting polished. They *had* to have lox from Zabar's, they *had* to be at Tiffany's when the doors opened."

"They were going to play tennis in Forest Hills, I told Ann."

"Perfect. The perfect explanation."

"Except I don't believe it."

"Make yourself. The alternative, your going to see Lise Story with your real motive the seduction of Vera Evans is too horrible to contemplate." Zimmerman uncovered the receiver. "Sorry to keep you waiting. How may I help you? . . . Hello, Darelle. . . . Good. . . . That fast? . . . Really? . . . You're absolutely sure? . . . Jesus. . . . Now be real cool on this, Darelle. Let us handle it. . . . No, we'll tell your sister's lawyer when it's time. . . . Thanks, Darelle. Remember, be cool. . . . So long." He hung up and got up and went to the door and closed it and sat back down.

"Yes?" Cullen said.

"Darelle's friend at the phone company ran Downtown's MUDS for the week before Deborah Dean got shot," Zimmerman said. "She's going to run more, but this was a start. There were three calls to Deborah's home number from one extension."

Sudden panic that the extension was his, Snake Cullen's, the man who didn't want everything under one roof, just the sex and the laughs and the Lyle Lovett albums and the *Hill Street Blues* reruns and the Buffalo chicken wings. Everything that goes around comes around, as Connie would say (*did* say), and so it was coming around that he who had done such things as have an affair with the midwife who was to deliver his second child ("Talk about in*ter*nal affairs, Joe. Good christ"), he who was unambivalent about being ambivalent about introducing his children to a woman who gave him head in the shower, he whose motive in wanting to ask Lise Story about her mystery tour on the LIE was very likely the seduction of Vera Evans, was on Downtown's MUDS as making calls to a rookie woman cop he'd been having an affair with and had shot in a lover's quarrel—never mind that not only were they not lovers, he didn't even know her. "Amato's extension, right? We've both got our favorite suspects, right, and mine's Amato. . . . Right?" Amato with the roving hands and the dangling conversations.

Zimmerman heard Cullen's nervousness and knew that he knew. He shook his head. "Not Amato."

Cullen got up and went to the window and looked down at the mad dogs and Englishmen out in the noonday sun. What goes around comes around. Sooner or later, everybody comes to Rick's. It's a one-horse world. Was that why the son-of-a-bitch didn't sweat? "Not Hriniak."

"Hriniak," Zimmerman said.

# 19

Somewhere back before his brain got fried, Monroe (World) Riggs learned this lesson:

. . . .

Shit. He can't remember.

Oh yeah. Here it is. Listen up:

You can sure as shit always front somebody and you can sure as shit sometimes front everybody but sometimes you can sure as shit never front nobody.

So the fuck does Bobby Liberty think he can front World that he didn't have nothing to do with ashing the Raleigh, nothing to do with popping that Benz in Queens, nothing to do with making a special delivery to some bitch on Riverside Drive, when World's got eyes to see Bobby Liberty was there all three of them times, on the scene, plain as day, big as life?

"Bobby, shit, homes, I *seen* you scoping the Raleigh, man, I live in the Cabot, brother, you ain't forgot that, did you? I seen all the homeboys and bitches lamping and scoping them poor fuckers jumping out the windows, splattering their brains all over the floor"—*Ice is nice, but on account of I had a taste of desire, gimme fire*—"then I seen most of the homeboys and bitches split the scene, but one homeboy I see keep on keeping on lamping, he's been lamping since the first fire trucks and cop cars showed up, in the middle of *Geraldo,* he ain't even hardly moved, except once he walked down the block to the deli and came back with a Sprite and a donut it looked like, and that homeboy, Bobby, is you. I seen you, homey. I *seen* you.

" 'Sides that, homey, I *seen* you slying out to Queens in the middle of the night, man. I am on your case, brother. You was in a booth in the back of Delbert's, homes, I was in a booth in the front, your beeper went off, you went and made a call, you was with two def bitches, you dissed both of them, homey, you split. I say to myself, 'Shit, where's the wack homeboy going leaving them two def bitches all by themselves.' I tagged along, bro. You slyed out to Queens, homes, I was like your shadow. You boosted a Aries, took the Triborough, cooped out by La Guardia. I boosted a Chevette, I took the Triborough, I scoped you cooping, brother. Bridge over the Grand Central, wire and shit all over it so wack fuckers don't drop rocks and shit down on the cars, you slyed through the fence, walking like a motherfucking gimp on account of the motherfucking rifle you got stuck down your pants leg, homes, a Benz comes by, you pop it, brother. Wow, solid. What a fucking shot. Marines teach you to shoot like that, man? Shit. I seen you drive down to Brooklyn baby, down by the bridge, drop a big sack in the river, sank like a stone. I seen you ditch the Aries, get on the subway, start housing some bitch like you was just a regular dude going to work.

"And that ain't all, homey. I *seen* you make that special delivery to some bitch on Riverside Drive. I *fol*lowed you, bro. I seen you slipping and sliding, looking this way and that way, acting like you didn't have nothing to do in the world when you sure as shit had something to do, homey, you had to make that special delivery to some bitch on Riverside Drive.

"You hopped on a crosstown bus, homes, I hopped on my ten-speed, hitched a ride on that same motherfucking bus all the way across town. You got off at Broadway, you went into a Pizza Hut, you made some phone calls, I slyed out of sight and scoped the *whole* thing, brother. You came out, you walked over to West End, you walked up a block, down a block, back a block, over to Riverside, cross to the park, back over to the other side of the street, down back the way you came, back up again, fronting anybody who might could be thinking you was up to something low, but not fronting me, homes. You wasn't even hip I was scoping you, motherfucker.

"I scoped you hopping that gate by that big apartment house, homes, I figured you to go up the fire escape, boost a stereo, a TV, a CD player. But you didn't, did you, homey? You went round back of that little building next to the big building, made that special delivery to some bitch who lives there, didn't you? I stayed out front with my ten-speed, so I didn't see nothing, brother. I thought I heard something, a bump, like, but I might not've, I might just've thought I did the way you sometimes think you might could hear something 'cause you was where you might could've heard it, you hip to what I'm talking about, homeboy?

"Fire trucks, the man, all that shit. I slyed over and lamped a while and heard the man talking, bro, saying somebody made a special delivery to some bitch lived in that building. You can front the man, brother, but you think I ain't no hard homeboy, you wack cocksucker, you can front me the way you front the man?"

Bobby Liberty took the toothpick out of his mouth, checked that it wasn't too soggy for further service, put it back. "So?"

Questions like that World's fried brain couldn't always handle, especially when he'd just dumped it of just about everything it contained. "Wha-wha-what?"

Bobby hefted his testicles. "So what're you, bum-rushing me, World?"

"Who? Me? Hey, no. Word up, Bobby."

"You gonna drop a George on me?"

"Shit, homes, I ain't gonna drop a George on you. I was just hoping you could help me get some hard hype is all, Bobby. To, you know, house the bitches."

"Hard hype?"

"I want to *ash* some place, homes. I need a mental."

"A what?"

"A mental. A guy who teaches you how to do something."

"A guy who teaches you how to do something is a mental?"

"I seen it on the tube. This homeboy wanted to learn how to play the violin, he needed a mental."

"You a faggot or something, World?"

"No!"

"Violins is for faggots."

"I ain't no faggot."

Bobby's beeper went off. "I got to go, World. You drop a George on me, I'll rip your faggot nuts off."

You can sure as shit always front somebody and you can sure as shit sometimes front everybody but sometimes you can sure as shit never front nobody. So fuck Bobby Liberty, World'll go see Marks himself, 'cause every def homeboy's hip it ain't up to Bobby Liberty to decide what buildings he'll ash, who he'll make surprise package deliveries to, it's up to Marks.

So World hopped on his ten-speed (boosted off a parking meter outside NYU, off some smart homeboy probably, except how the fuck smart could the homeboy who locked it there be if he ain't hip that the boosters are hip to the locksmiths, he needed a better lock than one of them old Citadels), and rode over to Marks's, who had this thing about people, he lived out in the fucking country practically, up by the Harlem River across from Yankee Stadium near where the old homeboys always said the other ball park used to be, the Polio Grounds.

"Bobby Liberty's fronting you, Marks," World practiced saying as he rode, "if he told you nobody's hip he ashed the Raleigh, if he told you nobody's hip he popped a Benz in Queens, if he told you nobody's hip he made that special delivery to that bitch on Riverside Drive. *I*'m hip he ashed the Raleigh, I'm hip he popped a Benz in Queens. *I*'m hip he made that special delivery to that bitch on Riverside Drive. *I*'m hip and *he* ain't hip I'm hip, so what kind of homeboy would you rather have doing hard hype for you, Marks, a homeboy who's hip to somebody trying to front him or a homeboy who thinks he's fronting somebody when he ain't doing nothing of the kind?"

But before World could say that, he had to reconsider everything, had to reassess, reevaluate, take it from the top, start all over again—which, when your brain was fried, was like getting toothpaste back in the tube. Because when World got to Marks's—just *before* he got to Marks's—he saw somebody coming out of Marks's who he wouldn't have imagined in a million years he would ever see anywhere *near* Marks's—not at three o'clock in the morning or any other time, not getting into a regular old car or any other kind of car, not wearing jeans and a T-shirt and Pumas or any other kind of threads—Mister Sidney Lyons, the motherfucking homeboy Mayor of the City of New York.

# 20

Commanded by Chief of Department John A. Walsh Jr., letters in basketball and baseball at Jamaica High School (and, after that, in baseball at St. John's; Purple Heart, Korea; medals and citations and honors of every description in thirty-two years in the New York Police Department), one hundred Emergency Service officers set out in launches into Jamaica Bay from Floyd Bennett Field and Bergen Beach Park and Canarsie Beach Park in Brooklyn, and Spring Creek Park and Rockaway Community Park in Queens, on the cusp of another ferocious pink dawn, and raided a nameless island in Pumpkin Patch Channel off Grassy Bay, two of the names young Tom Valentine had loved to say. (Others he'd loved—and still did: Big Fishkill Channel, Hassock Channel, Hassock Creek, Broad Channel, Big Channel, Beach Channel, Pumpkin Patch Marsh, Elders Point Marsh, Duck Point Marshes, Stony Creek Marsh, Nestepol Marsh, Yellow Bar Hassock, Little Egg Marsh, Black Wall Marsh, Rulers Bar Hassock, The Raunt, Winhole Marsh, Silver Hole Marsh, Duck Creek Marsh, East High Meadow, Joco Marsh, Ruffle Bar, Big Egg Marsh, Canarsie Pol.) Helicopters staged at Floyd Bennett flew in support; others from TV stations whose assignment desks had been tipped by phone calls at around midnight (''anonymous'' calls made in Walsh's well-known and unmistakable austere son-of-a-bitch cadence) swooped and spun recklessly, nearly making themselves news.

Seventeen people had been living on the island—seventeen *homeless* people, the press called them, while civil libertarians (including—it's a one-horse world—Jimmy Freed, counsel for Police Officer Deborah Dean) pointed out that the *island* was their home and therefore protected by the Constitution against warrantless searches and seizures. Eight of the seventeen were children, four were women, five were middle-aged or elderly men. None was Tom Valentine, lover of this place's place-names and fox to the raiders' hounds.

(A number of the raiders had served in Vietnam—like Tom Valentine, one-horse world that it is—and noted both to themselves and out loud the force of the sense of *déja vu* that gripped them as the ferocious pink dawn turned to white hot day. It was not simply an illusion induced by the watery landscape, by the stupefying heat; there was that old frustration they had felt so many times so long ago at setting out to look for Charlie and landing only mamma-sans, little kids, old farts.)

One of the women and the eldest of her three children, a girl of five, died. Depending on one's affiliation, the woman, Althea Dove, her daughter, Lamotta, in her arms, either panicked and ran right off the island into Pumpkin Patch Channel (*Pumpkin Patch Channel, Pumpkin Patch Channel*, young Tom had used to almost sing), *or* she was knocked down and possibly out by an Emergency Service officer whose order to turn the child over to his care (he'd been in Nam, this particular officer, and remembered what hell those kids had raised with their plastic bombs and shit, you couldn't trust the fucking pissants worth a good god damn) Althea had not heeded.

Depending on one's affiliation, it was either a predictable or a pathetic end to Althea Dove's pathetic story: once upon a time a registered nurse with a good job, a nice apartment, and a responsible boyfriend, she had lost first the boyfriend (in a car crash), then the job (when the crack with which she hoped to erect a barrier against her grief toppled over and buried her), then the apartment (when the landlord said he couldn't feed *his* children with her good intentions).

Althea left the kids at a cousin's and moved into a crack house. By chance, a former girlhood friend, now a social worker, heard about Althea's fall from grace and sent to her through a sympathetic fellow-addict a series of entreaties that finally persuaded Althea to meet with her at a coffee shop around the corner from the house.

The social worker, Joy Griffith (the same Joy Griffith—it's a one-horse world—who was Tom Valentine's old lady and was to die in the Raleigh fire), recognized right away that Althea was someone who was so far down that up was beyond imagining:

"How long you been in that house, girl?"

"Dunno."

Joy Griffith knew it had been four months. *Four* months. "Been out at all?"

"Yes."

Joy Griffith knew that Althea had not been out at all. Not once. "Let me tell you something, girl."

"What?"

"I have a dream. Doctor King had a dream. *I* have a dream."

The fuck's Doctor King? I dunno no Doctor King.

"You ain't been outta that house, girl, in four months. The brothers in that house leave two, three times a day some of them, maybe only two, three times a week some of the others, but they all of them, at one time or another, leave that house. They leave the house, they boost a car, a TV, they knock over a store, they get some bread, they come back and score more jumbo.

"You get bread to score more jumbo too, girl, but you don't leave the house to get it. You just stay indoors and party, 'cept you don't look like no party girl no more, girl, you look like shit. You just stay indoors and party with the brothers who leave the house, boost a car, a TV, knock over a store, get some bread, come back and score some pussy and some jumbo.

"Motherfuckers like that—*brothers* they may call themselves, but they are *mother*fuckers—motherfuckers like that, girl, you party with them, they don't stop to slip no rubbers on their johnsons. Bad niggers don't slip rubbers on their johnsons, girl, and those motherfuckers are *bad* niggers.

"But when you party with motherfuckers like that, girl, who ain't slipped no rubbers on their johnsons, this is what goes down: you get pregnant, you get AIDS, your baby gets AIDS and a crack jones; maybe the motherfucker gets AIDS too, but the fuck do you care about that?

"My dream, girl, is this: my dream is that black sisters, Hispanic sisters—all sisters anywhere, but especially black sisters and Hispanic sisters—will *just say no* to these motherfuckers. No pussy till you motherfuckers get your shit together.

"Just. Say. No.

"You dig, girl? You dig what it'd mean if you could say it, if all the sisters could say it? Say it and get the motherfuckers to *hear* it? It would be a new motherfucking world. That's my dream, girl. That is my dream."

That was Joy Griffith's dream, and in time, when she had dragged herself up to a point where she was no longer so far down that up was beyond imagining, it became the dream of Althea Dove. At first, Althea said no to the motherfuckers and the motherfuckers beat the shit out of her until she spread her legs for them, fuck putting rubbers on their johnsons. (This was an eventuality Joy Griffith had foreseen but hadn't mentioned because she knew the sisters she was trying to get to dream her dream along with her got the shit beaten out of them plenty already as it was; she feared that until the consciousness of the motherfuckers had been *created*, forget about raised, it might be necessary for the sisters whom she was trying to get to dream her dream along with her to do more than just say no to the motherfuckers but to cut themselves off from them altogether. "Or maybe we should just cut the motherfuckers' johnsons *off*," Joy Griffith would sometimes say when feeling frustrated by the intractability of it all.)

Interestingly, as time went by, the beating stopped. Surprisingly, some of the motherfuckers slipped rubbers on their johnsons. Miraculously, a few of them saw beyond that immediate issue to the necessity that *they* get *their* shit together. Being in the Raleigh helped move things along, for it was that vacant six-story tenement building that Joy Griffith made the laboratory for her little experiment in living (an experiment conducted on her own time, financed with her own money—and some of Tom Valentine's, independent of the work she did for New York City—and, frankly, behind New York City's back, for New York City didn't approve of free-lance do-gooding). To squat in the Raleigh, you had to get the okay of Joy Griffith, who had her eyes open for sisters with the potential to dream her dream along with her, to motherfuckers who maybe weren't motherfuckers after all, they *were* brothers.

To squat in the Raleigh, you also had to be straight, you had to be sober, you had to know where your children were all the time and take responsibility for what they'd been up to if what they'd been up to had riled someone else. Althea Dove managed to get *her* shit together sufficiently to manage all of those things.

Then the Raleigh burned down.

Althea Dove and her children, Lamotta, Vurnell, and Jamel, survived the fire. Joy Griffith, who wouldn't stop looking until she'd accounted for every dreamer, every brother, even every motherfucker, did not. Without Joy, Althea wasn't sure she could keep her shit together. She tried crashing here and crashing there, but there were too many motherfuckers around always wanting to blow some jumbo, to party. A friend, another Raleigh survivor, who wasn't sure she could keep her shit together either, heard about the people living on the nameless island in Pumpkin Patch Channel off Grassy Bay and suggested that maybe out there away from it all they could keep their respective shit together.

They arrived just two days before the raid, commanded by Chief of Department John A. Walsh Jr., letters, medals, citations, honors.

"Neil?"

Zimmerman looked up from washing his hands to look at Cullen in the men's room mirror. "Yeah?"

Cullen had already checked that the stalls were empty, but he checked again. He'd left the water in his sink running. "Did I say anything to you about Jamaica Bay? I know I didn't. You were out when I called Connie, and I had the door shut. That was the only time I mentioned it."

Zimmerman pulled down a towel and dried his hands and arranged the pieces until they made part of a picture. "You said something on the office phone to Connie—or she said something to you—about Valentine's old stomping grounds in the bay. You wondered—or she did—if maybe that's where he was. You wonder now if what you said got back to Walsh."

"There's no chance—none—that Connie repeated it to anyone—certainly not anyone in the Department. The cops whose wives she was friends with are all retired or dead. Or doing points."

Zimmerman wadded up his towel and shot a skyhook at the wastebasket. Swish. "Except Hriniak."

"Hey, Neil."

"More than once you've said how tight Connie stayed with Beryl Hriniak, even after you guys got divorced."

"Tight in a personal way. They don't trade Department gossip; they don't trade *tips*."

Zimmerman yanked out another towel, wadded it, skyhooked. Swish. "How long're you going to sit on this thing about Hriniak's calls to Deborah Dean?"

"We don't know Hriniak made calls to Deborah Dean. We know there were calls from Hriniak's phone."

"How long're you going to sit on it?"

"I'm not sitting on it."

"You haven't said anything to Maslosky. I don't know how long we can count on Darelle to stay buttoned up. He's got his sister's interests in mind—rightly."

Cullen turned off the water in his sink. If it had ever been true that water stymied electronic bugs, wouldn't the surveillance nerds by now have figured out a way around it?

"Joe?"

"What?"

"I don't know how long we can count on Darelle to stay buttoned up."

"I heard you."

"Did you hear me say you haven't said anything to Maslosky?"

"I know I haven't."

"Did you hear me say you're sitting on it?"

"Neil, get the fuck off my back, will you?"

"Among other things you're sitting on."

"I'm not sitting on the John Anthony thing. I'm going up to see Vera right now."

"Vera?"

"Vera."

"Christ." Zimmerman spun around and turned the water on in his sink and washed his hands of Cullen. He yanked down a towel and dried his hands and wadded up the towel and slam-dunked it into the wastebasket. He looked into the mirror at the back of Cullen's head. "You want a ride?"

"A ride where?"

"Uptown. I'm working behind the counter at Taubman's Pharmacy, on the chance our friend the Fourex lady'll drop in."

They went out the door and down the hall and got their jackets and took the elevator down to the garage. Keith Bermúdez was waiting to get on.

*"¿Que tal, hermanos?"*

"Hi, Keith." Shit, the Mets game.

"Berms."

"*Mira*, Joe, listen. I been calling you, homes. You're never home. I'm glad I ran into you. I said I couldn't work tonight 'cause my uncle's getting married? Check this out. The wedding's off. Last night, he goes to his bachelor party—bachelor, my ass, I *told* you he was a fucking *espada*, a swordsman—he falls in love with this *chica* delivers a strip-o-gram. I'm not kidding, man, it was love at first sight. She was *muy guapa*, homes, great tits, but still. My mother's going crazy. His ex-fiancée's mother's going crazy. I could use a stakeout, get some peace and quiet. You got something to do, enjoy. You got nothing to do, enjoy that too. How's Ann?"

How *was* Ann? Too much had been happening—or rather, nothing had, for he'd been sitting on so much—for him to keep tabs on her condition. And he *did* have something to do, didn't he—take Hoagy and the nerd to the Mets' game—and he'd forgotten all about it, hadn't he, for he was sitting on too much for him to keep tabs on his own life, wasn't he? "She's fine, K. I'm glad I ran into you. I owe you, buddy. Thanks."

"*De nada*, babe. So long. Later, Neil."

"Later, Berms."

Cullen and Zimmerman walked to the Saab.

"A job in a pharmacy's right up your alley," Cullen said. "With your knowledge of hair- and skin-care products, you'll be a star."

"I can sit on this stuff till Monday," Zimmerman said.

"That's fair."

Zimmerman stopped. "No, it's not fair, because I don't stand to gain anything. All the potential gain is yours. All of it. You stand to screw a movie star—"

"Neil."

"—and the best, the very best, that can possibly come of this from my point of view is that I don't get suspended, that I don't lose my gold shield, that I keep my job." He took his wallet out and took out a ten and gave it to Cullen. "For a cab. All the shit you've been sitting on, I don't want you in the Turbo.'' He put his wallet away and walked on.

So the *bottom* line wasn't just that Cullen was someone who didn't want everything under one roof, just the sex and the laughs and the Lyle Lovett albums and the *Hill Street Blues* reruns and the Buffalo chicken wings; the bottom line was that he was someone from whom people felt they had to protect their upholstery.

# 21

Nicky Potter said, " 'My more-than-assistant, my life-support system.' That's how Vera introduced me. Remember?"

Cullen nodded. "Sure." And he'd been The Old Friend of Chuck's I've Told You About. (Followed by that ambiguous The Policeman Who Helped When The Poor Driver Was Killed.)

"So it won't surprise you to learn that I know why you're here."

If that followed, Cullen didn't know by what curvy path. "I'm here to see Vera. To reminisce. I thought it was time."

Nicky smiled a smile that was a little aggrieved that he would try and smoke her. "You're here because someone saw Lise and Claire driving into the city the morning Story was killed."

Something in that flat, unadorned *Story*—no christian name, no title, no *Vera's brother, Lise's husband, Claire's stepfather,* not even a *your old friend*—made Cullen take a closer look at Nicky. That and the flat misstatement: Story—Charles Story, Commissioner Story, Vera's brother, Lise's husband, Claire's stepfather, Cullen's old friend—had been killed (a more-than-assistant-a-life-support-system's kind of verb, a better verb than *murdered*, certainly better than *polished* or *done* or *'fewed* [as in *curfewed*], the street verbs-of-choice of the moment) in the evening of the day whose morning was under discussion.

What Cullen's closer look showed him—and he had no idea what it was worth—was that for all Nicky resembled Vera, she was nothing like her; there was a defect in Nicky's beauty, something twisted, awry—not evilly, but as if by a mistake that both creator and created would forever regret.

"Your Ann Jones has been on the phone asking where they were going," Nicky said.

And after she'd promised him she wouldn't. Or had she? Well, he'd broken his promise to her not to broadcast her speculation about the flambéing of the Raleigh, speculation that according to Hriniak (who made phone calls, speaking of speculation, to Deborah Dean) was erroneous. Did that make them even, or . . . or what? "Ann is *her* Ann Jones. You *did* tell Vera I was here?"

Nicky smiled. She was enjoying this. "You go back a *long* way, the two of you."

"Do you and Vera live near each other, in Los Angeles?"

"Vera lives in Nichols Canyon. I live in Westwood."

"Where UCLA is."

She tipped her head, as if at a precocious student. "How do you know LA?"

"I know Westwood's where UCLA is probably from watching college basketball on television, otherwise I don't know LA. What were you doing in New York?"

She craned her neck. "I beg your pardon."

Something a more-than-assistant-a-life-support-system probably rarely had to do. "You were already in New York when Story"—he leaned on the name ever so slightly—"was killed, weren't you?"

"Nicky's bi-coastal," Vera said. "You probably hate that word." She came in from some other room like . . . well, like an *estrella de cine;* she put a hand on his shoulder to keep him from standing to greet her, leaned down to kiss his cheek (kiss at it; he wouldn't swear he *had* been kissed), sat opposite him, right on the edge of an off-white club chair, her hands clasped together down between her knees, a posture that said she'd waited for this moment a long time. "It's nice to see you off-duty, Joe, away from processions and distractions."

He couldn't speak, which was the point, wasn't it?

Vera unclasped her hands, sat back in her chair, crossed her legs. She wore a big loose white blouse, big loose white slacks, silver sandals. Hollywood smooth cool while outside it was New York gritty hot. "There's a lot of *stuff* going on in New York that needs constant looking-after. I have had people here looking after it full-time, but they didn't know enough about what was going on at Storyboard—that's my production company—and in the rest of my life. . . ."

(Cullen deduced—hey, he was a cop, after all; a detective—that what he was hearing was the answer to his question to Nicky.)

". . . . Nicky and I spent more time explaining things to them than they did representing us, so we decided it was more efficient—and even ultimately less expensive—for her to come here a couple of times a month. Her brother lives here, in the Village. He's a jazz clarinetist, and on the road quite a bit, and she usually stays at his place. This trip, he was in town, so she stayed at the Hilton. She got in Wednesday night and would've been here through Monday or Tuesday."

"I like big busy hotels," Nicky said.

Cullen said, "I'd like it if you'd leave now, please, Miss Potter." Nicky looked as if a big busy hotel had fallen on her, but Vera extended a hand to pull her from the rubble. "It's okay, Nicky."

Nicky found some things to do—picking up papers, putting them in folders, capping pens, searching for a hair comb that might or might not have fallen down behind some cushions—before she finally left. It was not okay with her.

Vera clasped her hands around a knee. "Well."

"Well."

"What did Phil Hriniak say? It's a one-horse world?"

"It's a one-horse world."

"Not quite like old times, though, is it, Joe?"

Old times:

*"Hey, Snake."*

*"Hey, Tommy."*

*"We're going to Forest Hills to shoot some hoops. You wanna shoot some hoops?"*

*"Nah."*

*"Come on, Snake."*

*"Like nah. Like I'm going over to Chuck's."*

*"Chuck's coming with us."*

*"Bullshit."*

*"Like his old man gave him the aft off, like he's coming with us."*

*"Yeah?"*

*"Yeah. So like come with us."*

*"Like nah. Like I got stuff to do."*

*"Like what "*

*"Like stuff."*

*"Hello, Joseph."*

*"Hiya, Mister Story. Chuck here?"*

*"I gave Chuck the afternoon off to play basketball with his friends. How come you're not playing?"*

*"Too hot."*

*"It's a very pleasant day. There's a delightful breeze."*

*"Yeah, like that's it. Too windy. . . . So like you're here all alone?"*

*"No, Vera's helping out. Vera?"*

*"Yes, Daddy?"*

*"Chuck's friend, Joseph, is here. What'll you have, Joseph?"*

*"Like I don't know. Like a cherry Coke."*

*"A cherry Coke for Joseph, Vera."*

*"Yes, Daddy."*

*"And like a Devil Dog."*

*"And a Devil Dog for Joseph, Vera."*

*"Yes, Daddy."*

*"Nice to see you, Joseph. I'll tell Chuck you were in."*

*"Like okay. Sure."*

*Then, when Vera brought Joseph (Snake) Cullen his cherry Coke and his Devil Dog, he would swivel on his stool so that his back was to her, his elbows on the counter, because as hard as he worked to be around her, Joseph (Snake) Cullen never let Vera Story know it. He was always leaving things at the Storys' house; always coming over to play Ping-Pong even though he'd hated Ping-Pong then and would hate it for the rest of his life; always passing by the candy store or the house on the way to or from school, even though neither was on the beeline between his home and school. But Joseph (Snake) Cullen never let Vera Story know that all that passing by was to be around her. Nor,*

*God knows, did he let anyone else. That wouldn't have been like cool.*

## Old times:

*Joseph (Snake) Cullen was afraid Vera Story had the hots for Tommy Valentine, otherwise why did she always think of a reason to come down to the basement when Tommy came over to play Ping-Pong with him and Chuck, she never came down to the basement when just Joseph (Snake) Cullen came over to play Ping-Pong with Chuck.*

*Tommy Valentine, big man on campus, always tossing the ball appropriate to the season in the air, always with a flock of adoring girls in his wake, wouldn't have noticed Vera Story if he'd tripped over her. Of that Joseph (Snake) Cullen was fairly sure because being sure of it was one of the reasons he hung around with Tommy as much as he did, to the dismay of his fellow rocks, to whom big men on campus tossing balls with flocks of adoring girls in their wakes were hopelessly square, hopelessly uncool:*

*"So what chick do you like like, Tommy?"*

*"What do you care, Snake?"*

*"I just want to like know, that's all."*

*"You trying to tell me you like like somebody, Snake?"*

*"Me? Right. I would like rank out my mother on the Ed Sullivan show before I would go out with any of the scags in our frigging school."*

*"Maida from Beta likes you, Snake."*

*"Maida from Beta's a scag."*

*"She's a nice girl."*

*"You trying to tell me you like like Maida, Tommy?"*

*"Maida's Barry's sister. I couldn't go out with a friend's sister."*

*"You couldn't?"*

*"You know, it would be like going out with your own sister."*

*"So what're you saying, that you couldn't go out with like Vera Story?"*

*"I just said I couldn't, Snake. She's Chuck's sister."*

*"Yeah, well, like pretend she's not Chuck's sister."*

*"Snake."*

*"So you don't want to go out with her; it has nothing to do with her being Chuck's sister. You just don't like her, that's all."*

*"Okay. You win. I don't like her."*

*"You don't like Vera?"*

*"Like who're we talking about if we're not talking about Vera?"*

*"We are talking about Vera."*

*"Okay."*

*"Okay."*

## Old times:

The moment that stands out in my memory, *Cullen had said to Zimmerman back on the Brooklyn Heights Esplanade while they waited for Darelle Dean*, was Vera's appearance in a play. God knows what play. One of those awful things young amateurs do—*The Late George Apley* or something. Vera'd been the stage manager, the girl playing the ingenue got appendicitis, Vera went on in her place. She was extraordinary—even thugs like me knew it. It was like *All About Eve:* wallflower to toast-of-the-town in one night. Except it was more like Cinderella because it was for one night only. There were other plays, but Vera wasn't in them; there were parties and dances and Vera wasn't at them. . . . I don't know why.

*There were other plays, but Vera wasn't in them, there were parties and dances and Vera wasn't at them, and Joseph (Snake) Cullen knew the reason she wasn't at them because right after that play Vera got a letter, an unsigned, typewritten letter with no return address on the envelope, that said:*

Dear Vera,

I am writing you to tell you something that I think that it is very important for you to know.

Tom Valentine has been telling all the other boys on the basketball team and all the other boys on the teams who use the boys locker room after school that he has been to bed with you and screwed you and you gave him a blow job.

I am writing this to you because I think that it is something that is very important for you to know.

A Friend.

*There were other plays, but Vera wasn't in them, there were parties and dances and Vera wasn't at them. Vera walked to school by herself in the morning, kept to herself between classes all morning long, ate her lunch in the librarian's office, where she had a job that earned her service credits, kept to herself between classes all afternoon, walked home by herself. Whenever Joseph (Snake) Cullen or any of her brother's other friends came by, Vera shut herself in her room.*

*"Hey, Snake, like guess what," Dave Cannell once said to Joseph (Snake) Cullen. "We went to Chuck Story's yesterday aft, like me and Blankenstein."*

*"Yeah. Like so?"*

*"I go into the kitchen to get some water, like Chuck's sister was in there getting a big pot like from under the sink. She went running out the other door with it when she saw me."*

*"Maybe she got a look at your face, Cannell."*

*"Ooh, rank out."*

*"Fucking A, I ranked you out."*

*"Don't you get it, Snake? That was the pot she pisses in 'cause she's afraid to come out of her room."*

*"Like the fuck're you talking about, Cannell?"*

*"I told you—Chuck's sister pisses in a pot in her room 'cause she's afraid if she uses the same bathroom as Chuck or his friends she'll get knocked up."*

*"Who told you that?"*

*"I heard it."*

*"You hear it from Chuck?"*

*"No."*

*"Who'd you hear it from?"*

*"Some girl."*

*"Which girl?"*

*"I can't remember. Ow! Hey, cut it the fuck out, Snake."*

*"Remember."*

*“Ow! Shit! You dumb fuck! What the fuck's the matter with you?”*

*“Nothing's the matter with me. What's the matter with you?”*

*“You practically ripped my fucking ear off, that's what's the matter with me.”*

*“Yeah, well, watch what the fuck you're doing then.”*

*“What the fuck's wrong with what I'm doing?”*

*“Fuck you, Cannell.”*

*“Yeah, well, fuck you, Snake.”*

*“Fuck you too.”*

“Fuck *you.*”

“*Fuck* you.”

# 22

Old times:

*"Excuse me. Aren't you Vera Story?"*

*"Yes."*

*"You probably don't remember me, but I'm from your neighborhood. Joe Cullen."*

*"Of course. You're a friend of Chuck's."*

*"How is Chuck? I haven't seen him for a couple of years. My folks moved to Florida—my Dad retired—and I'm living in Manhattan with some buddies—I go to City now. I hardly ever get out to Queens."*

*"Chuck's fine. Our Dad died—"*

*"Yeah, I heard. I'm sorry."*

*"Our mother'd been dead for years, you probably remember—and Chuck took over the store. He worked it for a while, and then decided to sell it. He made quite a lot of money and bought an apartment building and sold it, so he's doing very nicely, buying and selling buildings."*

*"He always was a pretty good salesman."*

*"Yes, he was. . . . Well, it was nice to see you, Joe."*

*"How are you, Vera?"*

*"I'm fine."*

*"You look . . . great. I didn't recognize you. You're . . . well, you're all grown up."*

*"That happens, I guess. Ha ha."*

*"Ha ha. You look great."*

*"Thanks. Do you work here?"*

*"Four nights a week. Is there something I can help you with?"*

*"There is, yes. I'm looking for the score to* Bye Bye Birdie.*"*

*"The album? The album's over here."*

*"No, the sheet music. I need the sheet music for a class."*

*"A music class?"*

*"Sort of. I'm studying at The Actors Studio."*

*"No kidding? I remember you in a play once at school. You were great."*

*"You really remember?"*

*"Sure. You were great."*

*"I have a job sort of like yours; I work at the Drama Book Shop. It's just down the street, but on the fifth floor, so not too many people know about it."*

*"I've heard of it. Does that mean you live in the city too?"*

*"I'm sharing a place with some other acting students, in the Village."*

*"I bet that's nice. I'm way up on a Hundred Thirty-fifth Street. Listen, it's time for my break. Would you like to have a cup of coffee?"*

*"Well. . . ."*

*"Or a Coke or a glass of milk or just a glass of water. Or we could take a walk around the block."*

"This *block?"*

*"Hey, no. It's safe. Really. A friend of mine's the cop on the beat this time of night. He's a jazz buff. He comes in here on his lunch hour to look through the jazz records. Phil Hriniak. This block's one of the safest in Manhattan because of him. You'll never guess what, Vera."*

*"What?"*

*"He talked me into going to the Police Academy, Phil, into becoming a cop. I was thinking about teaching—you know, English or something—but Phil convinced me that, well, you know, maybe I could make a little bit of a difference, you know, help people."*

*"You were sort of a bad kid, weren't you, Joe? What did they used to call you?"*

*"Aah, we were just kids."*

*"Snake, wasn't it?"*

*"We were just kids. What did we know?"*

*"You were a rock."*

*"Hunh, I'd forgotten that word. Yeah, I guess I was a rock."*

*"You used to read a lot too, though. I remember you were always in the library. I used to work in the librarian's office."*

*"You knew I was in the library?"*

*"How could I not? The librarian's office was right next to the reading room."*

*"But you never came out or anything."*

*". . . No. . . . And now you're going to be a cop."*

*"Yeah, well, we'll see. First I have to get into the Academy and everything else. . . . Can you have that coffee?"*

*"Well. . . ."*

*"Please."*

*". . . Okay."*

Old times:

*"I can't stop thinking about that movie, Joe."*

*"It's an amazing movie."*

*"I couldn't believe it when she killed herself."*

*"It had to happen though. Their friendship—Jules's and Jim's—is the really important relationship in the movie. Catherine was like this constant barrier between them."*

*"Well, here we are. You know you don't always have to bring me home, Joe."*

*"It's no trouble."*

*"Now you have to go all the way back uptown."*

*"You could invite me in."*

*"I can't, Joe."*

*"Just for a cup of coffee."*

*"Joe, I have roommates."*

*"That's not really it, is it? If someone were important enough to you, you'd tell your roommates and they'd be happy for you and you'd work something out."*

*"It's not that you're not important to me, Joe. I've loved our times together. The movies, the plays, the walks, the talks, the cups of coffee. We should get a coffee company to put us in a commerical, we drink enough of it."*

*"The ball game."*

*"The ball game. Did you ever see anybody steal home before?"*

*"Never."*

*"It was thrilling. I can still see it."*

*"You know what I'm talking about, Vera."*

*"Yes."*

*"To you, I'll always just be one of your brother's asshole friends."*

*"Joseph."*

*"Snake Cullen, the rock."*

*"Sit down here and listen to me. This is very important. I want to be an actress. No: I* am *an actress already; the studying I'm doing is part of my apprenticeship. I* am *an actress already; I'm going to be a* successful *actress and successful actresses, by definition, don't have time for family or friends or a life of their own, so forget about lovers."*

*"I love you, Vera."*

*"Oh, Joe, don't."*

*"You must love me too, or you wouldn't've said what you just said."*

*"Did you* hear *what I just said? I just said—"*

*"You said you don't have time for lovers, so you must love me."*

*"I said I don't have time for you, Joe. Did you hear that?"*

*"I'll wait."*

*"Joe."*

*"I will. I'm not going anywhere. I don't have anything better to do."*

*"Of course you do. You have a life to live. You have a career ahead of you. You've got your play."*

*"My play. My play's a joke."*

*"It's not. It's a wonderful play."*

*"For an asshole ex-rock who's thinking about being a cop and wrote a play on his summer vacation."*

*"For anybody."*

*"How can you say it's not a joke, my play, when it's about a guy who falls in love with his best friend's sister? A* shmuck *who falls in love with his best friend's sister."*

*". . . Because it can't happen in our case doesn't make it a joke."*

*"It's Tom, isn't it?"*

*". . . Tom?"*

*"You're still in love with Tom, aren't you?"*

*"I was never in* love *with him. I had a crush on him when I was in about the fourth grade."*

*"You've been keeping up with his career."*

*"Keeping up? I showed you a little tiny item in the newspaper that said he's in a summer basketball league in the Catskills. Is that keeping up?"*

*"An item in the sports section."*

*"So? Are you saying women don't read the sports section?"*

*"Vera."*

*"Joe, don't."*

*"Can't we try?"*

*"No."*

*"You won't even* try*?"*

*"No."*

*"Why? Why not?"*

*"Because."*

*"Because you're going to be a fucking* actress, *a* movie *star."*

*"Joe, don't. It doesn't have to end this way."*

*"Oh, it's over? Is that what you're saying?"*

*"It doesn't have to be over unless you make it be."*

*"Oh, right, it's* my *fault."*

*"It's nobody's* fault, *Joe."*

*"Yeah, well, I'd say* some*body's responsible for it and that somebody's* you.*"*

*". . . All right."*

*"All right, what?"*

*"I'll take the responsibility. You're right. We shouldn't see each other any more."*

*"Vera, Jesus."*

*"Well, it's what you want, isn't it?"*

*"No, it's not what I want. What I want—"*

*"What you want you can't have."*

*"Don't interrupt me, okay? Give me a chance to say what I have to say, okay?"*

*"I'm sorry."*

*". . . What I want . . . is what we have now."*

*"What we have now isn't—"*

*"Let. Me. Finish."*

*"I'm sorry."*

*"Can I finish?"*

*"Yes. I'm sorry. I said I'm sorry."*

*"Do I have your permission to speak?"*

*"Don't."*

*". . . What I want . . . is what we have now* and *something we don't have yet but that I think we can have if we just let ourselves. Not just you, me. Both of us."*

*"Joe, don't."*

*"Indulge me, Vera, for christ's sake. I don't want to walk away from you and have it be for the last time. If I'm deluding myself, let me delude myself."*

*"I can't do that."*

*"Do it!"*

*"I should go up. People're looking out their windows. They're going to complain to the landlord."*

*"I'll see you Tuesday, for the thing at City Center."*

*"Do you think we should?"*

*"I'll pick you up after class."*

*"Joe."*

*"Tuesday."*

*"Joseph."*

*"Six-thirty. Good night."*

*". . . Good night."*

*"No kiss?"*

*"Joe."*

*"On the cheek, Vera, for christ's sake!"*

*"Don't shout."*

*"A kiss."*

*". . . There."*

*"Good night."*

*"Good night."*

*"Tuesday."*

*"Good night."*

Old times:

*"Vera, I— Oh."*

*"Joe, why didn't you knock?"*

*"You said to meet you here."*

*"In the lobby. This is a private office."*

*"Well, you didn't say that."*

*"It says it on the door, Joe. Caleb, this is Joe Cullen, an old friend of my brother's. Joe, this is Caleb Evans. Caleb teaches my film acting course."*

*"Joe. Glad to meet you."*

*"Hi."*

*"I'll, uh, leave you two alone."*

*"Don't bother. I'll leave."*

*"Joe."*

*"Joe, you ought to listen to what Vera has to say."*

*"I don't need to listen to what she has to say. I have eyes, don't I? So what do I need to listen to what she has to say for if I can see with my eyes that she's sitting on your lap with your hand up her dress?"*

*"Joe."*

*"Fuck you. Fuck both of you."*

*"Joe!"*

# 23

"Not quite like old times," Cullen said, "but then I'm not terribly nostalgic, not one of those people who think the music stopped with the Dell Vikings."

Vera smiled. Nostalgically, hearing "Come Go With Me"? "Nostalgia's a symptom of dissatisfaction with the present, wouldn't you say?"

Talk radio. *Nostalgia: A Healthy Longing For Then Or A Kick In The Ass Of Now? Tune in to the next Larry King show.* "I've enjoyed your movies. I especially liked *Back East;* it was ahead of its time."

"Thank you. I'm glad. It was."

"And *The Losers* and *Reasonable Doubt* and *Brilliant City* and *My Enemy's Enemy* and *Nickel Curves*. That was ahead of its time too; much better than *Bull Durham*."

She was flattered. "My. You've seen a few of the forgettable ones. You always did like to go to the movies."

"I go maybe once a month now," Cullen said. "When I first separated, I'd go two or three times a week. . . . Remember *Jules and Jim*?"

Her eyes fluttered momentarily. This might not be nostalgia; it might be vendetta. "Of course."

"There was a time when I saw it every year, in the spring. I'd read *The Great Gatsby* and see *Jules and Jim* and feel rejuvenated. They're both about violent death, so go figure."

Vera was sitting forward in her chair, her hands together prayerfully. "You don't see it any more, or read *Gatsby*?"

Cullen smiled, nostalgically. "I met Truffaut. I was on a homicide. A woman who worked for the Lincoln Center Film Society witnessed a mob rubout. I went to interview her and wound up getting invited to a reception for some French directors. Truffaut was one of them. I summoned up some French and some nerve and told him *Jules and Jim* was my all-time favorite movie. He was embarrassed, and a little bit annoyed, probably, at being accosted by a stranger—one whose French was as bad as *his* English. But I think most of all he was impatient at having to discuss a youthful work. He'd just made a movie—that to him was undoubtedly his best work. He's dead now, of course, but I guess I don't see the movie anymore, or see it as often, in deference to his wanting to put it behind him. . . . Or am I wrong about all this? Do you finish something and *know* it's not your best work?''

Vera thought about it, her eyes inventorying objects in the room, as if she were the guest—skipping over him, by whom she was clearly baffled, he who talked of mob rubouts with one breath and waxed *cinéaste* with the next. ''Movies are collaborations.'' She finally looked at him. ''A director—especially a European director, an *auteur*—has more of himself in a work than just about anybody else involved, so it's possible that he can feel strongly that the work is *his* and that his last work is his best. Why did you come here, Joe?'' Her hands, still pressed together, extended toward him, entreating without entreating. ''You're not going to. . . . You don't—''

It was several seconds before Cullen registered that the sound that cut Vera off came from within the house, for it—the sound; a scream, a yell, a shriek, he didn't know what to call it—had a level and an urgency and a stridency that clashed with furniture and rugs and nice things. It was a street sound, a jungle sound. He had heard sounds like it twice:

Once, back in his uniformed days, as he patrolled the perimeter of a fire scene, keeping back the ghouls, the building began to buckle and a firefighter who sensed it sounded the sound close to Cullen's ear, imploring his buddies by the volume, the pitch, to get the fuck out. Once, shortly after he began working in clothes, Cullen had sounded it himself when a suspected perp who had just been tossed by Cullen's partner, Jacky LaRusso, threw down on Jacky with a derringer Jacky hadn't found in the perp's Converse hightops. *Jacky, No*, Cullen had screamed, yelled, shrieked. When he heard the sound now, in half-awake dreams on summer Sunday afternoons or for no good reason in a crowded elevator in the Criminal Courts building, full of felons and shysters and burnouts—each word—*Jacky, No*—lasted a good hour, hour and a half, about as long as the blast of Jacky's .38 Special had reverberated when he polished the perp, whose derringer jammed.

But enough nostalgia, that symptom of dissatisfaction with the present. The present sound—scream, yell, shriek—was sounded, there was no mistaking, by a woman, for it was plaited of every mother's urgent bellow ever and forever on discovering an empty cradle, a broken bough, a toppled tricycle, front wheel spinning slowly; a scream, a yell not of despair but of warning: Vengeful Mother on the Loose.

And there Lise Story was, at the top of the stairs that spiraled up from a rear corner of the living room to the second floor—a ladder, really, offering a shortcut should you not care to go out to the hall and up the grander, carpeted stairs. She gripped the iron railing as if she might tear it apart. If bare feet, distressed jeans, and a big work shirt over a tank top were for mourning, then mourning became her, but Cullen thought she looked like a mannequin from a Guess? jeans ad.

She said, "Claire is gone."

Vera, halfway up the stairs, uncertain whether to ascend all the way or coax Lise down to her, called Nicky's name.

Nicky appeared at the hallway door. "She knew he was here." She tossed a look at Cullen. "I found her listening at the top of the stairs. I put her back in her room and went away for just seconds. When I got back, she was gone."

Cullen, not sitting back with his legs crossed anymore, but not on his feet either, said, "Now just a sec. How can you be so—"

He let the question collapse, for Vera, lifting her feet, supporting her weight on her hands, riding the curled rail like an exuberant kid, was back down the stairs and heading toward the rear of the house. He got up and followed. What the hell? If enough people believed it was your fault, it was your fault.

A small hallway, a smaller one, a pantry, a hallway smaller still—she was fast, Vera, graceful, athletic. Then a storeroom—coats, boots, gardening things, old stuff in limbo between desuetude and the junk heap. A blast of hot white daytime as Vera yanked open a door to the backyard.

She did another one of her kid things, putting both hands on the wooden railing and jumping over all three wooden steps to the grass, browning despite the best efforts of the gardener to keep it from baking.

Cullen, Olympic hurdler *manqué* (just about everything *manqué* if you wanted to get real nasty about it), took the stairs without the benefit of the railing and nearly broke a leg. He staggered and flailed and gasped and followed after the spoor of Vera the gazelle, who was nearly in another country by now.

Across the yard, tiptoeing through a bed of hydrangeas (to Cullen, Joseph [Snake] Cullen, ex-rock, a child of concrete and asphalt and brick, *all* flowers were hydrangeas, except when they were tulips or roses, which any idiot knew. Or sunflowers), a tight, tight squeeze between some pieces of wire fencing, a rather sloppy patch on the backside of a billionaire's perimeter, out onto a square of rough cement behind a six-story apartment building that fronted on Seventy-first Street.

And there was Vera, Vera Story Evans, *estrella de cine*, a star so—what had Ann called her? and how *was* Ann?—so incandescent, down on her knees on the rough cement, her arms around Claire Langois, huddled up against the building wall.

Claire Langois, Cullen could say without hesitation, because who else could she be? But in fact, when many minutes later she finally stood, Vera's arms still around her, and let herself be guided back to the gap in the fence and through it—her mother waited there, and Nicky—and back across the sunblasted yard and into the house, Cullen could not have said for sure that she was Claire, or that a *she* was what she was.

She had cropped her hair, Claire, shaved it down to the skin except for a leechlike pigtail in the very back. The pigtail she had died jet black, the color of the eyebrow pencil she had used to draw new brows above where her own, now plucked, had grown. She had used black mascara and black eye shadow too, and a gray rouge on her cheeks. She wore a black silk slip under a black cotton shirt, worn unbuttoned with the sleeves cut off, and under the slip torn black fishnet stockings or maybe tights that didn't reach the tops of her black Doc Marten's boots. On her left hand were silvered brass knuckles, on her right five death's head rings. A swastika hung from the lobe of her left ear, a carriage bolt pierced her right.

* * *

"Where did she get the clothes, when did she do the makeover?" Cullen ignored Vera's glare at his flippancy. "You tell me so I can tell my bosses, because if my bosses find out about this before I can tell them they're going to ask you where and when—and why—and you're not going to like the way they ask."

"Don't threaten me, Joe."

"Where? When? Why? I've seen the log of the guard detail. No one's left the house since the funeral except servants and Nicky. The only guests have been friends of Lise's who shop on Fifth Avenue, not Avenue A. The only deliveries have been from florists and grocers. She didn't get those clothes at Dean & DeLuca."

Vera folded her arms tight against her belly and let out just enough to satisfy him. "The back way. It's her way—Claire's. She comes and goes when she wants. I can't stop her. Lise can't. She's an adult, practically. All right, I know she's a kid and I know she's screwed up. I *asked* her to stay in; I watched her as much as I could. And Nicky did. We have to sleep. We can't chain her up. She went out. Just once. Once was enough."

"Christ."

"What? You don't approve of her taste? It's not for you to say, for any of us. You're probably a *per*fect father, aren't you?"

Cullen looked at his watch. It told him it was 5:00.24 . . . 25 . . . 26 and that if he *were* a perfect father his daughter would probably have given him a watch he wouldn't have to break to keep the alarm from going off. "I have to go. *My* kids. I'm not reporting this"—*I'm sitting on it, along with all the other shit I'm sitting on*—"I'm going to the ball game with my kids and I'm going to sleep in my own bed for the first time in a long time"—How *is* Ann?—"and I'm going to come by here early tomorrow morning and you and I are going to have a long talk. Just the two of us. No Lise, no Claire. You know the questions I want answers to; make sure you have them. Clear?"

Vera's eyes got wet with pain. "Joe, can't we just—"

"Clear?" Cullen said.

Vera nodded. "Clear."

# 24

Same dream, different night:

*The creak of his bedroom door, the tap-tap-tap of his slippers, the whump of the bathroom door, the splatter of urine, the toilet's gasp, the bathroom door again, again his slippers.*

*And that sound. Like . . . ?*

*Then: the click of her latch.*

*Then: the hiss of his clothing, of his breath, by her bed.*

*Like . . . ?*

*Then: on her, in her, knocking her breath away, slamming, shoving, grunting.*

*Like . . . ?*

*Then: he's done.*

*Then: he's gone. Hiss, click, tap-tap-tap, creak.*

*Like . . . sleigh bells.*

# 25

Joseph (Snake) Cullen, ex-rock, imperfect father, didn't have wheels, of course; his car was at home (where *he* never was), gathering tickets. (Unless it had been boosted, or had a tirectomy; how would he know? He was never home; he slept on an exercise mat on his office floor, showered and shaved in the men's locker room, got clean socks and underwear from a supply he and Zimmerman had bought one day on Orchard Street, threw the dirty laundry in a bottom drawer of his desk.) Doug Aiello, though, Connie's husband, Hoagy's and the computer nerd's stepfather, already had his car back from the shop: "Good as new, didn't even need a new transmission. But here's the thing, Joe—the kids don't want to take the subway all the way out to Shea; it's not cool or something. So I was going to offer to drive you guys, and then, out of nowhere, I got this ticket. To tonight's game. Versus the Dodgers. A guy at work, George McMennamen. George and three of his buddies're supposed to go to the game. George can't go 'cause his wife's Aunt Patty's in town from Greensboro, North Carolina, or someplace, he offers me the ticket. I say I got a better idea, George, swap me you and your buddies' four tickets for the three tickets I've got, you were going to give me the ticket gratis anyway, there's no difference to pay.

"Now I know, Joe, they weren't *my* three tickets to swap, I know you mailed them here so the kids could look forward to the game. If you don't want to go along with it, I understand. But I called you, Joe, and you weren't home. Connie and the kids, they say—"

"I haven't been home much," Cullen agreed. "And it's okay, Doug. It's fine. It'll be nice to have a ride, especially if the game goes late. You did the right thing."

"We're going to have a great time, Joe, I know it. You and me and James and Tenny."

Who were James and Tenny? Oh yeah—Hoagy and the computer nerd. "It'll be nice, Doug."

The first nine innings *were* nice. The kids didn't ask who Ann was—how *was* Ann?—and how come he'd never introduced her to them or even told them about her. Doug told Cullen a history of the travel agency business, and Cullen, who for some reason had always thought Doug was an insurance agent, didn't have to think—think about Claire Langois's skin-head, her leechlike pigtail, her black eyebrows and black eyes, her gray-rouged cheeks, her brass knuckles, her death's head rings, her swastika, her carriage bolt. Neither the Mets nor the Dodgers scored any runs and got hardly any hits.

The next five innings were hectic. The Dodgers scored three times in the top of the tenth, the Mets three times in the bottom of the tenth; the Dodgers got one in the twelfth and so did the Mets. In the top of the fourteenth, a Dodger rookie, up in the show (Doug said) because another guy was on the DL, hit a three-run homer; in the bottom half, Doc Gooden, pinch-hitting because the Mets were out of hitters, hit a three-run double. Cullen didn't have to think about Claire Langois.

The next three innings were tedious: deep counts, long talks, heavy managing. Cullen struggled to keep from thinking about Claire Langois.

Then came just one of those things: Cullen was looking around at nothing special and saw a total stranger and just like that he knew the stranger was about to become part of his life. It had been like that with Vera, not a total stranger but . . . different, back in that Times Square record store twenty-five years ago; with Connie, in Washington Square Park fifteen years ago. It was happening now—differently, of course; Cullen wasn't going to tumble for him—with this uniformed sergeant—

"Dad, your watch is broken."

—this uniformed sergeant coming up to the top of the ramp and looking around the loge to get his bearings. "This is the right time, isn't it? Twelve-oh-one." Point 15 . . . 16 . . . 17.

"Yeah, but it didn't beep on the hour."

The sergeant checked with an usher, who thrust a thumb over his shoulder. "The alarm made me nervous, Ten, so I, uh, turned it off."

"Nervous how?"

"Just nervous."

"Come *on*, Kevin."

Doug leaned forward to see past Hoagy. "So what do you think of the Mets' chances to go all the way this year, Joe? Got a gut feeling?"

The vendors had reappeared when the game went into extra innings and the sergeant slipped past one spearing hot dogs with a fork. He smiled at a pretty brunette carrying too much stuff in a cardboard tray, and sidestepped her. "My gut feeling is they have too many Kevins."

"Da-ad." The computer nerd jounced in her seat. "They have *two*."

The sergeant reached the foot of the stairs that led to where they sat, about ten rows back, just under the overhang of the upper deck. "Sometimes it seems like more. Sometimes it seems like an all-Kevin lineup."

"Da-ad. Kevin *El*ster's cute."

"He's *mar*ried," Hoagy said.

The nerd punched his knee.

"Ow!"

"Kids."

"He started it."

"She started it."

Doug looked at Cullen and rolled his eyes.

The nerd put an elbow on the arm of Cullen's seat and her chin in her hand. "So, Dad, tell us about your girlfriend. Ann." *Ay-un*.

Hoagy groaned and rolled his eyes.

"Kids. Doug. Listen I left my seat number with my dispatcher. Just in case. This officer—"

"Sergeant Cullen?" the uniformed sergeant said.

"I'll be with you in a minute, Sergeant. This officer is here because of some kind of emergency—"

"It's a ten-thirteen, Cullen, so if you'll—"

"I said, just a minute . . ." Cullen tried to make something pronounceable out of the letters on the sergeant's nametag, but they were nearly all consonants. "Kids. Doug. I have to go. I'm sorry. Tenny, James, I'm really sorry. It's . . . it's work. Doug, I'm real glad you're here, because—"

"Hey, Joe. No problem."

"I love you, Ten. I love you, James. I *want* to tell you about Ann."

"When?" the nerd said, which meant she wasn't a nerd anymore, she'd become a woman, because only a woman, when you'd said—with sincerity, with *em*phasis—that you *wanted* to tell her something, instead of saying *Oh, good*, or *Whenever you're ready*, asked *When?*

"Soon." Cullen made passes at kisses. Hoagy and the nerd dodged and ducked.

"I'll see you guys."

"Bye, Dad."

"Bye, Dad."

"So long, buddy."

"Tell Connie I'll call tomorrow."

"So long, buddy. Hope everything's all right."

Cullen led the way down the stairs and along the aisle. At the top of the ramp he turned and faced the uniformed sergeant.

"Bermúdez," the sergeant said.

"Yeah?"

"He got polished."

Polished, done, 'fewed, drilled behind the left ear while sitting in his Omni outside 119, reading *Love in the Time of Cholera* in paperback (in English), with a bullet from a silenced 9 millimeter pistol fired at the closest range by an individual—oh, hell, *man*—who then took Bermúdez's keyring, let himself into 119 by the basement-level service door, went up to the third floor, crept into Nicky Potter's room, and woke Nicky by inserting the gun barrel between her lips and whispering that before he pulled the trigger she would pull his. He called her "Vera, baby," so he was in the wrong room.

The wrong room in more ways than one, for Nicky, the recipient of some training in karate, as befits a more-than-assistant-a-life-support-system, put a knee in the interloper's groin, yanked out a clump of his hair, and screamed for help so loudly that neighbors heard her up and down the block. The intruder got away before the cops who caught the nine-eleven got to 119, and when they finally looked to see how come the cop on guard duty outside hadn't reacted to all the commotion, they saw how come.

Hriniak, Walsh, Amato, Maslosky, Ruth, Ingram, Intaglia, Nixon, Pavonelli, Kean, Paltz, Winerib. Mayor Lyons, District Attorney Levitt. Cappy and Tippy and Mopsy and Suzie, the yuppie newshounds—newsbitches—yapping at the skirts of Deputy Commissioner Susan Price, fascinated, *fas*cinated at their glimpse of the shaven-headed Claire Langois being taken off by private ambulance, having been pushed all the way over the edge by this intrusion and needing serious round-the-clock medical care. Everybody was out on this one. Even Ann.

"How are you?" Cullen said.

She didn't say fine; her drawn and sallow skin said she'd had enough. She was sweating; he'd never seen her sweat, except healthily, moving atop him, beneath him, nostrils flaring, eyes not quite closed, watching him watching her, grunting with the pleasant effort. "Oh, Joe, I'm so sorry."

"Driving here, I was thinking about Martha's Vineyard." They'd gone there at Christmas, Hoagy and the computer nerd having gone skiing in Quebec with Connie and Doug. They had stayed mostly indoors for five days,—sex, laughs, books, seafood, naps. "You'd brought that biography of Clara Bow."

"The 'It' girl. Don't ask me why. I never opened it. I still haven't."

"I read a few pages—a part about how she'd gotten seriously depressed once in New York, but said she'd wait till she got back to Hollywood to have a full-fledged nervous breakdown, so she'd have it in 'the proper surroundings.' "

"That Clara. What a tongue."

"But it's New York that's the madhouse, isn't it? It's unrelenting. What made me think I could bring kids up here?"

Ann nodded. "Neil told me about the woman you saw hit by a cab."

"Neil?"

"He called to see how I was."

"Oh. I see. And I haven't called, so I'm a bad guy." The best defense is immaturity.

"I didn't say that."

"Neil went to get Keith's mother." Or change the subject.

"Keith wasn't married, was he?"

"No. He was seeing someone last winter, a nurse, but then they broke up."

"That happens."

"Yes, it does."

That dangled there in the hot wind and they watched it for a while. Then Ann said: "I know what you mean about New York. I was on the Broadway local today. It was like *A Chorus Line* for panhandlers; it's not enough to have a cup and a sore anymore, you've got to have a story. One guy had his ten-year-old daughter with him. He was upstaged by a woman with *her* ten-year-old daughter who she said had been raped by her teacher; she didn't want any money, she just wanted the number of a law firm that did *pro bono* work. She said *pro bono*, not me. I wanted to tell her the number she should call was 911 and that if she knew what *pro bono* was, she had a big edge on most everyone else in the car. I just looked at my feet. Then a woman getting on the train seemed to get her leg caught between the train and the platform; a man who helped her discovered that he'd had his wallet boosted, that it was all a scam. I know, I shouldn't talk like a player. . . . So why haven't you called?"

Cullen was able not to answer by making a production of watching Hriniak step out in the street to meet a whitetop with a stuttering siren. Hriniak opened the back door and handed out a dignified Hispanic woman, then a hysterical one: Bermúdez's mother and sister. The photographers and cameramen collapsed on them, splashing light all over them. Mayor Lyons tried to get in the pictures, but Hriniak stilled everyone with a gesture of going for a shoulder-holstered gun. Just a gesture, but a perfect one, and he got the two women up on the sidewalk and, with the help of Zimmerman, who'd followed the whitetop in the Saab, in the service entrance of 119. "They think it was Tom."

"That's crazy."

"Which doesn't stop them from thinking it. It's the same *kind* of gun that killed Story."

"But what was Tom's motive?"

"He was out to kill Vera. Vera's a Story, he's on a Story vendetta. He killed Keith to get in the house, he mistook Nicky for Vera."

"They do look alike."

He shook his head. "No, they don't."

"You would know. You can probably *smell* the difference."

Cullen took Ann by the elbow, carefully, so she wouldn't think he assumed that because she'd slept with him, she liked him. "Let me tell you a story."

"Joe. . . ."

"It's important."

## Old times:

*"I thought I'd find you here."*

*"Who gives a fuck what you thought?"*

*"I'm moving to California."*

*"Who gives a fuck where you're moving?"*

*"Next month."*

*"Who gives a fuck what month?"*

*"I guess I was crazy to think you might be glad to hear the news."*

*"Yep, you're crazy. A crazy whore."*

*"That's hardly fair."*

*"It was true, wasn't it? The things we heard about you in high school?"*

*". . . What things?"*

*"About your screwing Tom. Who else were you screwing, whore?"*

*". . . Oh, Joe."*

*" 'Oh, Joe.' "*

*"It wasn't you, Joe, was it?"*

*"You mean you don't even know who you were screwing? You* were *a whore."*

*"It was you. You wrote the letter, didn't you?"*

*"I don't know what you're talking about."*

*"You wrote the letter."*

*"I don't know what you're talking about."*

*"When I got the letter I went straight to Tom. I don't know where I got the nerve, but I went straight to Tom and said, 'Is this true?' and he read it and said, 'It's not true, Vera.' No 'I swear to God' or any of that shit; just, 'It's not true, Vera,' and I believed him. He wanted to get the police involved in finding out who wrote it. I didn't care who wrote it; it was written by someone too sick to punish. Their sickness would be the punishment. . . . God, Joe, you must've suffered."*

*"I don't know what you're talking about."*

*"If you wanted me, why didn't you try to have me? Why did you try to destroy me?"*

*"How long've you been seeing this guy?* Caleb. *And how the fuck old* is *Caleb? About a hundred and ten?"*

*"Why couldn't you? I knew you liked me. You were around so much—hanging out with Chuck but not really with Chuck. I knew you liked me."*

*"Big deal if I did, right, 'cause you'd've just gone off with somebody else."*

*"You're being silly, Joe. You're being a child."*

*" 'I'm going to be a* successful *actress and* successful *actresses, by definition, don't have time for family or friends or a life of their own, so forget about lovers.' "*

*"You're not making any sense. Why're you mocking me? Why're you behaving like a child?"*

*"What do you care? You've got* Caleb. Caleb*'s no child.* Caleb*'s about a hundred and ten."*

*"Oh, Joe."*

*Vera.*

*"Oh, Joe, Joe, Joe, Joe, Joe."*

*Vera, Vera, Vera.*

## Old times:

*Writing the play had been a blatant attempt to impress Vera, as had been reading plays, reading collections of drama criticism and biographies of playwrights and actors, saving places for Vera on lines for standing room tickets for plays and concerts and dance performances and operas and helping her mem-*

*orize and analyze material for class, reading—memorizing, practically—copies of* Backstage *and* Variety.

*Reading the latter was a nasty habit that persisted for another six months after Vera Story walked out of the bar where she tracked Cullen after he surprised her on Caleb Evans's lap. The habit-breaker was an item announcing the nuptials of Vera Story and Caleb Evans (which, presumably, entitled her to sit wherever she wanted, certainly entitled her to a starring role in Evans's next picture, Evans being considerably more than an occasional lecturer at schools for actors, being a director sometimes known as the American Bergman).*

*To commemorate the breaking of the habit, Cullen got the manuscript of his play out of his desk drawer, wrapped it in that issue of* Variety, *and dumped it into the Hudson River from the pedestrian walkway of the George Washington Bridge, after entertaining momentarily the idea of throwing himself in as well.*

Ann pushed herself off the fender of the whitetop that had been her perch for Cullen's reminiscence. "I get it. I mean, I get it, but I don't get it."

"Tom and Vera have stayed close over the years. She didn't tell me this; I just figured it out. Tom had a drinking problem; it ended his basketball career. The rehab, well, I think Vera was part of it—encouraged it, paid for it, whatever. I didn't understand her reaction when I told her Tom was a suspect in Chuck's murder. It wasn't simply skepticism, surprise; it was the total disbelief of someone who knows someone very well. He wouldn't mistake her, even in the dark. He *could* smell the difference, and he wouldn't be attacking her in the first place."

"So your little prank, intended to drive them apart, brought them together."

That needed no confirmation. "Here's the other thing."

"What other thing?"

"I was supposed to work tonight, for Keith."

"Oh, Joe."

"Originally, he was going to work for me. We made the arrangement on the phone: he was in the shop, I was on the street. He had a change of plans and we switched back. We made the rearrangement face-to-face."

Ann shook her head. "I don't get it."

"I had a conversation, on the same phone, the shop phone, with Connie, about Tom, about his fascination, when we were kids, with Jamaica Bay. Within days, came the raid."

Ann's forehead had a deep dent in it. "So what? I mean, things happen. Other people must've known about Tom and the bay. Plenty of other people."

"But none of them is working on the Dean thing."

Her brow cleared. "You think that's it?"

"I think that's it."

"So this. . . ." She waved at 119, at Bermúdez's Omni, its doors open, looking like a pair of pants with the pockets turned out, being crawled over by someone from Crime Scene.

"Smoke. That is, the bit with Nicky—or was it supposed to be Vera?—was smoke. The bit with Keith, that was real—except it was supposed to be me."

"Because of the Dean thing."

"Here's what I'd like you to do. Deborah Dean's brother, Darelle, is a cop in the One-Nine. He's been in touch with us, with me and Neil, to do what he can on his sister's behalf, and he did us a favor. A friend of his who works for the phone company found out that in the week before Deborah Dean was shot there were at least three calls to her home number from . . . from an extension Downtown."

"Business calls?"

"No. Those calls would come from the precinct."

"Whose extension?"

"What I'd like you to do is call Darelle—I'll give you his direct line; if he doesn't answer, don't leave a message—and ask him to ask his friend to find out if there're any Title III intercepts on IAU. Tell him I'll owe him a favor."

"Title III intercepts?"

"Wiretaps. I thought you were a player."

"That's mean, Cullen."

"I'm sorry. Make sure you say intercepts *on* IAU, not *by* IAU."

Ann looked genuinely astonished. "You guys use *wire*taps? On fellow *cops*? Jesus."

"Will you do it, Ann, or should I get somebody else?"

"That's mean. You're just a mean guy."

"I'm sorry."

"That was horrible what you did to Vera. It was the late fifties, right? To not be a virgin was to be damned. Did you apologize to her?"

"I wanted to today. Yesterday. We were interrupted. A little episode with Claire Langois."

"What's with her? She's gone hard-core."

"I don't think your phone call helped matters."

"There were several calls, actually."

"Right."

"Neil and I talked about all the things you're sitting on."

"Neil talks too much."

"Did Vera tell you where Lise and Claire were going on their little drive?"

Cullen rubbed at the knots in his neck.

"She did. And now you're sitting on that."

Worse than knots. Welds.

"Whose extension, Joe?"

"Hello, Commissioner," Cullen said.

"Hello, Joe," Hriniak said. "Ann."

"Commissioner."

"Hell of a thing, Joe. I'm truly sorry. Ann, would you excuse us? I have some police business to discuss with . . . with Joe."

"Later," Ann said.

Hriniak watched Ann walk back toward where the other reporters slouched, talking about the weather, telling lies. "Joe, what the fuck?"

"I know. People I'm with keep getting polished, or almost."

"You don't know the fucking half of it."

"Don't I?"

Hriniak rubbed his thumb with his first two fingers, calling in a debt. "Gimme everything on the Dean thing."

"The lawyers have it."

"Not any more. Deborah ate her off-duty gun."

It was too much: the heat, the dying, the three hot dogs he'd eaten at Shea, more dying, more heat. Cullen stepped to the gutter and vomited.

# 26

A one-horse world. Patrolman Lester Glatter, the sorry son-of-a-bitch who caught the nine-eleven when the PC got polished; who had worried that in his novitiate he might tromp all over the crime scene or glom up all the latents or forget to mirandize a suspect; who had been able to foresee no benefit to his career coming from his having his name somewhere on every single piece of paperwork generated by that unprecedented misfortune, the same Lester Glatter made a collar just before dawn that same morning that had the potential to put the young officer's name not just on a bunch of bureaucratic forms but on the front page of every newspaper in the land, maybe in that one-horse world.

Glatter was on loan from the Nineteenth Precinct (Deborah Dean's brother Darelle's precinct, it being a one-horse world), borrowed by a special borough-wide unit formed in response to reports by social workers of still more attacks on defenseless homeless people. In one case, a middle-aged man (the author of several midlist novels in his younger days) was beaten in a playground near the Great Lawn in Central Park; in another, a transvestite prostitute living in a Sanitation Department warehouse near the Holland Tunnel had his hair set on fire; in a third, a young woman squatting in a building undergoing renovation near Tompkins Square Park in the East Village was stabbed in the abdomen.

Neither the victims nor anyone else had seen the attackers (the former novelist told of spotting a band of six or eight teenagers before he lost consciousness, but he also insisted to detectives from the Midtown North Squad that there were two small men in saffron robes—Buddhists, apparently—riding on the hood of their car); the prostitute had as many enemies as he had neighbors in the warehouse—and maybe johns on the street, if any had discovered (his métier was oral sex and discovery wasn't inevitable) that he wasn't a woman; the young woman was a bone contended over by three young men who shared her living quarters. It was therefore entirely possible that the incidents were discrete, but it was just possible, given the widespread feeling that the down and out were too much with us in those days, that they were concerted, hence the formation of the special unit, known very unofficially as the Happy Homeless.

Lester Glatter (Duke to his friends because he did a pretty fair John Wayne imitation) and three dozen other young men and women officers were sent out into the streets to imitate the homeless and their habits, to become bait for those who were preying on them. Along with Officer Pauline Richards and Officer John Berkery, Glatter was assigned to hang around the World Trade Center and City Hall Park. The Vietnam veterans who lived in the park smelled the trio's paramilitariness right away, and confronted them.

"Cops?" said the vets' spokesman, who said his name was Judy and whose eyes warned against making a joke about it. "And you think—what?—that we're going to fall down and lick your boots and fucking thank you for showing the fuck up? We should all scoot over some so you'll have a place to lie down? We should toss another steak on the broiler? Get a grip, fellows and gals, 'cause the fucking fact of the matter is you want room and board we ain't got to give."

"Well, uh," the cops attempted.

"And anyway," Judy went on. "You see that tree there, right in the middle of the park, those six or eight brothers sitting around it?"

The cops looked and nodded.

"That tree is known as Loco Oak and the reason it is known as Loco Oak is those six or eight brothers and five or six more who aren't present and accounted for at this time have elevators that do not go to the top floor. Their dice do not have all their dots, they are not playing with a full deck, they are a couple of beers short of a six pack. They are moored ten feet from the dock, they are not playing on a level field, they are out where the buses don't run. They are on line without a ticket, they are a few bricks shy of a load. Do you catch my drift?"

The cops nodded and guessed they understood now why the six or eight brothers sitting under the tree known as Loco Oak were wearing combat boots and fatigue pants and field jackets and trench coats and watch caps and even, one of them, a balaclava—but not understanding *how* they could be wearing so much when wearing anything was to be overdressed.

"So what is to keep *them*," Judy said, "in the event of an enemy attack, from inflicting reprisals on their attackers? Put it another way, if somebody comes around here looking for trouble, we'll give it to them. And if you try and stop *us,* on the premise that you're *helping* us, we'll be obliged to give it to you. Am I still coming through without any major static?"

The cops nodded.

"Good," Judy said. "Since we understand each other, and since you fellows and gals just have a job to do, I know, my suggestion is you stay out of our way and we'll make a little room for you. Don't expect nothing in the way of food; we don't have any to go around. And don't go flaunting your Burger King take-out bags and your containers of Chinese food, you dig, or somebody's liable to cut your throat."

And then Judy was gone, having soaked them all over with his pungent smell and his indisputable logic.

The duty was tedious, hot and tedious. The sun started slowly sucking the air out of the world about an hour after it came up, and by high noon the only way to survive was to pretend to be dead. To relieve the monotony when he wasn't pretending to be dead, Duke Glatter played Being Visible: he sat on a bench along one of the pathways through the park and tried to will passersby to look at him, to acknowledge him as a fellow member of the human race, instead of looking around him or away from him or through him. Sometimes two or three hours and hundreds of people would pass before somebody would look at him and see a human being, albeit an eyesore. Once, his brother, Jim, who worked for the Customs Service in the World Trade Center, walked by and didn't look at him. When Duke called Jim that night to tell him about it, Jim denied that he hadn't looked; he contended he'd seen Duke and figured he was on assignment and hadn't wanted to blow his cover. "Bullshit," Duke said, and Jim changed the subject.

Overnights were best, for the sun still hadn't figured out a way to shine at night, the ranters at Loco Oak stopped ranting (or ranted less, anyway), the traffic dissipated, and the noise. You could think about something other than the white-hot electric drill boring into your forehead. You could think, as Duke Glatter was thinking just before dawn, lying on a bench near the east, the Park Row, side of the park, his neck over one metal arm, his legs over another, about intimacy. Physical intimacy. Physical intimacy with Officer Pauline Richards, who had a funny little scrunched-up face and a funny little lopsided body but who gave off a . . . well, an *attitude* that was driving the Duke nuts.

The Duke was hip to the perils of fraternization. Hell, every cop in town was, on account of the Dean thing. "Would you fuck one of the bad guys?" was the way the Captain at the One-Nine put it (in a talk to the troops delivered on one of Darelle Dean's days off, so as not to stir him up). "You would not, knowing bad guys to frequently carry loaded weapons that should they become hostile to you they might discharge in your direction. And for the very same reason you should not fuck one of the *good* guys, on account of once the honeymoon was over even minor domestic disturbances might be resolved in a violent manner."

First had come the word that rather than finger the brass she was fucking Deborah Dean wouldn't let the docs cut the bullet out of her and now came the word that rather than finger the brass she was fucking Deborah had eaten her off-duty gun, and how did she get a gun in her hospital room anyway since she was technically under arrest, wasn't she? So the Duke wasn't likely to actually pursue physical intimacy with Officer Pauline Richards, but that didn't mean he couldn't think about her.

Thinking about Officer Pauline Richards gave the Duke a hard-on, which was inconvenient and potentially embarrassing, since the Vietnam vets enjoyed ragging the cops at the least provocation and would love, if they noticed, to call attention to the lump in the Duke's drawers. They might all be asleep, the vets, and they might not, for they had a way, developed in Asian jungles, the Duke imagined, of watching when he was sure they were resting and resting when he was sure they were watching; but just for safety's sake, he ought to change his position.

Duke Glatter lifted his head and his feet and manoeuvered around on his side and finally onto his stomach, making the necessary adjustments so that his hard-on wouldn't hurt like hell against the slats of the bench. As he turned, he saw the movement in the bushes.

Just one man. He'd fantasized there would be several.

Paunchy. Out-of-shape. He'd fantasized they'd be swift and hard.

Bumbling, noisy. He'd fantasized they'd move like cats.

The paunchy, bumbling man was headed across the patch of park just to the south of Loco Oak, a road not taken by the rest of the vets (nor were the approaches from the north, the east, the west), because it wasn't worth their time or energy to get spat on or snarled at just for trying to pass the time of day, just for inquiring how everyone was doing. Some nights everyone was too drunk, too beat, too wasted to post guards, but when there were guards they never bothered to check around Loco Oak because they half-hoped someone *would* beat the shit out of the snarling, spitting assholes. So the paunchy, bumbling man wasn't a vet on guard duty. Nor did he look like a Loco Oak regular returning late to the hearth. Glatter had had a look around Loco Oak an hour earlier—getting snarled at and spat on in the process—and the place had looked to have just about a full house.

So who was he?

Duke Glatter rolled off the bench onto his hands and knees and went on all fours to a hedge, to a tree, to another, to a bush, to a tree. He peeked out.

The man was pissing on Loco Oak, pissing on the men asleep on the ground all around it.

Now he was lighting a match. To see where he'd—Oh, shit. No.

"Freeze. Police." Duke Glatter got his revolver out from inside his shirt and came out from behind the tree all in one motion. "I said *freeze! Police!*"

It was too late. The man had thrown the match after the lighter fluid or kerosene or gasoline or whatever it was he had doused on the ground, on the Loco Oak, on the sleeping men around it. The fluid ignited with a gasp.

"Fire. Help. Fire." Duke Glatter's voice sounded meek.

"Fire!" That was better.

*"Fire!"* Good.

Then: "Judy. Judy! *Judy!*" If Judy was sober he'd get things organized. *"Juuuudy!"*

"Here, slick. What the fuck?"

"Help those guys. I'm going after the son-of-a-bitch."

"What the fuck, man? What the *fuck*?"

"Help those guys. I'm going after the son-of-a-bitch." But Duke Glatter couldn't move. All he could do was watch the men around Loco Oak trying to shake the fire off their bodies, out of their hair.

Watch and smell the hideous smell.

Watch and hear the pitiful screams.

Then finally Duke Glatter ran after the paunchy, bumbling man. The man, who ran like a man parodying the run of a woman, elbows leading, wrists bent back, hips swiveling, knees swiveling, hadn't gotten very far in spite of his head start. He was just at the driveway that split City Hall Park in two like an asphalt moat; on one side of the moat lived the vets, on the other lay City Hall.

The paunchy, bumbling man crossed the driveway.

He crossed the plaza in front of City Hall.

He ran up the steps of City Hall.

He ran in the front door of City Hall.

In the front door of *City Hall*?

Jesus.

Duke Glatter went across the plaza and up the steps and in the front door, which was open, of City Hall.

Open?

There was a desk to the left of the door and seated at the desk, his arms folded across his stomach, was a fat cop, asleep. Behind the desk was a metal fence with a gate; the gate was closed, the hallway beyond it dark.

To the right was another hallway. Duke Glatter went toward it and along it and came to a room that looked like a press room: cluttered desks, stacks of newspapers, reports, press releases, computers, typewriters, Styrofoam cups, soft drink bottles and cans.

From outside came the sound of sirens—fire trucks, ambulances, whitetops.

From inside came the sound of breathing—paunchy, bumbling breathing.

From inside the room that looked like a press room.

From under a desk in a far corner of the room.

"Come on out real slow," Duke Glatter said. And added, "Motherfucker." He spread his legs and bent his knees and aimed his gun with two hands. He felt kind of stupid.

From under the desk came the sound of sobbing.

"Come on, buddy."

"I didn't do anything. I didn't. I didn't do anything. I didn't. I didn't do anything. I didn't."

"I saw you, buddy. I saw you."

"I didn't do anything."

"I saw you." Duke Glatter felt more stupid, arguing with this jerk like they were kids or something. He stood up straight and let his gun dangle. He looked over the edge of the desk and saw the soles of a pair of sneakers, red Pumas. He moved a little and saw the red Pumas' owner on his knees in the kneehole of the desk, his arms over his head. "Come *on,* buddy."

"I didn't *do* anything."

Duke Glatter holstered his revolver and moved all the way around behind the desk and took the man by the ankles and straightened him out with a yank.

The man wore black sweat pants and a black sweat shirt and a black watch cap pulled down below his ears. Not seasonal clothing, but the urban terrorist always has the problem of what to wear in the summer and still avoid detection. The man kept his hands clasped over his head.

"Get up, pal."

"I didn't—"

Duke Glatter kicked the man in the ribs, easing up at the last instant but still aiming to hurt.

"*Hey!*" The man let go of his head and pressed his hands on his ribs. He rolled on his side, then on his back, and glared indignantly at Duke Glatter. "You dumb punk cop."

Holy shit.

"Who the hell do you think you are going around kicking people?"

Oh christ no.

Groaning, the man sat up. He clutched his ribs and rocked back and forth. "I'll see you pay for this. Police brutality."

No.

The man pulled the watch cap off and used it to towel his dripping face. "You'll pay."

Why me?

The man began to sob. "Why me? Why *me*? Why *meeeee*?"

Mayor Sidney Lyons.

"Why, why, why me?"

Why me?

# 27

As welcome as a slasher in a horror flick to most folks those days *(One Hundred Two in the Shade—Part LXVIII),* the sun bulled its way up over the horizon. Molten light poured over the roofs of Harlem, killing everything. Cullen flipped down the Saab's sun visor so he wouldn't have to watch the destruction.

"Some bran muffin?" Zimmerman said. He didn't usually allow eating in the car, but these were exceptional times.

"I'll just have the coffee." Cullen tore a careful V out of the lid of his container and looked for a place to put it. The Saab's ashtrays were virginal; the gutter of Morningside Drive was deep with trash. He put it in the change pocket of his suit coat. It was the least he could do, having been allowed back in the Turbo.

Zimmerman unwrapped the muffin and with a plastic knife thinned the butter the deli counterman had dolloped on. He put the muffin on the dashboard, tore a V out of the lid of his coffee container, put the scrap in the empty deli bag.

Cullen took his scrap out of his change pocket and put it in the bag.

Zimmerman raised his coffee container. "To Keith."

"To Keith."

They sipped, thought, sipped again.

"To Deborah Dean," Cullen said.

"To Deborah Dean."

They sipped.

Zimmerman cut a piece of muffin with the knife and offered it to Cullen. "Sure?"

"Well, okay. Thanks." Cullen took it and waited for Zimmerman to cut a piece for himself.

They ate.

They sipped.

"I've got news," Zimmerman said.

Cullen tried to remember: had he told Zimmerman about Claire Langois's skin-head, her leechlike pigtail, her black eyebrows and black eyes, her gray-rouged cheeks, her brass knuckles, her death's head rings, her swastika, her carriage bolt?

"I haven't had a chance to tell you, what with everything else. I've been working at the drug store. Last night, seven, seven-thirty—I was in the stock room, fortunately, because she'd've been spooked if she saw me—who comes in to buy three Fourex condoms?"

Just tell me, Neil. "Who?"

"Mabel Parker."

"No."

"Taubman says she's the one who made the call in the thunderstorm. He's sure of it."

"Who's Taubman? Oh, the pharmacist. She *can't* be the Fourex lady."

"Can't she?"

"We told her we had a description, we told her we were going to stake the place out. Didn't we?"

"We told her a lot of stuff. We thought she was a good guy."

"Christ."

Zimmerman cut two more pieces of muffin and handed one to Cullen. "I tailed her to one-one-six East Seven-one. That's the six-story apartment building that backs on 119. She doesn't live there, she lives on York Avenue. She comes there two or three times a week—this is from the doorman—sometimes on weekends, usually Sunday night, goes to apartment five D-dog, to which she has a key. A guy comes a little later—an older guy, middle-aged. They stay three or four hours, the guy leaves first, then she leaves. Sometimes she stays overnight, but not a lot. Five D-dog is rented—are you ready for this?—by Norman Levitt."

Cullen shook his head. "I don't know a— No."

"Yes."

"Norman Levitt Leah Levitt's husband?"

"Norman Levitt Leah Levitt's husband."

"District At*tor*ney Leah Levitt."

"I don't know any other Leah Levitts."

"They haven't split up, have they?"

"Not that I know of, but then I don't run in prosecutorial circles. Or banking circles."

"Arbitrage," Cullen said. "So the apartment's a . . . what's the word?"

*"Pied à terre."*

"There's another word." Cullen had to laugh. "And we asked Mabel who in her office might've seen the woman leaving 119."

Zimmerman laughed. "We did ask her that."

"Christ. What else did we ask her? What else did we *tell* her?"

"We told her about the footprint."

"No matter, since she saw the print being *made*."

"We told her the call to the One-Nine was on an unlisted line. No matter."

"Since she made it."

"We told her Taubman made the caller as a customer who bought condoms."

"Fourex." Cullen laughed.

"What."

He laughed harder.

"What, goddamn it?"

Cullen got his breath back. " 'She's not worried about AIDS.' "

*"What?"*

" 'She's not worried about AIDS.' That's what Mabel said. Something about natural skins transmit the virus, and rubbers don't."

" 'Natural skins are pervious to the HIV virus. Rubbers aren't.' "

Cullen laughed. "And you said, 'Gulp, oh?' "

"What're you getting at, Joe?"

"Oh, admit it, Neil. You thought she was fresh."

"So?"

"Nothing. So nothing. She *was* fresh. *Is* fresh. I'm just a little whacked out, that's all. *Garçonnière* is the word I was trying to think of—an apartment for having an affair in."

Zimmerman folded his arms against edification.

"Did we tell Mabel anything else?" Cullen said.

"I don't remember."

Cullen sighed. "I remember. We told her Ann has a source who says the Raleigh was torched."

"*You* told her that," Zimmerman said.

Cullen ignored him. "Anything else?"

"I don't remember."

"Neil, I'm sorry I laughed, okay? Don't take it too hard. I'm a little hysterical. Something I don't remember, Neil: Did I tell you about Claire Langois?"

"About her skin-head, her brass knuckles, her swastika, her carriage bolt?"

"I did tell you. There's been so much going on. Vera said that the back way—across the yard and through the fence and out the alley next to the apartment house on the next block—she said the back way is Claire's regular way out."

"And you think—what?—that the kid's the woman Mabel saw?"

"I wish I knew more about Charles Story," Cullen said.

"Like?"

"Like did he fuck around? I never heard rumors, but I never hear rumors. You hear rumors; did you ever hear rumors?"

"No." Zimmerman put his coffee on the dashboard and sat sidesaddle to face Cullen. "We've got to tell somebody, Joe, about Hriniak." The car phone rang and he answered it. "Zimmerman. Wait one." He covered the mouthpiece with his hand. "Joe?"

"I hear you."

"Maslosky. Anybody."

"I hear you."

"Today. This morning. Now."

"See who that is, will you?"

"Promise me, Joe. Promise me that as soon as this line's clear, we'll call Maslosky."

"I promise. See who that is. It might be Connie." Wanting to know if that had been his idea of a nice night out with the children. No: that wasn't fair. Even though she'd never known Bermúdez, she'd been before his time, she'd want to know if there was anything she could do for his family. Connie was the only decent person in the whole wide world.

Zimmerman uncovered the mouthpiece. ''Yeah? . . . . Hi, Ann.'' He handed the phone to Cullen. ''Ann.''

''Thanks,'' Cullen said.

Zimmerman said, ''You promised.''

''I promised.'' To Ann, Cullen said, ''Hi.''

''You asked me to ask Darelle Dean to ask his friend about the Title III intercepts—''

''Oh, Ann, christ. That was be*fore* his sister killed herself.''

''I know when it was. I'm not some ghoul. I'm at Beekman Downtown. Walsh had a press conference. Darelle's under suspicion. Darelle was her only visitor yesterday and he could've brought her the gun. Darelle came up to me. How does he know you know me? Did you tell him?''

Had he? And what had Darelle thought of that, of an IAU homeboy's being involved with a reporter, Darelle who'd worried that a couple of IAU homeboys might think it wasn't such a good idea for him to, you know, fraternize, with a business representative involved in a special pilot program? Or had Cullen told Darelle it was cool, that he was an IAU homeboy who didn't want everything under one roof, just the sex and the laughs and the Lyle Lovett albums and the *Hill Street Blues* reruns and the Buffalo chicken wings? ''How's Darelle doing?''

''His friend from the phone company was with him,'' Ann said. ''Her name's Iris. Iris Hall. He's doing all right. I told them what you wanted and Iris went straight to a phone, made a call and got the answer. At five o'clock in the morning. They're in love. Iris looks like Flo Jo. She's fast like Flo Jo. There's a Title III intercept on your office phone. It's the only one inside IAU. It was authorized by a judge whose name Iris's contact couldn't make out and requested by Walsh.''

''Walsh?''

''What's going on, Joe?''

''I have to be going, Ann. I'll call you.''

''You son-of-a-bitch, Snake.''

''Thanks for your help.''

''You son-of-a-bitch.''

Cullen hung up. He took a sip of coffee and dumped the rest out the window. ''Drink up.''

Zimmerman shook his head slowly. ''You promised.''

''Drink up.''

# 28

High noon. Striding down Canal Street, backpack slung over one shoulder, damn the heat and his fugitive status, full speed ahead, six-feet-six and hard as hell to hide, Elmhust-Elmhurst High-Syracuse-Nam, big man on campus, varsity hoops and baseball, president of this club, treasurer of that one, most likely to, most inevitably, most assuredly, always tossing the ball appropriate to the season in the air, always with a flock of adoring girls in his wake, listening through Walkman headphones to WINS, all the news all the time, you give us twenty-two minutes, we'll give you the world, Thomas George Valentine.

And what a world: to the regular lineup of Famine, Pestilence, Destruction, and Death let's have a big hand for our special guests, Inhumanity, Indifference, and Incompetence. Twenty-two minutes, hell. Twenty-two *hours* would be barely enough to scratch the world's battered, grimy surface.

A surface baked to adamancy, scorched nearly free of habitants. Tom Valentine had hitched a ride in through the Holland Tunnel on a rig hauling swinging meat from Godawful, Maryland. The rig had headed north up to Little West Twelfth, that area, and Valentine had been faced with a long hot walk on a long hot street that was auditioning for the part of main drag of a ghost town. No buses ran, no taxis passed, the few pedestrians slunk along the building lines, vying for what little midday shade there was. Valentine thought passing out might be a useful thing to do. Someone would call an air-conditioned ambulance. Or then again, they might not.

Then a magic carriage materialized—a police whitetop standing at the curb at West Broadway, its windows rolled up, its occupants cooping in air-conditioned comfort. Tom Valentine walked over and tapped on the window.

A cop maybe fourteen years old looked up from the *Daily News* in his lap.

Valentine made roll-down-the-window circles in the air with his forefinger.

The cop looked down at his newspaper. His nametag said *Kiss*.

Valentine tapped with a knuckle on the window.

Kiss turned the page. To a photograph, fairly recent, of Valentine.

Valentine slapped the window with the palm of his hand.

Kiss jerked the paper into a wad between his knees and cranked the window down three inches. "What the fuck, mac?"

His partner, a sixteen-year-old, leaned across from the driver's side to see out the window. "Just move along, pal. Windshield's clean." His nametag said *Monday*. He sat back and sipped a container of coffee. Kiss cranked up the window and straightened out his newspaper.

So they thought he was a squeegee guy, hey? He'd give them a squeegee-ing they'd never forget. He slung his arms through both straps of his backpack and climbed up on the hood of the whitetop. The hood was hot enough to cook on and Valentine was glad that, hot as the weather was, he was wearing blue jeans, having thought long and hard about it and having decided that to one's surrender on murder charges one wore long trousers. Valentine pressed his face against the windshield.

Monday leaned on the horn with the heel of his hand. Kiss beat with the side of his fist on the inside of the windshield. Valentine could read his lips: *Hey, you crazy fuck!*

Sensing an accumulating crowd, a crowd hoping for a little violence, a little bum-bashing (one and a half of the twenty-two minutes of famine, pestilence, destruction, death, inhumanity, indifference, and incompetence had been about the setting on fire of several homeless Vietnam vets in City Hall Park by an unidentified assailant captured red-handed by a cop of a different breed, clearly, than Kiss or Monday), Valentine pointed exaggeratedly at Kiss's lap. Kiss put a protective hand on his *Daily News*.

Monday was on the radio. . . . *request immediate backup*.

Valentine waved at Kiss to get his eye and pointed at his own face, then at the newspaper, then at his face, then at the newspaper. He mouthed: *I'm . . . Tom . . . Val-en—*

Oh, shit. Somebody had him by the ankles. "Hey."

"Off the car, mister."

Somebody strong. "Hey, take it easy, man."

"Off . . . the . . . car."

Very strong. Valentine thought about grabbing the wipers for purchase, but they'd break and there'd be a *huge* fuss about that: destruction of public property and all that shit. "Okay, okay, okay. Let go and I'll get off."

The puller stopped pulling but didn't let go. "Get off."

"Let go of my ankles."

"Get off."

"I can't unless you let go."

"Get . . . off."

"Let . . . go."

The puller let go. Valentine spun on his hip, ready to kick the puller in the chest. But the puller wasn't there any more. The puller was right next to his head, holding a gun barrel against Valentine's cheek. "Nothing fancy, mister."

This cop's nametag said Steele. She had long blond hair in a ponytail. Her pale blue uniform shirt had come unbuttoned in the pullathon; beneath it she wore a dark blue bra.

"Nothing fancy," Valentine promised.

Hriniak, Walsh, Amato. (Maslosky, Ruth, Ingram, Intaglia, Nixon, Pavonelli, Kean, Paltz, and Winerib were out in the hall, wondering what was so important that the three top brass were grilling a perp.)

Jimmy Freed, the civil libertarian's civil libertarian (formerly—it's a one-horse world—lawyer for Deborah Dean, now representing her brother, Darelle), was there too, in a windowless room in the basement of One Police Plaza, sitting a little farther from his client than was his custom, very aware that the distance symbolized a reluctance to be identified with his client but aware too, civil libertarian's civil libertarian or not, that identification in this case was something he could, as his wife had put it, "die without."

Lester (Duke) Glatter was there too, *certain* that identification with Freed's client would mean an end to life as he knew it: a life of mostly work, of handball at the Y; a computer course at the New School; *Wiseguy* on Wednesday nights; softball Sunday mornings in Alley Pond Park; early Sunday dinner at his Mom's in Bayside—except when he had to work, in which case he drove by and picked up a care package; lately, the occasional thought about intimacy, physical intimacy, with Officer Pauline Richards with that funny little scrunched-up face and that funny little lopsided body and that *smell*.

It was one thing to have pulled the nine-eleven when the PC got polished, to have had his name somewhere on every single piece of paperwork generated by that unprecedented misfortune; it was quite another to have collared the mayor of the City of New York for torching some homeless vets and on top of it to have kicked him in the ribs while making the collar, just to express his personal abhorrence of that kind of antisocial behavior. Not that he wouldn't, if this weren't a country where you were presumed innocent until proven guilty (or if the brass's backs were turned) gladly kick Lyons again—in the ribs, in the groin, in the teeth—anywhere to stop his horrible whining.

"Whhhhhy meeeeee?"

"Mister Mayor," Hriniak said, leaning in to try and penetrate the shroud of moans and groans in which Lyons had swaddled himself, "we'd like to go over this from the beginning. I want to be absolutely sure that you understand the nature of these allegations."

"Why, why, why, why *meeeeee*?"

"According to the eyewitness testimony of Officer Glatter here—"

Lyons whirled in his chair, pointed a quivering finger, shrieked. "He *kicked* me."

Glatter sat up straighter, ready to explain himself, but Jimmy Freed slammed a hand down on the table in front of Lyons. "Sid! Shut up! Please! Goddamn it!"

An angel passed, one with more sense than to hang around with *this* bunch. Then, with all the rationality in the world, Lyons said, "The allegations stemming from Officer Glatter's eyewitness account do not begin to encompass the crimes that I have committed—"

"Sid!" Freed had a rogue client on his hands now, instead of an unctuous one. "Sid, this is neither the time nor the place to be saying these things."

"I de*tested* Charles Story."

"Sid."

"He re*vol*ted me."

"Mister Mayor."

"I fooled him, though. He was supposed to be so *clever,* but I fooled him."

"Com*miss*ioner Hriniak—" Freed turned away from his client. Did he move a little farther away from him too? "I think it would be to everyone's advantage—"

"*I* fooled him. *Me*. He was supposed to be so *clever* and *I* fooled him. Fooled you too, Hriniak. Com*miss*ioner Hriniak. I faked you out of your jock. I looked you in the eye and told you Story was working undercover in his own department. A weasel—you said you cops called what he was a weasel. I looked you in the eye and told you Story dreamed it all up, but it was *I* who dreamed it up. *Me*. Me, me, me. It was brilliant. Incredibly brilliant.

"Do you know what I told him—the *ass*hole? I told him—the *ass*hole—that I had a tip from one of my people—*what* people? My people don't know shit, but Story doesn't know that—I told him I had a tip from one of my people that someone in my administration, someone high up, had a *huge* gambling debt. To pay it off, he made a deal—I mean, shit, I got this stuff from watching *mov*ies, *tel*evision, and you guys, you pro*fess*ionals, bought it—he made a deal with a loan shark, a mobster: he would let them know in advance about decisions affecting the real estate market."

Lyons lurched backwards in his chair and laughed. "God, how trite, how pa*thet*ic. Can you i*mag*ine anyone *fall*ing for that?"

Freed leaned across that symbolic distance and put a hand on Lyons's arm. "Sidney, please."

Lyons took Freed's hand in both of his and patted it gently. "I can look you in the eye, Jimmy, and say that I have always done what's best for the colossus among cities we live in. Done what's best. Done what's best. I had to protect it—the City of New York—from Charles Story. It was the only way. He'd have bought it up the way he bought up buildings and yachts and companies and . . . and everything. Airlines. He was going to buy an airline. An *air*line. It was the only way. It was up to me. It was up to me. It was up to me.'' Pat, pat, pat.

''I told Story,'' Lyons said, recapitulating now for the benefit of the slower studies, ''that I'd gotten a tip that someone high up in my administration had a gambling debt, that to pay it off he was passing information about the real estate market to some unspecified businessmen with connections to organized crime. I suggested to Story that we use *his* real estate connections, Story's connections, to our advantage, that we make it look''—pat, pat, pat—''as though *he* was being unscrupulous and was passing information to the trust administering Corinthian Holdings. Surely, the rotten apple in my administration would get wind of Corinthian's interest in some hitherto unappealing chunk of real estate, and would nibble at the bait by making purchases of its own. The SportsDome was the ideal morsel for our trap—*my* trap.''

Pat, pat, pat. Everyone was being lulled by the gesture, and by Lyons's voice, which had gone from singsong to birdsong.

Everyone but Walsh, Chief of Department John A. Walsh Jr., letters in basketball and baseball at Jamaica High School (and, after that, in baseball at St. John's; Purple Heart, Korea; medals and citations and honors of every description in thirty-two years in the New York Police Department). Lighting another in the chain of cigarettes that stretched all the way back to Asia, Walsh struggled to keep from grinning, for he could see where this was headed: There had been speculation that the SportsDome would be built on landfill downtown; Lyons proposed to Story that Story tip Corinthian that Lyons had decided instead on a site in Clinton. Corinthian reacted to the tip by buying several Clinton properties, including the Raleigh. Since there *was* no ''someone high up'' in Lyons's administration, there was no other reaction.

Lyons then arranged (''It's all right, Jimmy.'' Pat, pat, pat, ''I did what was best.'') for a hood to burn down the Raleigh. At the same time, he leaked to Ann Jones of *City* magazine so-called information about an anticipated increase in arson in Clinton. As garnish, Lyons had his hood toss a harmless but dramatic Molotov cocktail into Ann Jones's apartment.

Lyons *didn't* polish Story (''I want you guys to understand that. I hated the son-of-a-bitch, but I didn't kill him. You've got to believe me. You've got to."), but he took advantage of Story's getting polished, and thoroughly confounded things, by having his hood take a potshot at Story's sister's limo and leaving behind the graffito *Raleigh 2*.

And Hriniak had known all about it. Or some. Enough. Not when it was hatched, but nevertheless before now, before it was aired, soon enough for the question to be asked, Why hadn't he aired it himself, why had it had to come to this? No wonder Hriniak was sweating.

Without pushing his chair away from the table, as only the lean and lank can, Walsh got up and slipped close to Hriniak, who had his chin propped in his hands, watching a whispered consultation between Lyons and Freed. "Phil, I—"

*"What?"* Hriniak started and snapped, for Walsh had been that stealthy.

Walsh kept his mouth close to Hriniak's ear—so Amato would wonder. Get them all wondering, and while they're all wondering, stick 'em. "I thought I'd look in on Valentine, see what's up there."

Hriniak felt like taking a handful of Walsh's perfectly pressed lapel and jerking him down onto his perfectly creased knees and putting a foot on his perfectly groomed neck, like telling him he knew every fucking thing Walsh was thinking, to watch his every fucking move; but he just nodded.

# 29

"I was standing about three feet from him. He was sitting in a swivel chair at his desk, tipped back a little, his hands clasped over his belt. His left leg was crossed over his right knee." Tom Valentine was able to tip back a little in the cheap metal folding chair, and to cross his left leg over his right knee, but with his hands cuffed behind him he could only look down at where his belt would have been if he'd worn one with his jeans. "I shot him once, in the left chest. He jerked back, grabbed the chair arms, then reached for the desk to pull himself up. He knocked a folder, a manila legal-size folder, onto the floor. The papers in it spilled out. He took two or three steps, not really going anywhere, just side-to-side. Then he kind of reached for me and fell forward. His feet caught on the legs of the swivel chair and he twisted as he fell. He ended up on his back. . . . None of this has been in the papers, so I had to have been there."

Tony Lippo, from Crime Scene, gave Cullen a look that said, *I wasn't there either, but that's the way it could have gone down.* Cullen nodded his thanks, and Lippo left.

"Do me a favor, Tommy," Cullen said.

Valentine frowned sincerely. "What's that, Joe?"

"Don't fuck with us, all right? Don't tell us what's been in the papers and what hasn't and what your knowing what hasn't has to mean."

Valentine smiled. "Nicely said."

"I don't buy any of this," Cullen said. "I don't buy that you polished Chuck. I don't buy that you polished Janofsky, I don't buy that you polished Bermúdez."

"Janofsky was Vera Evans's driver," Neil Zimmerman said. "Keith Bermúdez was our partner."

"I know who they were," Valentine said. "I'm sorry it had to work out that way, but I know who they were."

"I don't buy it," Cullen said. "Where've you been, Tommy? Where've you been since a week ago Wednesday?"

"Down the shore, as they say in Jersey. Not right on the beach—inland a little. Around Forked River."

"The Pine Barrens."

"The Pine Barrens."

"You went down there a week ago Wednesday?" Zimmerman said. "After you polished Janofsky?"

"I'd been hoping for a shot at Vera. I settled for the driver."

"But you went to Jersey right after that?"

"I went up to Van Cortlandt Park to visit some friends, then I went to Jersey."

"By car?"

"Bus. I took a casino bus headed for Atlantic City, got off at a rest stop in Forked River."

"A bus from the Port Authority?"

"From a street corner in Riverdale. Those buses leave from all over."

"Still. You're six-six."

Valentine shrugged as much as a man can whose hands are cuffed behind his back. "Remember, years ago, those guys who stole the jewels from the Museum of Natural History? Murph the Surf and the rest of them?"

"Before my time, but I've read about it."

"They had to leave a rope hanging from the roof for a couple of hours while they were inside. They took the risk because they noticed while they were scouting the job that people don't look up."

"This is all bullshit," Cullen said. "I don't buy any of it. How did you know Vera's route? Five or six people knew Vera's route."

"Joe, I gave you guys the gun I shot Chuck with. What more do you need? The guns I shot Janofsky and Bermúdez with I threw away."

"Bullshit. All bullshit. You went up to Van Cortlandt because you wanted to be seen, you wanted to set up that friend of yours from Nam."

"Monsky," Zimmerman said.

Cullen said, "Well?"

Valentine shrugged. "His name's Monsky, that's right."

"Monsky was busted," Cullen said.

"So?"

"So you went to see him because you wanted to set him up."

"Why would I do that?"

Cullen thought about it. There comes a point in an investigation where there's nothing new to know, where all you have to work with is what you already know, maybe have known for days or weeks. Or months. Or years. The arrival of that point, for Cullen, was signaled by the echoes and reverberations:

*The piece was a nine millimeter Glock,* he heard himself saying to Hriniak in the parlor floor hallway of 119 around 4:47 . . . 19 . . . 20 . . . 21 on the fifth of July. . . . *A serious piece. Could mean a contract hit—the mutilation to throw us off.*

"Where'd you get the gun, Tommy?"

"Around. There're people on the street who can't get food, but they can get guns."

"You know the make, Tommy?"

Valentine shrugged. "It's a gun."

"No, it's a Glock, and anyone who has a Glock knows he has a Glock."

Valentine shrugged.

Cullen listened, but there were no more echoes, no more reverberations. "I don't buy it."

"I'm not selling it, Joe. I'm giving it away."

Cullen got off a table he'd had a leg up on and took a step toward Valentine. Zimmerman moved between them.

Valentine laughed. "Jesus. You guys're right out of a B movie."

Cullen went off into a corner and leaned against the wall, his arms tight around him as if he were straitjacketed.

"In the Pine Barrens," Zimmerman said, "what'd you do for food?"

"There's a Roy Rogers at the rest stop I got off at. I lived out of the dumpsters. The things people throw away."

"And you came back when?"

"Yesterday morning. I hitched a ride on a rig on the Turnpike. I spent the afternoon in Riverside Park, in the train tunnel underneath it. After dark, I went over to 119."

"And polished Bermúdez."

"I was after Vera. I told you. I'm sorry, but Bermúdez was in the way."

"Bullshit," Cullen said from his corner.

"Tell us about that," Zimmerman said. "About how you polished Bermúdez. Where you were standing, all that."

Valentine slumped in his chair. "Fellows, I'm guilty. I don't have an alibi. I gave you the only gun I kept. The Winchester I got rid of in a sewer in Queens somewhere. I'll try and remember where, you can go look for it. The handgun's in a trash can on . . . Lexington, I think, or maybe Third. In the Seventies. Unless they picked it up, in which case. . . . So just lock me up and throw away the key and stop wasting your time and mine with questions about method."

"How'd you get in the house, Tommy?" Cullen said. "How'd you get in 119?"

"Which time?" Valentine said.

"Fuck you."

Valentine shrugged.

"How'd you get in 119, Valentine?" Zimmerman said.

"The first time, Chuck Story let me in. I called him, said I wanted to talk, went over. I'd more or less accused him in public of being responsible for the Raleigh fire, and I said I wanted to apologize, that I'd found some new information about who was responsible."

"Who was responsible?" Zimmerman said.

"It was just talk. I wanted to get the son-of-a-bitch alone."

"Called from where?" Cullen said from his corner.

"From . . . from the street. A pay phone."

"You had to think about that a minute, didn't you? You know—even if you don't *know*—that there'd be a record of a call from your house. You didn't make a call from anywhere, but especially not from your house."

Valentine sighed.

"How'd you get in 119 the second time?" Zimmerman said.

Valentine smiled. "Remember when we were kids, Joe, and Chuck had this idea that we should all have keys to one another's houses? And remember at his wedding—"

Cullen smiled back, a crazy smile. "Shmuck. That's the wrong answer. You didn't use the key Chuck gave you. You took Ber*múd*ez's keys. Remember?" He came out of his corner, arms still crossed, as if restraining himself. "It wasn't in the paper, but you *must* remember."

Valentine shook his head wearily. "Your routine needs work, Joe."

In his mind's eye, Cullen kicked the chair legs out from under Valentine, and when he hit the floor kicked him in the head, the loins, the crotch. In reality, he leaned over and put his hands on Valentine's shoulders. He could go to sleep like that, so weary was he, go to sleep with his head tipped over on his elbow, his old friend's face just inches from his. "Tommy, what do you know about Chuck Story, about his life? You spent time with him, worked with him, you on behalf of the homeless. What do you know? Can you tell us anything?" Did any of this make sense? He couldn't tell from looking at Valentine, who seemed only disarmed that Cullen's face was so close. "Who would want to kill him?"

A laugh, hard and austere, not from Valentine, from the doorway, where Walsh stood with one hand in his pants pocket, the other bringing a cigarette to his lips, carefully, gently, as if bestowing a benediction. "Go home and get some rest, Sergeant. You're over the edge." Walsh put the cigarette in his lips again and left it there, one eye closed against the smoke. He came across the room, a hand in his coat pocket, feeling for something.

Cullen panicked. Walsh was going to polish him. He'd put a tap on his phone and now he was going to—

"What in hell is the matter, Sergeant? You're sweating like a goddamn pig." Walsh had his hand out of his pocket now and was opening a blade of a small Swiss Army knife. A scissor. He wasn't going to polish Cullen, he was going to trim Cullen's hangnails.

Walsh smiled a hard, austere smile. "You're not forgetting, are you, Sergeant? Nicky Potter got a handful of the son-of-a-bitch's hair." And, snip-snip, Walsh got a small sheaf of Tom Valentine's. He shut the scissor blade against his hip, slipped the knife in his uniform jacket pocket, and took out a glassine evidence bag. He dropped the hair in the bag, sealed it, twirled it into a handy cylinder, and put it in his pocket.

Cullen wanted to ask him to please do it all again, so he could look for seams in Walsh's performance.

"I'll drop this by the lab myself, Sergeant. I want both of you—this is an order—to get two hours' rest." He looked at his steel watch. "Bermúdez's funeral's at noon. We can't have the pallbearers passing out. Oh, and, uh, Dean's funeral's tomorrow, in Brooklyn, somewhere. We're not going whole hog, but you guys should be there and, you know, wear suits. I'll send a guard in. We'll get back to this son-of-a-bitch this afternoon." And then Walsh was gone. A swirl of smoke marked where he had been and twitched in his backwash.

Cullen put his hands on Valentine's shoulders again and smiled. "A little problem for you, Tommy, *n'est-çe pas*? Because the hair Nicky Potter pulled out isn't going to be your hair."

Valentine couldn't look at Cullen. Then he could, and did. Cullen looked back for a moment, then looked away. Then he looked back and their looks didn't waver and Cullen saw it all plain and clear and bright and shining.

*People don't look up.*

He squeezed Valentine's shoulders. "I'll be back soon." He stood. "Neil, I'll be back soon."

Zimmerman didn't say *You promised*. He didn't say anything.

# 30

The lab was in a sub-sub-basement, at the end of a hallway bisected, for no apparent reason, by a pair of swinging doors. Cullen didn't get down here much, but whenever he did he was reminded of the sets of medium-tech horror flicks.

Not that he went to medium-tech horror flicks, or to any kind at all. He supposed it was an aspect of his—what did they call it?—his cultural literacy that he made the associative leap, or whatever the fuck it was. All he knew about horror flicks he knew from the writing of Joe Bob Briggs—or actually from writing *about* the writing of Joe Bob Briggs.

Though they cannot have been installed for *that* reason, the swinging doors *were* handy for tailing someone. You could sneak up on them from one side while they were on the other, never suspecting that sneaking up on them was what you were doing. Was that what they called it—*tailing*? Or was it *trailing*? Or something else altogether, something snappy and slangy, like . . . *bird-dogging*? Cullen was so weary he couldn't think at all, forget about straight.

Cullen got up close to the swinging doors and looked through the thick shatterproof windows. The doors were still trembling slightly: he was that close on Walsh's trail.

Out the door of the interrogation room and down that hallway to the stairwell and down, down, down the stairs, Cullen had been that close on Walsh's trail, close enough to always hear Walsh's heels on the concrete floors, Walsh's light, Fred Astaire soles on the metaled stairs, to always smell Walsh's bitter cigarette.

Joseph (Snake) Cullen had been a cigarette smoker, and the

smell of Walsh's bitter cigarette had a certain Proust-like effect on him; the cigarette was a wobbly cobblestone, a piquant cupcake, that tweaked his memory.

Joseph (Snake) Cullen had smoked Lucky Strike. Lucky Strike Means Fine Tobacco. L/S/M/F/T. Snake would light up his first cigarette—his first butt—going downstairs to the street on the way to school in the morning. He would smoke it and another on the walk to school and have a third butt and maybe even a fourth while hanging around outside with the rest of the rocks, making themselves deliberately late because that was the rocky thing to do. It was the rocky thing to do to go to the boys' bathroom in the basement outside the boys' locker room and have a butt after first period and to go to the boys' bathroom on the fourth floor next to the metal shop and have a butt after the second.

After the third period, the rocks and the rocky girls—Diane DeFeo, Suzie Handshaw (Suzie Handjob), Barbara Zalenski, Myra something, Bonnie Bender (Bend Her Over)—would sneak out of school and go to Sid and Cy's Nosh Box on Queens Boulevard for hamburgers and french fries and cherry Cokes and Devil Dogs. The girls would rest their arms on the tables and rest their high hard tits on their arms and the boys would stare at their high hard tits and get hard-ons and have to flick their fingers at the hard-ons under the tables to make them go away so they could stand up and leave, otherwise someone would notice and everyone would rank you out. They would smoke three or four butts apiece before sneaking back into school.

After study hall, after shop, before and during and after gym, the rocky thing to do was to go to one boys' bathroom or another and smoke a butt. After school, the rocky thing to do was to go to Chuck and Vera Story's old man's candy store—did it have a name? It was always just *the candy store*—on Elmhurst Avenue and get a Coke (in a bottle; there weren't cans then, if you can believe that) and a Devil Dog and sit on the fenders of cars outside and stare at the rocky girls' high hard tits (You never got a hard-on outside. That was interesting. You only got them sitting down inside. Very interesting; maybe it was the cold) and rank each other out and smoke butts.

Very interesting. Cullen stood close to the swinging doors in the medium-tech horror flick hallway of the sub-sub-basement and wondered what was so interesting about smoking butts.

No. It wasn't smoking butts that was interesting. It was sitting on the fenders of cars outside the candy store staring at the rocky girls with the high hard tits and ranking each other out.

No. What was interesting was sitting on the fenders of cars outside the candy store.

Sitting on the fender of a car outside the candy store.

Like a Chevrolet Bel Air.

Like a charcoal gray and pink Chevrolet Bel Air.

Like looking up.

(On top of the Proust-like effect of a bitter cigarette, echoes and reverberations: Tommy Valentine, ex-big man on campus, now suspect in the polishing of his onetime high school pal, talking, for some fucking reason, about a jewel heist: *They had to leave a rope hanging from the roof for a couple of hours while they were inside. They took the risk because they noticed while they were scouting the job that people don't look up*.)

Sitting on the fender of a charcoal gray and pink Chevrolet Bel Air outside the candy store, smoking a butt, rocky girls right there in front of you if you wanted to stare at their high hard tits, but not staring at them, looking up.

Looking up at a third-floor window. It was a six-story apartment house, like every other goddamn apartment house in Queens, just about, so . . . one, two, three. Yep, third floor.

Sitting on the fender of a charcoal gray and pink Chevrolet Bel Air outside the candy store, smoking a butt, rocky girls right there in front of you if you wanted to stare at them, but not staring at their high hard tits, looking up at a third-floor window.

A window of the apartment where Chuck Story and Vera Story and their mom—until she died—and their dad lived.

(. . . Echoes and reverberations:

*(''Hey, Snake, like guess what. We went to Chuck Story's yesterday aft, like me and Blankenstein.''*

*(''Yeah. Like so?''*

*(''I go into the kitchen to get some water, like Chuck's sister was in there getting a big pot like from under the sink. She went running out the other door with it when she saw me.''*

*("Maybe she got a look at your face, Cannell."*

*("Ooh, rank out."*

*("Fucking A, I ranked you out."*

*("Don't you get it, Snake? That was the pot she pisses in 'cause she's afraid to come out of her room."*

*("Like the fuck're you talking about, Cannell?"*

*("I told you—Chuck's sister pisses in a pot in her room 'cause she's afraid if she uses the same bathroom as Chuck or his friends she'll get knocked up.")*

Looking up at a third-floor window of the apartment where Chuck Story and Vera Story and just their dad now because their mom died lived, the apartment whose bathroom Vera Story wouldn't use because she was afraid she'd get knocked up if she used the same bathroom as her brother and his friends.

A third-floor window with someone in it.

A third-floor window with two people in it.

Vera Story.

Chuck Story.

Bare-ass naked.

Because people don't look up.

Then, like smoke, they were gone, he pulling her away from the window, it looked like, tugging her sharply, making her lose her balance, taking advantage of her disequilibrium to make sure she stayed away from the window. A lace curtain trembling.

Like smoke.

Cullen, just Joe Cullen now, not Joseph (Snake) Cullen anymore, looked through the thick shatterproof window of the swinging door again.

Walsh was hanging himself. By his hair.

No. Walsh had his back to Cullen, both his arms raised above his head. One hand held a sheaf of hair straight up, the other the Swiss Army knife, scissor open.

Walsh snipped the sheaf of hair, shut the knife blade against his hip, slipped the knife in his uniform jacket pocket, and took out a glassine evidence bag. He unsealed the bag, removed the sheaf of Tom Valentine's hair and put it in his pants pocket. He dropped his own hair in the bag, sealed it, twirled it into a cylinder, and put it in his pocket.

Walsh walked on down the hall to the lab, rang the bell, stood where the closed circuit camera could see his face, waited to be buzzed in.

Darelle Dean came down the hall from behind Cullen *so* fast that it was all Cullen could do to recognize him, forget about stop him. Darelle went through the swinging doors like an act of God and was right up on top of Walsh before Walsh's instincts could sound the alarm.

"Darelle!" Cullen fought his way through the swinging doors, which beat at him as if he were an interloper.

Walsh had gotten the picture by now and was fumbling with the buttons of his uniform coat—all those medals—to get at his gun. Darelle had a handful of Walsh's necktie and collar and his gun in Walsh's mouth.

"Darelle!"

Darelle pulled the trigger.

Cullen stopped and stood very still, eyes closed, until the waves of echoes stopped rolling over him. He breathed in and out, in and out, in and out through his nose.

He opened his eyes.

Darelle's arms were at his sides. From one hand dangled his gun, sizzling—or so it seemed, from the other Walsh, a lolling rag doll. As an afterthought, almost, Darelle let Walsh fall, and brushed his aura from his fingertips with a thumb, like crumbs.

Darelle said: "Remember, the other day, me telling you and your partner about the call to the One-Nine, the call during the thunderstorm?"

Cullen nodded. "I remember." Why was Darelle dressed in his best suit, a banker's gray double-breasted too formal for the hour, too warm for the weather—and too formal and too warm for detonating someone's head? Hadn't Walsh said Darelle's sister's funeral was tomorrow, somewhere in Brooklyn?

"Remember the call was from a woman who said she saw someone coming out of Story's house—a woman—the night he got polished?"

Cullen nodded.

"Remember the captain told me to call Walsh?"

Cullen nodded.

"Remember I called here first, Downtown, then remembered Walsh'd be at Story's funeral? I finally got him in his car."

How long would they be able to stand there chatting uninterrupted? If anyone in the lab had heard the shot—if there was anyone *in* the lab to hear the shot; lots of people were planning to go to Bermúdez's funeral—they hadn't investigated. Sounds—even gunshots—from the sub-sub-basement might never reach inhabited regions of the building. So *this* was the place to commit the perfect crime—the bowels of Police Headquarters.

"Remember you told me Deborah'd made regular calls here, Downtown, to the main number, and you asked me if my friend, Iris, at the phone company, knew a way to check Downtown's MUDS to see if there were regular calls to Deborah's home phone?"

Cullen nodded.

"Remember I called the other day—I didn't talk to you, I talked to your partner—to say Iris ran Downtown's MUDS for the week before Deborah got shot and found three calls to Deborah's home number from extension nine-oh-four?"

"Hriniak's extension," Cullen said, to show he was with the program.

Darelle Dean nodded this time. "That's what it says in the Green Book and on the Roster. But then this morning your lady, Ann Jones, asked me and Iris about Title III intercepts on your phone and Iris found one and it was authorized by a judge whose name Iris's friend couldn't read and applied for by Walsh. Just for the hell of it, after Walsh had his news conference saying I slyed Deborah her off-duty piece so she could polish herself, I went with Iris to her office and looked at the application for the Title III intercept on your phone and the judge's name was Marconi and I won't insult you, Sarge, by asking if you know Judge Marconi died last year, six months before the date on the intercept application, I know you know it. Attached to the application there was a copy of another application. It was attached because it was also requested by Walsh."

Cullen wondered if Darelle Dean would mind if he lay down on the tiles and took a nap, just a short one, nine or ten years. He wondered if Darelle Dean had a cigarette; he hadn't smoked since college—L/S/M/F/T—but he wanted one now. He wondered if Darelle Dean would think it . . . ghoulish . . . if he searched Walsh's pockets for one of his bitter cigarettes. He wanted a Proust-like hit, a wobble on the cobblestone, a taste of the cupcake, a memory—anything but to keep on standing here on sleep-starved legs, looking down (trying not to but not able not to) at the bile (it had to be bile, didn't it?) seeping out of Walsh's one-time former erstwhile say good-bye to Hollywood ex-head.

And who was it who had recently said *I'm not some ghoul*? Ah yes—Ann. Your lady, Ann Jones, defending herself against his charge, Joseph (Snake) Cullen's charge, that in light of his sister's death, she ought not to have brought the matter of the Title III intercepts up to Darelle. How *was* Lady Ann?

"Sergeant Cullen?" Darelle Dean said.

"Yeah, Darelle?"

"Did you hear what I said, Sarge?"

Cullen sighed. Had he? He had. "Walsh had a Title III on Hriniak's phone."

Darelle flicked a hand. "Not a Title III, a cut-in. The phone on Walsh's desk rang when Hriniak's did, Walsh could pick up if he wanted, he could make outgoing calls on Hriniak's extension. It's right there in the file; anyone could see it if they were looking for it. I guess he figured—"

"He figured people don't look up."

Darelle frowned. "Sarge?"

*Don't call me Sarge.* "So, Darelle, was Walsh's being cut in on Hriniak's phone reason to polish him?"

That impatient gesture again. "Deborah kept a diary. Ever hear of a man who kept a diary? I never did, but women do, for some reason. Deborah gave me her diary—she called it her 'journal'—after she got shot—'cause she was afraid Walsh would boost it, I realize now. She told me if anything happened to her I should read it so I'd know the kind of pressure she'd been under. That was what she said—'the kind of pressure I've been under.' I thought she was trying to house me: what the hell kind of pressure? What the hell was going to happen to her? She had a slug in her shoulder, but it was a superficial wound; she could've walked around for the rest of her life without having it out."

Lady Ann kept a diary—and called it a journal too—in a kid's composition book that resided in the drawer of her teak bedside table, underneath her diaphragm case and her tube of killer jelly. The temptation to peek at it was one Joseph (Snake) Cullen had to resist every time Lady Ann left him alone in her bedroom. That he'd been successful she of course didn't know (unless she armed the composition book with booby traps of strands of hair or slivers of wood), but if she did she would undoubtedly be distressed that he viewed it as a triumph of will rather than a flaw of character.

"Deborah met Walsh last spring at a civil rights demonstration out at Brooklyn College. He housed her, made her promises—first black this, first woman that—and when she finally saw that all he wanted was *his* first black woman and told him it was over he told her if she wanted to stay in the Department he'd be the one to say when it was over. Her last entry was the week before he shot her. He kept a gun to her head while he did it to her that time, which I call rape and him a rapist. What do you call him, Sarge? He boosted her off-duty piece and threatened to bust her if she reported it stolen. It was the piece she polished herself with, except she couldn't have because he'd boosted it. *He* polished her with it"—a kick in Walsh's ribs there, for emphasis—"he went to the hospital overnight when security's for shit, when everyone knows the cop on duty outside Deborah's door's been playing johnson, johnson, who's got the johnson, with the night nurses, and he polished her." Another kick.

Cullen wished he would stop: he was afraid the bag of bile might burst. "The diary, the phone set-up—it's evidence, Darelle. You just had to be patient."

Darelle laughed. "White smoke."

"White, yes—there's nothing I can do about that. Smoke, no. It's the way things work."

Darelle snorted. "What city you live in, homeboy? I live in a city where a fourth of the people're poor and most of them're black or brown, where a homeboy lamping on the corner's a felon, where a sister dressed to party's a whore, where any black who stands before a court of law is not only not presumed innocent, he's assumed guilty, condemned, damned." Darelle wafted his gun under Cullen's nose, as if it were an expensive cigar whose aroma he was flaunting. "*This* is the way things work.'' And before it occurred to Cullen that he might—but then what was new about that? So many things happened before it occurred to Cullen that they might, before Cullen figured out that Darelle was dressed for his *own* funeral, Darelle put the barrel against his head behind his ear and pulled the trigger.

Cullen put his back against the wall and let himself down onto the tiles and shut his eyes. After a while he opened them and looked at the opposite wall and said, ''MUDS.''

# 31

''Iris Hall?''

''Yes?''

''I'm Joe Cullen.''

''. . . Sergeant Cullen?''

He nodded. His mufti had never been much of a disguise; he was a guy people—guys, anyway—looked up and down and said, ''You a cop?''

''What's wrong?''

''Can we go somewhere?''

''What's happened to Darelle, Sargeant?''

''I'd just like to talk to you privately.''

''What about?''

''Is there someplace we can go?''

''*What* about?''

''. . . A case. A case I'm working on.''

''The case involving the Title IIIs?''

''Another case, but related.''

''We can go in here.''

Cullen followed Iris Hall into a conference room, remembering Darelle Dean on the Esplanade, walking the walk that had looked at first almost like a pimp-roll but was the walk of a man who was fraternizing with a supremely competent woman.

Iris Hall turned to face Cullen, hands on hips. ''Well?''

''I'd like the Message Unit Details for 119 East Seventieth Street the week before the fifth of July.''

''Of this year?''

''Of this year.''

''The calendar week or the seven days up to and including or not including the fifth?''

"Uh, the, uh, seven days, give or take a day at the beginning."

"I'll start wherever you like, Sergeant. You just have to tell me where to start."

She being supremely competent, he about a step away from passing out. "I'm interested in calls to California—Los Angeles."

"Only those calls?"

"For the moment, yes."

"That shouldn't take long, if you care to wait."

"I would like to wait, yes."

"You can wait here if you like, but there's nothing to read. There're magazines at the receptionist's, if you'd prefer to go out there."

"If you don't mind, I'll stay in here."

"I don't mind." But her eyes said she minded. Oh, how she minded.

"Sergeant Cullen. . . . Sergeant Cullen? . . . Sergeant *Cul*len!"

"What? Yes? I'm sorry. I guess I fell asleep."

"Sound asleep."

And, thank God, dreamless. "I'm sorry."

"Here's a printout of the calls. There're three separate phones at the address you gave me. Calls to California were made from all three."

"Yes, I see." Saw two dozen numbers that connoted nothing. "These numbers, do you—"

Iris Hall handed Cullen a second printout. "These are the addresses and the customers' names."

Among them the names and addresses of Vera Evans, Nicky Potter, Storyboard Productions. "Thanks very much. Modern technology." He looked around the room, but there was no place to go and nothing to do but tell her. "I have bad news."

"You're a son-of-a-bitch, Sergeant Cullen. Did anyone ever tell you that?"

Cullen played with the perforations of the fanfold paper for a moment. "Chief Walsh was having an affair with Deborah Dean. Things went sour, they had an argument, he shot her. My partner and I pulled the investigation. As you know, Walsh had a Title III on our phone. He must've thought we were closing in on him, although I have to say honestly that we weren't. He killed the cop on duty outside 119 thinking it was me. To cover it up, he got into 119 and pretended to be Tom Valentine—you know who that is—out to get revenge on Commissioner Story's sister. That's not important. What's impertinent . . ." *Easy, Snake*. ". . . What's im*por*tant is that after Deborah died Darelle read her diary—her journal—read what she'd written about her and Walsh. He came Downtown—to Police Headquarters—and found Walsh and shot and killed him."

"You son-of-a-bitch."

Cullen nodded. "Then Darelle killed himself."

"You goddamn motherfucking son-of-a-bitch."

Cullen backed toward the door. "I'll get someone to be with you—one of your, uh, colleagues."

"Bastard. You goddamn motherfucking son-of-a-bitch bastard."

"Sergeant Cullen? I'm Doctor Persons." Anne Persons, her nametag said, and she looked a little like Lady Ann without an *E*. Same efficient physique, same level look, same Show Me set to her mouth—show me you're *not* a goddamn motherfucking son-of-a-bitch bastard who doesn't want everything under one roof. Different hair—a lighter blond, short, brisk.

"This isn't an official visit, but I don't have a lot of time, so I showed the nurse my badge. I apologize if that caused you any anxiety. I'm a friend of Miss Langois's aunt, and of her late stepfather, and, well, I just wondered how she's doing."

"Well enough. She's going home today."

And just how *good* a friend would you say you were, Sergeant Cullen, if you didn't know that? "Oh. I didn't know that. I've been pretty busy."

"Her mother and her aunt thought she'd be more comfortable there and I couldn't disagree," Doctor Persons said. "She's doing as well as can be expected given the alarming frequency with which she's been proximate to violent death. I'm sure as a police officer you're somewhat inured to death by firearms, but the rest of us, despite our exposure to television mayhem, are rather virginal."

"Somewhat inured," Cullen said. "Did Claire say anything about the attack on Miss Potter, her aunt's assistant? Claire's reaction was so extreme that I wondered if she felt *she* was the intended victim. Had she received any threats, for example?"

Doctor Persons drew in her neck defensively. "You said you're here *un*officially."

"I'm never entirely off duty, Doctor Persons," Cullen said. "I wanted to know how Claire was *and* I want to know who's responsible for her having been here."

Doctor Persons thought a moment. "Miss Langois was under sedation. She talked in a rambling way about things I'm constrained by privilege from telling you. I'm not unaware, however, that you're looking for a murderer—someone who killed a colleague—and I think you should know, therefore, about the jewelry."

"Jewelry?"

"The man—I assume it was a man, you must assume it too, it's assumable—the man who attacked Miss Potter wore jewelry. It made a jingling noise. Claire didn't see him, but she heard him. She talked—this is drugged half-gibberish we're talking about, remember—as if she'd heard him before."

"Jewelry." Cullen couldn't swear to it—and knowing for sure would mean going back to the sub-sub-basement of Police Headquarters where he had left the bodies of Chief of Department John A. Walsh Jr. and Officer Darelle Dean (not because *he* was a ghoul but because everybody Downtown was on his way to Bermúdez's funeral, it seemed like)—but he didn't think Walsh wore any jewelry but his steel watch. Medals Walsh was festooned with, but jewelry. . . . Possibly he wore a ring, a class ring, but Cullen couldn't swear to it, wouldn't bet on it, didn't know.

"I would imagine bracelets," Doctor Persons said, and freed her bracelets from under the sleeve of her lab coat and shook her wrist so that they jingled.

Echoes and reverberations. But of what? "Did Claire—"

Doctor Persons covered her bracelets and folded her arms. "That's all I can say."

Cullen nodded. "Thanks."

"Please see yourself out. I must get back to my rounds." And Doctor Persons took one more look before she turned her back on Cullen and he saw in it that she knew that his had been only an official visit and knew too that he *was* a goddamn motherfucking son-of-a-bitch bastard who didn't want everything under one roof.

''Doug, it's Joe Cullen. Connie's ex-.''

''Hey, Joe, what do you think, I don't know who you are? Hey, Joe, Jesus, I heard about your partner. That's rough, Joe, really rough.''

''Doug, I need a favor. Can—''

''Anything, Joe. Anything.''

''. . . Can you track down the pilot of a charter flight from Los Angeles to La Guardia on the fifth of July? It got in around seven A.M., so I guess it would've left around . . .'' He looked at his computer nerd watch and tried to make the calculation, but couldn't. His body wanted sleep and was inciting his mind to go on strike.

''Probably about eleven or so on the fourth, Joe, depending on what kind of plane. Do you know the charter line?''

''Air something. I'm sorry, Doug, I'm whipped. Air Deluxe—could that be it?''

''Air *Trans*lux is a big transcontinental charter line.''

''It was a big plane—not jumbo jet big, but more than one passenger, more than twenty passengers, probably. . . . I'm sorry, Doug, I don't know what kind of plane it was.''

''Hey, Joe, what's a travel agent for? I'll get right on it. You want the pilot's current whereabouts, I guess. Where can I call you?''

''I'll call you, Doug. Thanks.''

''No problem, buddy.''

''Hello, Sergeant.''

''Hello, Miss Parker.''

''Ah, it's 'Miss Parker,' is it? No more 'may we call you Mabel?' Where's your good-looking partner?''

''Please close the door. We wouldn't want Norman Levitt's wife to hear us.''

''Ah.'' It came out as if it punched her in the stomach.

''Please close the door.''

Mabel closed the door and motioned Cullen to a chair and went back behind her desk. He didn't sit so she didn't either. She held the back of her chair like an old lady with a walker.

"Describe the woman you saw leaving 119."

Mabel reached for her bag and took out a pack of Carltons. "That all gets farther away every day."

"I'm sure you see her more clearly every day," Cullen said.

Mabel smiled. "You're right. I do." She pinched out a cigarette and lighted it. She was ready for this moment: handy in her desk were vodka, cocaine, Eskalith, Xanax, and Sinequan—and her new favorite, for when all else failed, Ritalin. "Tall—five-eight. Thin—one-twenty, one-twenty-five. A raincoat—tan, long, almost ankle-length. A hat—brown, soft-brimmed, old-fashioned. A fedora. Hair up so I couldn't see the length or color, but my guess is she was . . . blond. Blond hair, blond complexion. Light. White pants—jeans or painter's pants. Blue shoes—sneakers or espadrilles." She smiled, hoping he would say how good she was being, saying all this over again without saying she'd said it all before. He just waited. "Very graceful—like a dancer or an athlete. Confident—not bumbling or stumbling or feeling her way, even though it was getting quite dark." Mabel picked an imaginary flake of tobacco from her lower lip. "Norman once said that a man knows the instant he sees a woman, even from a block away, even from behind, whether or not she's a woman he wants to fuck. He says it has something to do with primal instinct, survival of the species, all that. Is that the way it is for you?"

Cullen waited, going up and down on the balls of his feet to keep from falling flat on his face. A goddamn motherfucking son-of-a-bitch bastard he might be, one who didn't want everything under one roof, one from whom people felt they had to protect their upholstery; but he wasn't going to tumble to the seductiveness of a material witness.

Mabel smiled and sucked in some smoke. She puffed it out bit by bit as she spoke. "She looked like a woman a man could see from a block away and want to." Mabel waved away the smoke so she could see Cullen clearly. "Did I say something wrong? Oh, my God—you don't . . . ?"

Cullen went up and down on the balls of his feet.

Mabel kept fanning her hand, as if she could dispel the

notion. "I heard—on the grapevine—that you and Vera Evans used to. . . . You don't think . . . ?"

Cullen heard Cullen say: "Was the woman you saw Vera Evans, Miss Parker?"

Mabel shut her eyes, then opened them. She shook her head, she shrugged, she giggled, she shrugged again. She inhaled smoke and blurted it out. "It was dark."

"Not pitch dark. Dusk."

"A rainy day dusk."

"But dusk."

"You should be a lawyer, Sergeant. You're a good quibbler."

"Was it Vera Evans?"

Mabel breathed out through her nose. "I don't think so, but I'm not sure. I think she was thinner, younger. The raincoat—it was big. It wasn't just long, it was big—in the way that a grownup's clothes are big on a child, an adolescent child."

"She wasn't a child?"

". . . No."

"But it might not've been her raincoat?"

Mabel smiled, relieved he'd put it together. "Yes."

Cullen held out a hand. "Give me your key."

Mabel stammered. "The . . . the key to . . . to the apartment?"

Cullen nodded. "What's going on between you and Levitt is between you and Levitt—and between you and your boss. I don't care to publicize it. But you're a material witness, and if it comes to it, you'll testify. I'll leave the key with the doorman."

Mabel nodded. She put the cigarette in her mouth while she fished in her bag for her key case. She took a key from a clip and put it on the desk. "Just the top lock."

The smoke made her eyes water and when she had blinked them dry, the key and Cullen were gone.

Standing in the bedroom of apartment 5-C at 116 East Seventy-first Street, beyond fatigue, looking—falling, it felt like—out the window that was the stokehole on another blast furnace of a day, Cullen realized he hadn't asked Mabel Parker if she had been seen by the woman she saw, though he knew the answer was no: people don't look up.

And looking down, there wasn't much to see—just backyards

in a city where backyards don't count for much, it's what's up front that counts. One-nineteen looked benign, not like the funhouse he knew it could be: a maid dusted in the parlor, near a window closed to keep in the conditioned air.

Might as well go down and join her.

Cool off.

''Saints preserve us, you gave me a start. Coming in the back way like that.'' The maid was lightly freckled and brogued.

What the hell—so many people went *out* the back way of 119, Cullen had thought he'd go *in*—through the gate with the panic lock (opened by the superintendent of 116 East Seventy-first, who had just enough English to understand Cullen's Spanish), down the passageway next to the building, across the cement courtyard behind it, through the hole in the fence into the backyard of 119, across the yard, up the back steps.

''I'm sorry I frightened you. I'm a police officer.''

The maid took Cullen's badge and studied it, front and back, then handed it back. The super had done the same thing, which had interested Cullen, since native-born Americans tended to bend forward from the waist and peer at the badge as if it were something rare and breakable; he couldn't think of one who had ever touched it. ''You were here t'other day, when our Claire had her upset.''

Was that what they were calling it below stairs? In that case, which upset was she talking about? ''I knew Mister Story and Miss Evans. Years ago. We grew up together. In the same neighborhood.'' It was easier to talk in shards of sentences than to form whole big long ones that stretched on and on and. . . .

''Mrs. Story and Miss Evans have gone to hospital, to fetch our Claire.''

Cullen knew that; he'd phoned from apartment 5-C, 116 East Seventy-first Street. Would it someday confound somebody to find on that phone's Message Unit Details a call to 119? Indeed, it would. ''And Miss Potter?''

The maid put a finger to her lips. ''Upstairs napping. It gave her quite a turn, the brute sneaking in on her like that. The doctor gave her something to help her sleep.''

Help? There were people who needed help to sleep? ''The

day Mister Story was killed. Afterwards. Did anyone. Did you. Was anything stolen? Anything at all."

"Stolen? I don't think so. Not that I'm aware."

"Not necessarily anything important," Cullen said. "Maybe something . . . unimportant. Something. . . ." Trivial? Inconsequential? Come *on,* Snake. ". . . Something you might not even mention to the police. Like, oh, a . . . a coat, maybe, or a hat, or. . . ."

The maid was staring at him as if he were a toy in need of winding up but without a key apparent anywhere. "A coat?" She brightened. "A coat. A raincoat. Oh, Sergeant, was it *your* raincoat?" She touched his arm as if moved by his predictable male ineptitude at living.

"M-m-my raincoat?" There was always that suspicion, that fear, when you'd done this kind of work long enough, that *you* were the one you were looking for—the ultimate perp.

She frowned and removed her hand. "It couldn't be now, could it? It was a lady's raincoat."

Cullen took a deep breath. "I'm sorry, I'm very tired. I've been working a long time without any sleep. I'm not sure . . ."—what the *fuck* you're talking about—". . . what you mean."

She pursed her lips. "T'was you who mentioned the raincoat, Sergeant. I only concluded that if you mentioned it, it must be yours."

"No. I mean, it isn't mine. But I'm still not sure. . . . Could I *see* the raincoat?"

She smiled, as if he'd sprung a tender but tenacious trap. "Indeed, you mayn't, since it's missing too, which makes it all the more mysterious."

Cullen tried to tug free, but couldn't. "Missing from . . . ?"

The maid clasped her hands in front of her and led the way, back out the way they'd come in—through the parlor, down a small hallway, then down a smaller one, into a pantry, down a hallway smaller still—

(Echoes and reverberations: but of what? Ah, yes—following Vera, swift, graceful Vera, as the hue and cry went up for Claire.

(Swift, graceful. Echoes and reverberations: of . . . ?)

—down a hallway smaller still to the storeroom by the back

door: coats, boots, gardening things, old stuff in limbo between desuetude and the junkheap.

"There!" The maid pointed an accusatory finger at . . . nothing.

"There was a raincoat there?" Cullen attempted.

"Indeed. Himself's raincoat. That's why you gave me such a start. I thought for a moment it was himself knocking at the door. You see, that's the way he liked to go out sometimes—across the yard and through the fence and out the alley next to the block of flats there—late at night to pick up the morning papers, or to walk the dog before the dog died and our Claire decided she didn't want no more dogs."

"And he kept an old coat there, Mister Story, for when it was raining?"

"Yes, sir. A Burberry."

"And then there's a second raincoat. A second raincoat that was. A second raincoat that was . . ."—Come on, Snake, you can do it, put a little power to it—"that was hung where the Burberry was hanging, but now it's gone too."

"A Donna Karan," the maid said.

Cullen nearly asked who Adona Karen was, but all his time in the car—in the *Saab*—listening to Zimmerman—how *was* Zimmerman?—drop brand names paid off. "The Donna Karan raincoat appeared when?"

The maid thought. "I first noticed it the morning after himself was murdered."

"And was that when you noticed that the Burberry was gone?" Cullen said.

She hissed, conspiratorially, "Yes."

Cullen smiled. "Thanks."

"Will that be all, then, Officer?"

"It will. I would, though, like to wait for Mrs. Story and Miss Evans to get back. May I do that?"

"I suppose," the maid said, but her eyes said it would be better if he didn't.

"Thank you," Cullen said.

"Follow me, then," the maid said, and led him back to the parlor, glancing over her shoulder at him once or twice now, knowing as everyone eventually knew that he was a goddamn motherfucking son-of-a-bitch bastard who didn't want everything under one roof, who might stab her in the back if she weren't careful.

The maid made Cullen a cup of tea and then, on the one hand very, very reluctantly, on the other very, very gladly, left him alone.

Cullen drank one sip of the tea, then sneaked upstairs.

# 32

Bedrooms.

Scrumptious bedrooms with delectable beds.

Like a kid in a candy factory, Cullen crept from one to the next, peeked in, wanting to devour them all. Somehow, he resisted, moved on.

Moved on on a carpet so soft who needed a bed? He could lay himself down to sleep right out here in the hall, where the air was chilled to perfect sleeping temperature; he would take just a short nap—till Christmas. Would they cancel Christmas if the heat hadn't broken by then, or would they all celebrate it in the buff? A tough question: he should sleep on it.

Hold on—who's this sleeping in my bed?

Nicky. Nicky Potter, Vera Evans's more-than-assistant, her life-support system, looking life*less* right now, thanks, no doubt, to that little something to help her sleep, just a sheet over her, shoulders bare, nude probably; looking, in spite of the defect in her beauty, nice to snuggle up to. Joseph (Snake) Cullen thought about slipping out of his clothes and under the sheets.

*(Where did you meet her?* Connie would say. *Well, I was an old friend of Chuck's* and *I was the policeman who helped when the poor driver was killed.)*

The Policeman Who Helped When the Poor Driver Was Killed. Echoes and reverberations: of . . . ?

Creep, peek. Creep, peek. Bedroom after bedroom after bedroom. Cullen was on the third floor by now, or maybe it was the fourth. Did the very rich count the first floor as a floor? Did the very rich *count* anything, or did things—floors and bedrooms, money and cars, clothes and jewelry, maids and more-than-assistants-life-support-systems, scones or were they sconces—just accumulate?

Aha. Eureka. Excelsior. The place you've been looking for. Tantara. Vera's room.

Now how did he know that? Years of experience, years of creeping and peeking? Not really. In his line of work he did less creeping and peeking than he did pounding on doors, then kicking them in when nobody answered. (Not that he did all that much of that. What he mostly did was make phone calls, drive around, make more phone calls.) Her stuff? Not really: to tell the truth, for all his—let's face it, Snake—practically lifelong preoccupation with Vera Story Evans, he didn't have a strong sense of what kind of stuff she'd have. This was the first time, remember, the *first* time, he'd ever been in a room she slept in.

The stuff on the table beside the bed, the stuff he could see through the open bathroom door on the sink and in the medicine cabinet, whose sliding door was half-open, the stuff in the clothes closet (another sliding door, also half-open)—it didn't look like special stuff, like the stuff of the very rich or the very famous, stuff that can be produced only by killing endangered species. It didn't look ordinary either; it looked like the plain and simple that can be produced only at considerable expense.

Take this plain simple wooden jewelry box, for instance. Or this plain simple leather address book. Or this—

Hey, Snake. Remember why you're here?

Why was he here?

Raincoat.

What?

The *rain*coat.

Right. The *rain*coat. Adona Karen.

Cullen found it so quickly that, shit, she wanted him to find it, didn't she?

Not the Donna Karan. The Burberry.

Cullen found the Donna Karan too, hanging in the closet, where raincoats live when it's not raining. The Burberry wasn't *hanging* in the closet, but it was *in* the closet, in a suitcase (Zimmerman—how *was* Zimmerman?—would know the brand of the suitcase, but Cullen didn't) on the floor up against the wall—not hidden or anything, just pushed out of the way. The Burberry *was* sort of hidden in the suitcase, for it was folded up as small as possible and tucked into the big pocket under the lid.

*Pocket*. *Lid*. Cullen knew he didn't have any of these names right. Zimmerman—how *was* Zimmerman?—would know the right names. Zimmerman knew that the inside button on a double-breasted coat is called the *jigger button,* that the things of a mop are *thrums,* the ends of a necktie *aprons,* the ends of suspenders *findings;* that the movable dial on a watch is a *bezel,* the round pin at the end of a window shade roller a *gudgeon,* the flat pin at the other end a *spear,* the top of a fire hydrant a *bonnet,* the brace for a lampshade a *harp,* the tail end of a lobster a *telson,* the tail end of a dog a *croup,* the tail end of a tape measure a *true-zero hook,* the valley between lip and nose a *philtrum*—knew more goddamn—

"What the *fuck,* Joe? What the *fuck* are you doing here?"

Except that. Zimmerman wouldn't have known what the fuck Cullen was doing there, wouldn't have known from a handsaw. "Hello, Vera."

Vera Evans, *estrella de cine,* elbowed past him and jammed the coat back in the whatever it was called of the suitcase and shut the whatever *it* was and hurled the suitcase back in the closet. She turned on him, nostrils flaring but (echoes and reverberations) graceful, athletic. "Get out."

He didn't. He sat on the bed, so as not to collapse in a heap. "I haven't put it all together yet, but enough of it to make sense."

"Get. Out."

"Or what? You'll call the cops?" Cullen laughed. It was funny, right. *Right?*

She backed away from him, so maybe it wasn't a funny laugh, maybe it was a weird one. Backed and backed (gracefully, athletically) until she was at the window, at the center of a halo of fire that burned so much brighter than she that she all but vanished.

"People don't look up," Cullen said.

Vera frowned. *What?*

"You shouldn't think someone'll see you at the window and think you're in distress and come and help you. People don't look up."

She took a step toward him, a hand out. "Joe, are you all right?"

If she'd sustained the gesture, carried it all the way out, gone to him and comforted him, it might have turned things around, for all he wanted to do was lie down and sleep till Christmas, and while he slept she could have run and hid. But he pulled himself back from her reach and pulled himself together. "I haven't put it all together yet, but enough of it to make sense."

"You said that. I don't know what you're talking about."

"You can save me a lot of time by telling me when I go off track," Cullen said. "The Wednesday before Chuck died, you flew here from Los Angeles—not on a charter, on a commercial flight; not under your name, under Nicky's. You have a problem most of the rest of us don't, namely that you're too famous even to be disguised. Those pictures of Michael Jackson with a fright wig and sideburns looking like nobody else in the world but Michael Jackson with a fright wig and sideburns? You and Michael have the same problem.

"But you *can* disguise yourself as Nicky—and Nicky as you. I bet you've done it before. Haven't you? You've had to go to something you just couldn't get up the enthusiasm for—an opening, a groundbreaking. Something. You haven't had to speak, just smile a lot, so you've sent Nicky. Haven't you? Shades, a hat, a scarf—in this case, a first-class seat to insulate you from your fans, a flight at an off-hour to cut down on the chances you'd run into somebody in your line of work, somebody from show biz. Even if you did, even if they weren't on the cellular phone or tapping away at the old laptop or reading the morning's faxes, you could fake it: you could do a few hours of Nicky as easily as she's done a few hours of you."

Cullen never took his eyes off Vera as he spoke. He hadn't studied her this closely the other times he'd been with her. In the limo, with Lise and Claire and Mayor Lyons around, he hadn't wanted to stare at her; on the verge of the Expressway, under one umbrella, she'd been so close that her breast had touched his arm and distracted him; in the parlor below, just before Claire's breakdown, they had already become adversaries, and their looks had been thrusts and parries. He was at just the right distance now, not too near, not too far, and though they were still opposed, she wasn't, for the moment, fighting back. She really was lovely, starlet lovely but not brittle, not cold. Dowager lovely too, although she was nowhere old enough, of course, to be called *that*. But along with her gracefulness, her athleticism, she had pomp and dignity—more dignity, God knows, than Cullen had, hunched over on the edge of the bed, looking and smelling like someone—some *thing*—in need of serious fumigation.

"When you landed in New York, you took a cab to a hotel—the Hilton. No limos, no receipts, no major record-keeping. First-class, yes, but not Maharajah-class. Maharani. This was Nicky's trip, not yours. 'I like big busy hotels,' Nicky said. You like them too, because you stayed there for almost a week, probably not going out all that much, until the evening of the Fourth. The evening of the Fourth, you came here. Lise and Claire were on Long Island for the long weekend. Sagaponack? Sag Harbor? I keep getting them mixed up. Chuck was with them for part of the weekend, but he came in to do a radio interview that morning."

Vera had been a captive audience at first, but by now she was beginning to be interested, attentive. Was it because he was so far so right or so far so wrong? Whichever he was, should he keep on going, getting righter or wronger?

"You came in the back way, Claire's way. Chuck's way too, it turns out. Through the service gate of the apartment building on the next block, down the alley next to the building, across the courtyard behind the building, through a gap in the fence into this backyard. There's a panic lock on the service gate—a lock that opens from within without a key and stays locked once you're through the gate. I just came in that way and I figured I'd be able to pick the lock, to work the bar with a clothes hanger or something. But I couldn't; it's a good lock; the super had to let me in.

"The super said—I think he said; I have to get a Hispanic officer down here to confirm this—that the lock can be disabled, and that he sometimes finds the catch wedged with a small piece of wood or a rock. That's what Claire and Chuck would do when they went out that way—so they could get back in. That's what Claire—or maybe Lise—was supposed to do so you could get in.

"They forgot.

"They had to drive all the way in on the morning of the Fourth and take care of it."

How still Vera stood, like a bird on a wire, balanced by the very currents and vibrations that could unseat her. She barely blinked, hardly breathed.

"I've been thinking what a big risk it was to come in. What if Chuck came back from the interview? What if the interview were cancelled? Then I realized that there was no risk at all; all they'd have had to say was that they'd been bored and decided to come in to town. It wouldn't be the first whim they'd ever acted on. It was no risk because the plan was that Chuck die; he wouldn't be giving testimony. And the plan succeeded. That evening, you came through the gate, down the alley, across the courtyard, through the back fence, across the yard, in the back door. You hung up your raincoat, you found Chuck, you shot him. The gun Nicky probably got for you—your more-than-assistant-your-life-support-system. It's probably not traceable. You checked the bag you packed it in and anyway it's plastic—a designer gun. You went out the back door, taking Chuck's raincoat by mistake—you were shaky, and went back to the Hilton. The next morning, Nicky, wearing dark glasses and mourning clothes, arrived here from Los Angeles on a chartered jet—chartered by Vera Evans. A limousine took her into town. My partner and I were assigned to guard her—you. We had nothing to do until she—you—got to 119, so we went out to the airport and followed her—you—back to Manhattan. We saw the limo go off the road, the driver shot. When I told you, out on the Expressway in the rain, that that was me pounding on your window, you didn't know what I was talking about. You *didn't* know what I was talking about because *you* didn't know what I was talking about. You made a nice recovery, and passed it on to Nicky, but at first you didn't *know* what I was talking about."

Vera was getting tired of this. She shifted her weight, sighed through her nose, touched her face, her hair. *Wrap it up, Snake.*

"Susan Price, the Department's spokesperson, had met Nicky—you—at the airport. Her driver brought Nicky—you—here, and a little while later, *you* arrived, pretending to be Nicky, the more-than-assistant-a-life-support-system ready to help her mistress in her time of need. Nobody wondered—except me—how come Nicky Potter happened to be in New York or how she got here or when. She's the kind of person who can get anywhere, anytime. It was pretty good, as scams go, but what you should've realized, what you *must* realize if this is how you're going to live your life, is that there's a record of every phone call, *every* call, that you or anybody makes. There's a record of the calls back and forth between 119 and you and Nicky and Storyboard setting this all up. There's a record of the call Nicky made from the limo to you at the Hilton—I don't *know* that there was such a call, but I'll bet my life on it—to say she'd arrived safely.

"Juries love records of phone calls. Love them. They're circumstantial, a lot of the time, because they're only records of numbers and dates and times, but juries love them anyway, and disregard judges' instructions to disregard them, because we all know, I guess, about the calls we make, and how we rarely—*never*—dial the wrong number when we call our bookie or our phone sex service or our hit man or. . . ."

*Okay, Snake, enough.*

"The Hilton. At the Hilton there's someone—a bellhop, a desk clerk, a maid, a porter—who the evening of the Fourth saw 'Nicky Potter'—you—leave her room wearing a raincoat, a hat, white pants, blue shoes—sneakers or espadrilles. And there's someone who sometime on the night of the Fourth saw 'Nicky Potter'—you—come back to the hotel wearing a raincoat, a hat, white pants, blue shoes—sneakers or espadrilles. Maybe there's even someone who noticed that the raincoat 'Nicky Potter'—you—went out in wasn't the raincoat 'Nicky Potter'—you—came—"

Cullen ducked, for Vera came right at him, right at his throat, hand thrust out killer karate-judo-jiu-jitsu-kung-fu-aiki-jo-jen-jutsu-aikido-tae-kwon-do style (Zimmerman—how *was* Zimmerman?—would know the name), aiming for his . . . larynx? Trachea? *Pomum adami?* Come *on,* Zim—how *are* you, Zim?—help me here.

But all she did was take Cullen's hand and make him get up off the bed and follow after her. To Paradise? To the Heartbreak Hotel?

# 33

Up another flight of stairs, to Claire's room.

How did he know it was Claire's? Well, it was quite a place, a little shrine of anarchy on the posh (as they say in the tabloids) Upper East Side, a chapel of Heavy Metal and Speed Metal and New Wave, the décor mostly black with a dash of iron and steel. If he was hairy and ugly and wore ball-squeezing leather and had his tongue hyperextended, Claire had pushpinned his picture up on the wall; if she was tattooed and ugly and outrageously shorn and tinted and dressed for pain, Claire had pushpinned her picture up on the wall. If the lyrics were offensive, ugly, hostile, immature, stupid, Claire had scrawled the words on the wall in black nail polish. In red nail polish, in letters three feet high, she had painted a motto of her own devising:

FUCK THIS SHIT

Painted it on the panels of a black lacquered screen placed directly in front of the window, blocking any light that dared to sneak in through the high-tech blinds, screwed tightly shut.

Vera let go of Cullen—abandoned him, it felt like, to be nibbled at by the hostility that growled in the dark angles of the room, had its lair under the bed—if you could call it a bed: the mattress was half on the floor; the sheets—the black sheets—were knotted and contorted, as if thrashed. Vera let go of Cullen and reached behind the lacquered screen and unscrewed the high-tech blinds and let in a little light—not a lot of light, for it was as if some light held back, lest it reveal unspeakable things.

With difficulty, Vera hauled around the lacquered screen, which was made of some heavy, primitive wood. When she had yanked its reverse side to face the room, and had lured in just a little more light, she stepped back and invited Cullen with a sweep of her hand to examine it.

Lots of us have bulletin boards, refrigerator doors—temporary display spaces for cartoons, recipes, odd newspaper stories and photographs, playbills, reminders, tips, stubs, hints, notes—transient stuff that has just a little more staying power, a little more right to life, than the stuff we throw directly away. Claire Langois had her lacquered screen. Asserted with plastic push-pins (the silvered, ugly kind), from the top of the screen to the bottom, from the left side of each panel to the right, were photographs—newspaper photographs, magazine photographs, magazine covers, photographs from the dust jackets of books, family photographs, a photograph torn or somewhat roughly cut from a high school yearbook, a photograph from the program of some business convention, photographs new and old, big photographs and small, professional photographs and amateur snapshots, solo and in groups, on and on and seemingly forever on, of Charles Story.

There were drawings of Charles Story too—newspaper cartoons, caricatures flattering and insulting, an idealized silhouette for the cover of some holding company's annual report, a photograph of a T-shirt with Charles Story's likeness silk-screened on its chest, another photograph of a formal, old-fashioned, larger-than-life oil portrait of Charles Story.

In each and every photograph, each and every drawing, caricature, likeness, portrait, the surgery probably performed *(Way to go, Snake—good police work)* with a compass whose sharp pivot was driven—driven deep—into the wood of the screen in one of the few places not occupied by a photograph, a drawing, a caricature, a likeness, a portrait, the subject's, Charles Story's, eyes had been gouged out.

Cullen's eyes ached sympathetically and he winced and blinked and turned away, looking for Vera, who had gone to a far corner of the room while he studied the screen, got its message. He startled, for there between them, looking very curious to know if he *had* gotten it, stood Claire, who had come from somewhere on bare feet. "Hello," was all Cullen could think to say.

"Hi," Claire said. "I feel I know you. You've been through a lot with me. On the LIE, at the cemetery, the other day in the yard. Thanks.'' He had thought at first that the white cotton shift that was all she wore—no slip, no fishnet stockings, no evil boots—was a hospital gown, but he saw that it was merely fashionable, suited to the weather and her slender body. Her face was unsullied by mascara and eye shadow and rouge and in their absence her cropped hair, her pigtail, her plucked eyebrows, looked less menacing. No silvered brass knuckles, no death's head rings, no swastika, no carriage bolt. The hair and the shift made her look childlike, virginal, like an extraterrestrial, like one of those photographs of fetuses afloat in amniotic fluid, large-headed and preternaturally wise. And then again, the hair and the shift and her narrow cheeks made her look like an invalid, a radiation-therapy patient, a concentration camp inmate. Except that her eyes were clear and her voice was strong, whatever sedative she'd been under having lost its hold.

''You're . . . You're welcome,'' Cullen said.

Claire took a step toward the lacquered screen, bent toward it for a moment as if it weren't her creation at all, as if she were seeing it for the first time, then stepped back and looked right into Cullen's soul. ''The first time was a year ago Memorial Day,'' Claire said. ''The bed was a kid's bed then, the room was a kid's room. I was on the road, playing tennis. I was getting worldly, getting sophisticated, but my room was where I kept my childhood intact. Dolls, stuffed animals, ruffles. When he started fucking me, it started looking like this. Mom thought it was the influence of the boys I was hanging out with. Metal heads, stoners, euro-trash.

''I didn't tell anyone. What do you say? How do you say it? Who to? Mom heard the bracelets. He wore two bracelets on his wrist, his right wrist. One Mom bought in Africa on a tennis tour; she gave it to him for a wedding present. The other was copper, for arthritis. When he moved his arm, they jingled, like bells, like wind chimes. I have a dream about them. If it's as real as can be, is it a dream?

''Last month, the twenty-second, Mom heard them through the door, the bracelets. She knew the sound from . . . from making love with him—when he, when he, when he touched her. She waited outside. She hid outside. She was the criminal, right—the peeping tom. Out he came. So she knew.''

Cullen struggled to keep his eyes from going to the devastated bed, the knotted, contorted, thrashed black sheets. He succeeded, but his mind hurt like hell.

He looked at Vera.

Vera was looking at Claire, talking more to her than to Cullen, as if inspired by her, given permission. "The molesting started when I was ten. Mother was still alive. The rapes started when I was twelve, the day mother was buried. Sometimes he raped me after school, while Dad was working downstairs in the store. Sometimes he raped me at night, after Dad went to bed: Dad went to bed very early and slept very soundly. Sometimes he raped me Saturdays, on his break from working with Dad. Sundays I was usually safe. He usually went with Dad to visit our uncle, Dad's dead sister's husband, on Long Island. I think—I'm sure—he raped our cousin, Barbara. I haven't seen Barbara in years. I hoped she'd come to the funeral. If she had, I would've tried to talk to her about it. She didn't come. She found her own way to . . . to celebrate, I hope. . . .

"Dead mother, passive father, aggressive son, shy daughter—it was classic. You know all this; you've read about it. Multiple personalities. Acting saved me. I could be multiple personalities professionally. I don't think that's an oversimplification. A therapist helped, a woman who saw that acting could be a useful tool. . . . Ruth—the therapist, Nicky, Lise, Claire. They're the only people I've ever told. Perhaps my mother knew, perhaps my father: who knows? And Tom now knows. You left Tom out of your scenario. You haven't figured out how he fits in. When you wrote that letter back in high school, you threatened me, without knowing that that's what you were doing, with exposure, which I could not have borne. I confronted Tom not because I was afraid he was saying *he'd* slept with me but because I was afraid he—others—had been saying I'd slept with my brother. I knew—I don't know how I knew, since I knew so little, but I knew—when he said the letter was a lie, that he didn't know, that no one knew.

"You didn't know, Joe."

Vera was looking at Cullen now and it wasn't a question, it was a directive; it meant that she *had* seen him, Joseph (Snake) Cullen, sitting on the fender of the charcoal gray and pink Chevrolet Bel Air outside the candy store, smoking a butt, rocky girls right there in front of him if he had wanted to stare at their high hard tits, but not staring at them, looking up *(up!)* at the third-floor window with two people in it, her and her brother, Vera Story and Chuck Story, bare-assed naked. She had seen him looking and she was ordering him not to think he had known, not to think he should have known, because, hey, people *don't* look up.

Still, echoes and reverberations: Outside 119 the morning after the night Story was polished, talking to Ann, Ann touching his hand to calm him down after having questioned his old friend Chuck's integrity. *"You're right, and I'm not trying to impugn your friend, but I spent a month with him, and I noticed one thing. I noticed that like a lot of men, he did one of two things when he got angry: he was silent or he raged."*

Vera had moved to stand close to Claire, her hands on Claire's shoulders. Sisters, friends, warriors. "What else do you want to know, Joe? What else do you need to know? You need to know that Tom and I got to be good friends when he was in rehab. Caleb and I were working on a picture in New York—it was sixty-eight, right after Bobby Kennedy was killed—and I heard Tom was in a hospital in Brooklyn. I went to see him. He was very grateful. We stayed in touch after he got out, after his career got going. It was obvious to him that I was estranged from my brother, but he never asked why and I never told him. . . .

"Lise called me the day she found out. I got off the phone and told Nicky and we stood there in the middle of my living room and planned my brother's murder. No—we didn't plan it; it just . . . came out. Everything happened just as you said it happened, Joe—except that right after I shot my brother—you were right about the gun; Nicky did get it and it isn't traceable—right after I shot my brother, in walked Tom.

"Tom's friend, Joy Griffith, died in the Raleigh fire. Tom heard things that made him think my brother, or my brother's company anyway, had the Raleigh burned down. He more or less said so publicly. Then he found out something that made him think differently. He called my brother—one of those phone calls you can trace—and invited himself over that evening, the evening of the Fourth, to talk. When no one answered the bell, he let himself in. With a key my brother had given him. Remember how you guys all used to swap keys? Some macho rite. I don't know why, but to me it says something about how fearful you all were. Of something.''

*Of having everything under one roof, clearly.* Cullen had slowly, slowly become aware of a . . . a. . . . He didn't know what to call it. A sen*sa*tion—internal, intimate, ancient, the logical (with twenty-twenty hindsight, what isn't?) outcome of this summer of heat and death: his blood was boiling, boiling away. Soon, very soon, it would be altogether gone, and then his veins and arteries and . . . (Zim, how *are* you and what are they called, those little blood vessels?) . . . *cap*illaries would sear and melt and char. The fire would spread to his bones and they would burn and crack and collapse and without their armature *he* would collapse and the fire would spread to the sack of skin and hair that held all the rest of the shit together and *it* would burn and the wind would stir up the ashen what-was-left-of-him and strew it about and that, thank God, would be that.

Claire murmured something to Vera, and just as she'd come she was gone, answering some summons from the Mother Ship, perhaps. Cullen looked at Vera closely for the first time. In a tan cotton shirt and white cotton pants, leather huaraches, her wild hair held up by combs, she belonged on a coffee plantation in Kenya, not in a shrine of anarchy in New York City. Maybe, before his blood cooked away, he could rush to the nearest Bananas ''R'' Us, pick up a bush shirt, some shorts; race to a travel agent and book two tickets: New York-Amsterdam-Nairobi, liftoff at fourteen-hundred hours, just seconds before he was to have incinerated.

He'd be saved, she'd nurse him back to health, they could pick up where they'd left off, start a new life, shoot elephants for breakfast, buzz terrified gazelles in the old Stutz Bearcat (or was a Stutz Bearcat a car? Zimmerman—how *was* Zimmerman?—would know), order the beaters and bearers about in fluent Swahili, have everything under one palm frond, the sex and the laughs and the Lyle Lovett albums and (on videotapes made by friends stateside) the *Hill Street Blues* reruns and the Buffalo ostrich wings, be glorious, gorgeous, golden pains-in-the-ass. Couldn't they?

Vera was looking at Cullen strangely, as if *he'd* stopped talking. Her calm, easy voice turned to chatter: ''He was glad for me, Tom—sorry for Claire, sorry for Lise, sorry about all of it, but ultimately glad for me. And he saw an opportunity: he'd always been troubled by the violence. These people. The Hopeless. They killed those people, they cut off their fingers. He thought if it were made to look as though they killed my brother, they'd all be rounded up, or driven so deeply into hiding that they'd lose their . . . their force. He cut off my brother's finger. He wrote 'Raleigh' on the wall.

"But Tom had miscalculated. My brother's death inspired someone to try and kill me, it looked like. Tom had never imagined that. And the backlash—the woman and her baby in Jamaica Bay, your friend's death, Detective Bermúdez—I'm sorry, Joe, about Detective Bermúdez. . . . Tom turned himself in—he called me this morning before he came in; another phone call to be traced—because things were getting out of hand. He—"

"Let me finish up. Please," Cullen said. "Tom'll be charged with Chuck's, with your *brother's,* murder because he has the gun, because he was seen coming in here, because he had a motive—revenge for Joy Griffith's death. But he'll never be convicted because other than his momentary confession, there's no evidence but that circumstantial evidence. It'll be thrown out, and your brother's real murderer will never be found. Never. Never, never, never."

"What?" Vera took a step toward Cullen. "What, Joe? Why're you shaking your head like that?"

To prove to himself that he could still move *and* to say to Vera that it wouldn't wash, no one would buy it, it was what his computer nerd daughter called beneath belief. But while his head shook on, his brain stayed gyroscope-steady and said, *Hey—why not? People* don't *look up.*

# 34

"Lyons?" Cullen said. Talk about beneath belief. Talk about a one-horse world.

"I can look you in the eye," Zimmerman said. "Lyons and a mid-level punk named Hector Piñero, street name Marks, and a torch and occasional polisher named Robert Southey, street name Bobby Liberty."

*"Lyons?"*

"It's lonely at the top, I guess," Zimmerman said. "Stressful."

They were sitting in the Turbo, air-conditioner on *forte,* parked down the block from 119. Zimmerman had been waiting right outside when Cullen, an arm up against the sun like a wise guy ducking paparazzi, came out the front door. "I thought I'd find you here," Zimmerman had said. "That's because you know everything, Zim," Cullen had said. "Jigger buttons, thrums, findings, bezels, gudgeons, spears, bonnets, harps, telsons, croups, true-zero hooks, philtrums." Zimmerman had just stared at Cullen and chewed the inside of his cheek.

"How are you, Neil?" Cullen said now. "It's good to see you."

"I'm okay. Walsh is dead, and Darelle; I guess you were there for that. More funerals."

"How was Keith's?"

"Okay. Hot. Word got out about Walsh and Darelle, so people were kind of distracted. Keith's mother didn't notice, though, so I guess it was okay."

"More funerals."

"More funerals. Deborah's *was* tomorrow, but I don't know if they're going to change that because of . . . Oh, fuck it.

Your . . . I was going to say your brother-in-law, but he's not your brother-in-law, he's your ex's husband—"

"Doug."

"Doug called. With a name and a number. A west coast number."

"If I tell you to lose it, will you lose it, or will you ask me why?"

Zimmerman looked at Cullen. The front seat of the Saab had never been so wide. "How're you, Joe?"

"I could use a nap. You think anyone would notice if I slept till Christmas?"

"Christmas is off this year. The Humane Society won't let the reindeer fly in this heat."

Cullen wept.

Zimmerman squeezed his shoulder. "It's okay, Joe. Let it go."

And wept.

Until Hriniak's Lincoln pulled up alongside, his driver going the wrong way down Seventieth Street so that Hriniak and Cullen were face-to-face. They rolled down their windows.

Cullen blew his nose on a Kleenex from the glove compartment. "I know. 'What the fuck?' "

"What do you hear about Detroit?" Hriniak said.

"Darelle Dean polished Walsh, then killed himself," Cullen said. "In case nobody figured that out. In the left hand pocket of Walsh's pants, you'll find some hair he cut from Tom Valentine's head. The hair in the evidence bag is Walsh's hair, and it'll match the hair Nicky Potter removed from the guy who polished Bermúdez."

"That guy being Walsh."

"That guy being Walsh."

"That all went down on the doorstep of the lab, practically, so we've been able to put a lot of it together, but thanks for your eyewitness account. I assume you were on the scene."

"It all happened real fast," Cullen said. "But I'm going to resign anyway, because I basically booted it."

"In the movies cops resign when they boot something. In real life they stick around and boot something else." Hriniak lifted his chin at 119. "What's been going on in there?"

"Just a social call," Cullen said.

"Yeah. And I'm the prince of fucking Wales."

"Did you know he never carries money?" Cullen said. "Prince Charles? One of his . . . equerries or something carries it for him. Zim told me that. Is that what you call them, Zim—equerries?"

"Commissioner, uh . . ." Zimmerman leaned across the wide front seat. "With your permission, sir, I'd like to take Sergeant Cullen home. He hasn't slept in a long time."

Home? The plants the computer nerd insisted would balance his ecosystem would be dead; the bills and supermarket flyers and missing children and sweepstakes prizes would be knee-deep behind the door; there would be dust on the dust on the dust; the leftovers would have escaped from the refrigerator and would be playing the Lyle Lovett albums and making the Buffalo chicken wings. "Drop me at Ann's."

"Before you go, Sergeant," Hriniak said. "Thanks."

What had he done? Oh, yeah—sat on the calls from Hriniak's phone to Deborah Dean. "Sure."

"And before you say anything more about resigning, get some rest."

"Yeah. Sure. I will. Thanks."

"So long, Joe."

". . . So long, Phil."

Hriniak said something to his driver and the driver put the Lincoln in gear and went down the street toward Park.

Zimmerman put the Saab in gear and eased out from the curb and went to Lex and turned downtown. "You know something else I know?"

"What?"

"The fountain at the Plaza where we saw the homeless woman get hit by the cab?"

"Yeah?"

"The one the cop was chasing?"

"Yeah, Neil, yeah. How many homeless women have we seen hit by cabs?"

". . . Fuck you, Cullen."

"I'm sorry."

"Yeah."

"I am. I'm sorry. Neil, I haven't slept in—"

"I haven't slept either, you egocentric son-of-a-bitch. I can't remember the last time I slept in my bed. I slept on the floor under my desk . . . yesterday, I think. So fuck you and your fucking not sleeping."

"I'm sorry, Neil."

"Yeah."

"I am."

Zimmerman turned right on Sixty-sixth, heading toward the transverse road through the park.

"What a*bout* the fountain?" Cullen said.

Zimmerman said, "Nothing."

Cullen said, "Vera killed her brother. He raped her when they were kids. Repeatedly. For years. When she found out he'd been raping Claire, she killed him. By the purest coincidence, Valentine dropped in just after she shot him. Valentine rigged it to look like the Hopeless had done it, but when the backlash got out of hand he decided to take the rap himself."

From Park to Fifth, Zimmerman thought it through. "So the woman who got off the plane and into the Benz was Nicky. Vera was already in town."

They weren't questions, so Cullen didn't answer.

"And Valentine'll walk, probably, because other than his saying so, there's nothing to nail him with."

"Nothing," Cullen said.

The park was a joke—brown trees, brown grass, brown dust that clung to the sweating metal and turned all the cars and buses brown. On the sidewalk there was a lunatic on a bicycle; going the other way there was a lunatic jogging. They waved at each other as they passed—the lunatic high sign.

At a red light at Central Park West, Zimmerman said, "They're going to renovate the fountain. There was something in the paper. It's called the Fountain of Abundance. I just thought it was ironic, given what we saw there, that's all."

"It is," Cullen said. "It is ironic. The Fountain of Abundance?"

"It's called the Pulitzer Memorial Fountain too, but the other name for it is the Fountain of Abundance."

"The Fountain of Abundance."

"The Fountain of Abundance."

They sat there, even after the light changed, saying *The Fountain of Abundance* at each other over and over, for hours, it seemed like. Until the driver of a cab behind them, getting no action by leaning on his horn, got out and rapped on the driver's window.

Zimmerman lowered the window two inches. "Yeah?"

"Nothing. Forget it," the driver said, and went back to his cab.

Zimmerman watched him in the rearview mirror. "Nice guy."

But Cullen was asleep.

"You look exhausted," Ann said. She wore red running shorts and a sleeveless navy T-shirt that said *Where's the party?*

"I feel okay," Cullen said. "I had a nap in the car." A three-minute nap. "You got a new rug."

"Pottery Barn." Ann moved a big floor fan so it blew on his chair, and sat cross-legged on the couch. She tipped her head toward the backyard beyond the open French door. "I thought I'd be afraid to come back here so soon, but I really haven't thought about it much. I've been distracted by all the extraordinary news bulletins coming out of my radio."

"I forgot. You aren't even supposed to be here. You're supposed to be with Rita and Bruce."

"It's too hot to be a house guest. Or have one."

Cullen sat forward. "I'll be going."

"That isn't what I meant, you asshole."

He sat back. "Could I have an iced tea or something?"

"Lemonade?"

"Umm."

Ann went into the kitchen and Cullen fell asleep.

He woke up on her bed, under a sheet, nude, much later. Ann heard him stretching and came to the door, carrying a Walkman, the headphones down around her neck. "I did something I maybe shouldn't have. I called Connie just to say you were okay."

He wondered how she'd gotten the number, but he knew she'd say it was her job to find things out as much as it was his job, that she *was* a player. "Thanks."

"I talked to James. He's very sweet."

"I guess he is sweet. I don't think of him as sweet, but I guess he is sweet."

Ann sat on the bed and picked his watch up off the end table. ''You had this set to beep on the hour. I'm surprised. It's not like you. Remember that time we had dinner at Betsy and Frank's and there was that couple who had watches that went off thirty seconds apart? I thought you were going to stab them with the carving knife.''

''I thought the alarm was broken.''

''It went off while you were sleeping.''

''Now that it's not broken, I don't know how to unset it.''

''I unset it.''

''I'd like you to meet James,'' Cullen said. ''And Tenny.''

Ann nodded. ''I'd like that. Thanks.''

''Neil's figured out the answer to the question that stumped Freud. It's 'Everything under one roof.' ''

Ann nodded. ''Sounds right. Good for Neil.''

''I want *some* things under one roof.''

''Such as?''

''The sex and the laughs and the Lyle Lovett albums and the *Hill Street Blues* reruns and the Buffalo chicken wings.''

''Sounds like a fraternity house.''

''I suppose . . . Vera Evans killed Charles Story.''

Ann nodded. ''Incest?''

''With Claire Langois as well.''

''I think I knew that. It's silly to say, but I think I knew it. . . . Thanks for not saying, 'You didn't hear it from me.' ''

''It has to stay secret—I'm not saying you were about to run to the phone—but it's too bad it has to. Too bad he goes down as a victim.''

''Thanks for not saying I was about to run to the phone.''

''I seem to be saying some of the right things for a change. Or not saying them. For a long time there, I was Snake Cullen.''

Ann tumbled down into the rabbit hole of her mind for a while. When she came back, she said, ''Did you know that the cop who busted Lyons was the same cop who caught the nine-eleven when Story was polished?''

Oh, go ahead—talk like a player. ''Hriniak likes to say it's a one-horse world.''

''That stuff you said up at 119, after Keith was killed—the stuff about Vera and Tom being . . . close. . . . By taking the rap, Tom is. . . . Well, I'm no lawyer—and I can't seem to say what I mean—but . . ."

"I'm no lawyer either. But he'll get a *good* lawyer and he'll get off."

Ann fiddled with an earphone. "I'd like to get in that bed with you, but I'm not sure after somebody says 'incest,' that it's possible to just go on about one's business. You keep hearing the . . . the echo."

Echoes and reverberations. Cullen touched Ann's arm at the elbow, made contact for the first time in years, it felt like. "Soon."

She shook her head. "You didn't have to say 'soon.' "

"I'm trying to get it right, Ann. I'm trying to get it *all* right."

She nodded. "Isn't everybody? Remember that sign by the Ear Inn that we liked? 'Water Spilled From Source To Use'?"

Cullen nodded.

Ann cocked her head. "Well?"

Cullen nodded. "Yeah."